Pennies from Heaven

by Marjorie Malinowski

Copyright © 2013 by Marjorie Malinowski
First Edition – July 2013

ISBN
978-1-4602-1591-3 (Hardcover)
978-1-4602-1592-0 (Paperback)
978-1-4602-1593-7 (eBook)

All rights reserved.

No part of this publication may be reproduced in any form, or by any means, electronic or mechanical, including photocopying, recording, or any information browsing, storage, or retrieval system, without permission in writing from the publisher.

Produced by:

FriesenPress
Suite 300 – 852 Fort Street
Victoria, BC, Canada V8W 1H8

www.friesenpress.com

Distributed to the trade by The Ingram Book Company

Dedication

This book is dedicated to my family: my husband of thirty five years, my children – my son Todd, his wife Alisa, his son Kolby and my daughter Vanessa, her sons Jake and Carter and to my sisters – Corinne, Brenda and Sharon along with their children all of whom have provided me with a wealth of stories.

I also dedicate this book to Troy – even though he is no longer with us in the flesh, his spirit and love of life will live in our hearts forever. Troy – I believe sends me messages from Heaven on a regular basis.

Chapter One

Amy feels herself floating in a small tight room, she reaches over and touches the wall, it's warm and slippery. She's completely submerged in this wonderful warm liquid, somehow she's breathing calmly and silently in the quietness of her surroundings, for some strange reason she's not afraid.

She can hear sounds, straining she listens, it sounds like a train coming closer and closer. She has no idea where she is.

Suddenly Amy's sure there are other people in the room. She clearly hears two heart beats, getting louder and more rapid. She struggles to turn around in this very tight space to see if she can see something, anything, in this darkness.

The first heartbeat's right in front of her now and she can almost feel the second one behind her, she again reaches out hoping to touch something that she can identify.

Still nothing, nothing but liquid.

The wall encapsulating her is soft and flexible to her touch. Amy feels the wall where the first heartbeat appears to be coming from, she can sense the distress in the heart, it seems to be slowing down and eventually it stops. She can still feel the second heartbeat, growing weaker as the sound of the train grows stronger. She hears the sounds of thunder and rain.

Eventually the storm and the train both pass and Amy relaxes as the sound she's sure is a heartbeat continues in a soft and constant pattern.

Drifting off, Amy falls into a gentle sleep. Suddenly, she feels herself being ripped from the secure surrounds she's become accustomed to into a strong light that hurts her eyes. She shudders from the sudden drop in temperature; she's freezing cold and very wet. Closing her eyes as tight as she can, she feels a blanket being wrapped around her. She's being held by someone very large and feels herself being passed over into the arms of someone gentle and protective. Against the pain of the light, she struggles to force her eyes open, but as she succeeds, she can't see anything. She seems to be a dense fog.

Amy rolls over and finds she's in her own bed. She sits up only to realize she's had the dream again. She's had this same dream many times in her life. She wishes someone would help her to understand this dream. Maybe someone would if she'd only share it, but she has such a sense of peace and love she always decides to keep it to herself. She hopes the same will happen tonight. She gets up for a drink of water from her large ensuite bathroom. Quickly, she crawls back into her very warm and comfortable king size bed, quietly scolding herself to get some sleep.

Amy closes her eyes and reopens them to find herself in the middle of the corridor at the Rock Valley Hospital, where she's currently head of the Cardiology Department. The corridor leads to several operating rooms for the cardiac unit of the hospital. Someone's holding open the door. She runs through the door and stops. A patient's on the operating table waiting for his surgeon, and she realizes she's the surgeon. Hearing her pager go off, she hesitates. The tone of the pager tells her it's her mother's heart monitor. Her mother's in distress. She looks around in search of her pager. She's being pulled in two different directions.

Her attention shifts as she hears her name being called. It's her mother.

"Amy, Amy dear, you're having a bad dream." She feels a warm hand on her shoulder as someone's nudging her awake.

Amy sits up in bed with tears flowing down her cheeks. Her mother gently pulls Amy into her arms.

"It's okay princess," her mother comforts her. Princess is the nickname her parents often use when she's upset.

Unable to speak, Amy just hangs on to her mother.

"You need to let go, Amy. You need to understand you're human and can only make decisions you think are best. You can't change the past or the course of events that happened, it was my turn. You've got to remember, even as one of the best surgeons and cardiac specialists you're not God and you don't make His decisions, only He does. You have to let go of the guilt. You're not responsible for my death. I'm safe and happy."

The tears have slowed down and Amy relaxes in her mother's arms.

"Now hear me and hear me well, Amy Elizabeth Green Murray. (Amy goes stiff since her mother only ever uses this tone when she's angry). You let the guilt go and get on with your life. You have a wonderful and fulfilling future, but only if you allow yourself to follow your heart. Promise me you will do this."

Amy looks into her mother's eyes, "It's so hard, I'm not sure how."

"Start with the list I gave you. The list will help you learn to live again. Promise to start working on the list," Ann pleads with her daughter.

"I promise." Amy struggles with the words.

The sound of the alarm clock ringing wakes Amy up. She realizes she's had yet another dream. It's Saturday and her day off. She's sure she shut off the alarm last night, but obviously she didn't, since the alarm did in fact go off. That part doesn't appear to have been a dream.

Amy dresses quickly, she needs to go to the one place she feels safe and secure to think. She'd felt her mother's arms and heard her voice, but that's impossible. That's what her logic tells her, but her heart tells her otherwise. Amy brings herself back to reality as she backs her new autumn red Lincoln Navigator out of the garage and into the street. Traffic's quiet this early in the morning and she realizes she needs to pay attention to the road, but all the time, her mind keeps taking her back to her dreams.

In no time she's reached her destination. The sun's bright and high in the sky and the air's so quiet and still Amy does not hear the crunch of the fall leaves under her feet. It's a beautiful autumn Saturday, but Amy pays no attention to her surroundings; she's come to contemplate.

Reaching for another drink of water, she realizes her oversized water bottle's empty. Amy checks her watch; she's shocked at the time. She's been here much longer than she's planned. *What has she accomplished? Not much*, she shakes her head to her own silent question. Sitting, thinking, and crying. She's gone over her dreams and the events of the past year.

Slowly she stands up, shaking off the stiffness from sitting so long. There are no more tears to shed and Amy's exhausted. She stands in front of her adopted mother's headstone, Ann Marie Murray. It's a small family plot where her birth parents are also buried. Jeff and Mary died in a tornado on the same day she was born. She's visited many times over the years as she grew up with Ann, the only mother she has known, the woman who raised her from birth. She's never felt the same emotions when standing in front of the headstones of Jeff and Mary.

It's hard to believe it's been over a year since Ann's funeral. Amy has felt drawn back several times over the past several months. Each time, she feels her mother telling her to move forward with her life and she feels this is a safe place to think about her life and what she should do to move forward.

She reflects on the last three nights. The same dreams every night, her dreams have been so real. She knows they're dreams, and yet she's sure that her mother's sending her messages. She made a promise in last night's dream. Now she has to figure out how to keep such a promise. It's great to have someone tell you to get on with your life and she's had everyone encouraging her to do just that, but Amy has no idea what that means or how to go about it, much less figure out what her future holds. If she can piece together all the parts of the dreams she's had, maybe she can structure a plan and find some answers to her questions.

Again, Amy relives the day her mother died. She'd convinced her mother to put her heart monitor bra back on and had connected it back into the system. Amy was in surgery when the monitor went off indicating heart failure but as usual when she's in surgery she leaves her cell phone in her locker. The Central Emergency Dispatch Centre responded immediately, dispatching an ambulance to her parent's home where they found Ann, in her lounging chair in the back yard, dead. An autopsy showed she'd died peacefully as the result of a massive heart failure. Amy's good friend Sophia Charter, CEO and Hospital Administrator, personally reviewed the autopsy reports and has told Amy several times that her mother would've died even if she'd been in the hospital. It was so rapid that nothing could've been done to change the results. Regardless, Amy continues to carry a burden of guilt and the intense pain of losing her mother.

Amy's so envious of her older brother Jake; he's started to figure out his life. He shared the details of the conversations with their mother he'd had in dreams with Amy to try to help her as they had helped him. Amy seems to have missed the message. For some reason, he's now at peace and looking forward to the future. Amy seems to be stuck in neutral. She's doing her job, but there's no life to her, she feels like a robot. Maybe if she can keep the promise she made in last night's dream she can figure out how to move forward as well. Maybe she needs to talk to someone about the dreams and get help to figure out what to do next.

Ann came often to the cemetery, and Amy still remembers sitting in her little red wagon and hearing stories about her parents. One thing Ann did was make sure Amy knew her family and heritage. Amy begins to understand why she feels an odd comfort in this place. Most people dislike and even fear cemeteries, but Amy knows this is the place where only the body remains since the spirit and soul have passed on.

Sitting back down on the soft grass, Amy takes out the letter her mother left her. The letter's accompanied by two pages entitled "To do List". Amy's never paid much attention to the list, only ever focusing on the letter. She reads the letter one more time. She knows it by heart, but seeing her mother's handwriting is soothing. In the letter, her mother tries one more time to explain to Amy that she has to make a life for herself or she'll be very lonely as she grows older. Amy's heard that so many times. She remembers seeing the concern in her mother's eyes in her dream last night and she knows she's seen that same concern in her father's face. Amy just has no idea what to do next, she wants to find someone to share her life with, but right now she can't seem to figure out how to know when the right man comes along. Amy grew up in a home full of love, with no harsh words and a strong faith in God. She knows this is the kind of home she wants and she wants a loving partner and soul mate, but Amy's at a loss to figure out how you know the man you meet will be the love of your life. She's pretty sure that she hasn't had that experience yet.

Amy starts to review the list with an eye to what she needs to do to complete it. She actually sees a couple of items on the list she's already finished and others that she could work at without much time. Item #5 *Finish decorating all the rooms in her house*, Item #9 *invite friends for dinner parties*, Item #4 *call Dad at least once a week*. Maybe if she focuses on one or two items on the list things would make more sense to her. Item #3 *Find true love* - now that's one thing Amy has no idea about, but for the time being she'll keep her promise and try to work on the simple and easy items on the list. Item #1 – *No more tears* -, now that is one Amy knows she'll never achieve since she cries during the Hallmark commercials on TV.

Contemplating her life for a few more minutes, Amy aimlessly picks at some blades of grass. Another penny; how many pennies she's found in the last few weeks. She hears her mother telling her to pick up the pennies, *they're good luck*. Suddenly, Amy jolts up; she picks up the letter from her mother. In it, Ann tells Amy she'll send her messages. Could the pennies be the messages? No, that would be just plain silly.

Still, the pennies start to nag at her. She's found pennies where no pennies should even be. When would she have ever put a penny in her jewellery box or on her makeup shelf or under her chair at her desk or beside the center piece on her dining room table, so often and in so many places? Amy decides to talk to her father about it. Maybe he's got the answer. In fact, Amy decides her father's the perfect person to talk to about her dreams.

With a new sense of direction and determination, she gathers up her sweater, empty water bottle and her leftover snacks, and pops her mother's letter back into her Coach bag. Amy has some supplies in her car for Dad.

She worries about him being all alone in that big house. *Is he sleeping properly? Is he eating properly?* Amy can't even bear to think about something happening to her father.

Ed's outside in the front yard taking advantage of the nice fall day. He's busy getting his plants ready for the long winter ahead. He's a bit behind due to the continuous rash of company that constantly drop in. He shudders at the thought of spending his life alone in the house. He'd promised Ann he wouldn't make any changes for at least one year after she left him. They'd both known her time was limited even with all the positive tests from the hospital. He still hears Ann's voice telling him, "When it's your time, it's your time; God makes the decision, not the doctors."

He can't imagine leaving the house with all his wonderful memories of their life together and then there are his friends down the street. No, he's decided he'll live out his life in this house, tending his garden and plants, and spending time with his friends and family.

A horn sounds. Ed rises up from his plants and a smile forms on his face when he sees Amy. "This is a surprise, why didn't you tell me you were coming out; I would've made dinner for us." Ed searches her face and can tell she's recently shed some tears. He's not surprised since he knows she's having a real struggle coming to grips with her mother's death.

"I thought I'd surprise you and bring you something. I figured you might not stop to eat. It's good to see you." Amy gets out of her car and hurries over to hug him.

"Well, come on in; let's have a bite while we catch up on the news." Ed opens the car door and picks up several bags of groceries. "You know, we have stores here."

Amy laughs, "I know but I like my local Safeway, I can find everything I need. Besides, if I shop here, it'll take forever. I always find so many people I know shopping at the same time and they always want to talk."

"I know that feeling." Ed grins as he opens the house door for his daughter. "I can spend a whole day uptown when I go to get the mail. You meet someone who wants to go for coffee, and then you run into someone else who wants to go for lunch."

Amy's not sure what she expected, but the house is still the very same, everything in its place. "Boy, you sure can keep the house tidy. Mom must be proud of you."

"Yep, easy when it's just one person. I can't blame anyone for any messes, although I do believe someone sneaks into the house when my back's turned. I see all sorts of dust bunnies and dirt collected in the corners."

"Maybe you should find a housekeeper."

"Funny you should mention that. I was checking the list your mom left; seems she had already interviewed a couple and left telephone numbers for me to call. I've been meaning to call, but right now the yard keeps me busy. Well, that and the guys wanting to play golf and go for lunch. Not to mention your aunts and cousins who suddenly seem to find themselves in the area. You'd think they have nothing better to do but to keep me company."

Amy laughs. "I hear you; it's funny how many times a week I hear from mom's friends Joyce and Connie along with Aunties Katherine and Sara. Cheryl's finally finished up my renovations but she always seemed to want to hang around after hours to have dinner with me. I asked her yesterday if Bert left her or something. She confessed that Mom asked her to keep an eye on me."

Amy opens the fridge to put some juice in and sees it's full. "You expecting company? You sure have a lot of food in here."

"It seems both Joyce and Connie are determined to keep me fed and fat. Joyce was over last night with a couple of bags of stuff. With all the casseroles people from the church have brought over, I still have food in the freezer and I could eat for at least a month without leaving the house."

"You have to admit it's great to have friends who love you so much."

Amy bends down to put the plastic bags in the holder in the pantry. As she moves to close the door she finds another penny. "Dad, do you have a hole in your pocket. I found another penny. Just a little while ago I found one while I was visiting mom."

"Strangest thing, I'm finding them everywhere. I'm beginning to think someone's messing with my mind. I'm all alone in the house and I'm pretty sure Joyce isn't dropping them."

"Dad, is it possible they're coming from Mom?"

"Well, you know, Mom and I always talked about making sure whoever was left behind would get messages from the other. I've always believed that angels leave messages for us."

"A penny for your thoughts. She always used to say that." Amy's eyes mist over.

"You know, I'm just going to believe they're messages of love for us from your mother. Does that work for you?"

Tears form in Amy's eyes and the flood gates open. Ed, a typical man, hates to see any woman cry, much less his daughter. He gathers her into his arms and together they cry one more time.

Amy washes her face and starts rummaging through the fridge to see what treasures lay within. It doesn't take long and they find themselves sitting in front of a feast.

As they sit, Amy shares her dreams with her father. She tells him about the first dream; he listens quietly, not interrupting until she's finished.

"Interesting you should share this, we've been studying the dreams of the Bible in Adult Sunday School at church and there's a little handbook I found online to help me prepare for the classes about how to interpret your dreams " He gets up and walks over to the kitchen island where the family study Bible and mail sits. He picks up several sheets of paper he's printed off the internet.

"There are a total of 10 steps to this process." Ed starts reading from the first page.

"Since ancient times, the Greeks and Egyptians believed that some people have the power to draw meaning from dreams. As long ago as the second century, works were created on how to interpret our dreams. In modern times, we understand better that the world of dreams is simply another reality with which we can interact, and yet, as we grow older, it can be all too easy to dismiss the value of dreaming. Nonetheless, dreaming deserves to hold a special place in our lives because it is an important part of who we are. Dreams provide us with signposts and differing perspectives on our waking problems, all offered to us nightly, free of charge, if we only care to stop and take note of them. Interpreting dreams is for everyone, not just those already attuned to spending time exploring the psychic and subconscious. Self-decoding dreams can enable you to gain access to a wealth of intuitive wisdom."

Ed hands the papers over to Amy. "Here, why not just take it home and read it yourself. As you can see, it's a very easy read.

"You're right, it's a very fast and easy read, give me a couple of minutes and I can read it over."

"Of course." Ed smiles, "By the time I've made tea and cut this fresh apple pie from Joyce, you'll have it in your memory." Living with two kids with photographic memories has always been a challenge to him.

Giving her time, Ed proceeds to make up a fresh pot of Earl Grey Tea, cuts two very hardy pieces of apple pie and adds two big scoops of vanilla ice cream to each plate.

Amy sets down the papers as Ed brings over the tray of tea, cups, and pie for them.

"Dad, this is exactly what I need. I should've thought to Google dreams myself, but this looks like it's a good place to start. Maybe I should try to decode my dreams using this process."

"We're using it in our study of the Prophetic Dreams of the Bible and how they relate to current times and the future."

"I remember studying the dreams of famous people. Did you know that both Joan of Arc and Abraham Lincoln dreamed of their own deaths just days before they died? Hannibal based his battle plans against the Romans according to a prophet's dreams. There are even stories that Jack Nicklaus found a new way to hold his golf clubs in a dream. So I guess I should take some time to study my own dreams."

Amy takes her first bite of Joyce's famous apple pie. "Joyce never fails when she delivers apple pie, does she?"

"Nope," Ed replies with his mouth full. They laugh as they finish up their dessert and tea, and continue to discuss options for Amy to figure out her dreams.

They finish out their afternoon together with the latest stories from Sara and Owen on their recent trip to visit Trevor in Arkansas where they experienced their first ever tornado sightings.

Ed regales her with the story of the tornado that took her birth parents. He tells her about how loud it was with the sounds like a freight train and the thunder and hail storm that followed. Even though Amy knows the stories off by heart, she always listens knowing how painful and bittersweet these memories are to her father.

The grandfather clock in the living room chimes four o'clock. Much as Amy would love to take her father up on the offer to spend the night, she has to make plans to leave soon. Her friend from school and her brother Jake's old law partner is on business with Jake's firm here in Calgary and they are planning to get together later tonight. Christopher and his sister Victoria have been friends with Jake and Amy since they first met during their school days. She explains to her father that she has seen Christopher a few times since her mother's funeral. He has been a good friend to her during these past several months.

"I'm not sure if I can find any room left in my tummy after this enormous lunch we just consumed." Amy starts to clear up the leftovers and help tidy up the kitchen.

"You sure seem to spend a lot of time with Christopher when he's out here. Anything serious I should know about?" Ed teases.

"If you are asking if I think that he's the one, I don't see it. Christopher will never leave Toronto and I have never liked that city. Besides I can't see myself leaving Calgary, so unless one of us caves, it's unlikely we'll ever be more than just friends," Amy confesses.

Secretly, Ed's relieved. Even though Christopher seems like a nice enough fellow, Ed does not believe he's the one for his princess.

Chapter Two

Amy heads back to Calgary. She's enjoyed her outing. Leaving the house and not working on her scheduled day off is just what she needed. She's anxious to have some time to work on her dream analysis to see what she comes up with. Finally, she's got something positive to look forward to.

She checks the Navigator' clock and sees she has lots of time to get home and change before Christopher arrives.

Christopher's been so kind to her since her mother's funeral. It was a total surprise when he showed up at the cemetery. Jake seems to think Christopher's the one for Amy, but Amy's not sure. They continue to go out whenever he's in town; she enjoys his company but can't imagine living with him for the rest of her life. She's pretty sure she's not in love with him, but she's spent so long doubting herself she's not sure about much in her personal life.

As she drives back to the city, she remembers how she was reintroduced to Christopher on a trip to Yale to visit Jake. His sister, Victoria, and Jake both went to school there. They had actually met years before when all four of them had gone to elementary and high school together at Huntersville College. It was a special project for kids with photographic or eidetic memories. All four of them were part of the Booster Mind Team, as it was called. Her friend and boss Sophia Charter was also part of their group, along with twenty or so other kids. It always seems like a small world whenever she or Jake run into a member of their school since it was such a tiny class of kids.

She'd lost touch with Christopher and Victoria over time. Both siblings had left the project earlier than her and Jake because their mother had become ill. Christopher and Victoria finished off their primary education by home schooling with a series of special tutors and nannies their father had arranged. Both of them were left pretty much to their own devices since their father was a successful lawyer and businessman who travelled the world, leaving them at home for extended periods of time.

Victoria and Jake had always kept in touch and Victoria had convinced Jake to attend Yale with her. It was on a break from her last year at Booster Mind School that Amy spent a week with them. Victoria helped her sort through the list of medical schools and it was her recommendation that convinced Amy Yale was the place to go. It wasn't until she had already moved into the dorm at Yale that she realized Christopher had also chosen Yale to finish his law degree. It was no secret that Victoria wanted Amy as a sister-in-law.

Victoria had recently come to Calgary to work with Jake in his law office. Together they were working on a very large corporate merger that involved their mutual clients. Victoria split her time between her office in Toronto and Jake's office in Calgary and Christopher chose to remain in his much loved Toronto. It seems to have worked well for all involved, and Amy smiles at the thought of all the time Jake and Victoria have spent together and how often they try to drag her along.

Back in Yale, Christopher and Amy were close. It was the first time Amy had been away from home and she was very focused on her education. Medicine meant everything to her, even back then. Christopher was equally determined to get his law degree with higher grades than his father.

Amy shakes her head; she'd always felt sorry for Christopher and his relationship with his father. It's so different than the relationship she and Jake share with their father. Christopher is in constant competition; who got the best grades, who's the best athlete, who makes the most money in a year. She realizes that Victoria refuses to be pulled into competition with the two men. She prefers to play referee and keep peace. Amy had never heard much about the rest of Christopher's family, if there is one. He's never mentioned any cousins or other family. Amy just assumes it's a small family and if he ever wants to talk about them she'd always be prepared to listen.

Back then, neither one of them thought about marriage; that was an unnecessary burden. It would've stood in the way of their career dreams and plans. In fact, they were just friends and used to go to events or special occasions as each other's date when the need arose.

The only time Christopher showed real concern for her was when she'd been attacked. Amy fought off her attacker before he could rape her, but she'd been badly beaten before she'd managed to fight him off and scream loud enough for campus police to hear her and respond.

Christopher raced to the hospital and didn't leave her side until she was ready to go home. It was at the end of that semester that Amy decided to finish her medical degree at the University in Edmonton. Christopher blamed himself for not being there on time. They'd agreed to meet for a movie, but he was, as usual, late. Amy was mad he had stood her up yet again and decided not to wait. She was taking a shortcut through the campus park when she was attacked. Amy never blamed him, but she grew tired of his demands on her time after that.

Victoria and Christopher formed their own law firm in Toronto. Christopher hasn't wanted to be part of his father's law firm, wanting to make a name for himself by himself. Jake had been a partner with them for a while. Amy never asked what happened. She knew when she'd gone out to Jake's farewell party that there was some serious tension between them, but Amy was busy with her own life and didn't bother to inquire. She knows that Jake's involved in some kind of large oil and gas acquisition and that Christopher and Victoria are representing the associated money people. Now every time Christopher comes to Calgary he arranges to meet Amy for dinner. Tonight they have plans to go out to dinner and a movie.

Amy finds Christopher to be good company and she enjoys their time together, but she's just not ready to be serious with him.

Chapter Three

Once she returns home, Amy puts away her supplies for the week. Time seems to have gotten away from her as she thinks about her dreams and the process she's going to develop to analyse them. She's going to have to hurry or she won't be ready when Christopher gets to the house. These days he's almost always on time and sometimes even early.

Amy pulls the brush through her wavy strawberry blonde hair. She really has no idea how attractive she is which makes her even more beautiful. Amy sees her hair as an annoyance. The natural waves and the colour has been a problem for years. Amy tried once to colour it, but the results were disastrous. Since that time, she lets it stay its natural colour. She prefers it long since she can tuck it up into her surgical cap quickly. Often, she wears it in a simple pony tail, wearing the same style for as long as she could remember. When it used to get shaggy, her mother would make an appointment and together they'd go for a day out, mother and daughter. Since her mother's death, Amy's just let it grow out. She stops and puts a note into her cell to make an appointment for a haircut.

Amy changes her clothes and quickly pulls on an emerald green top and slides into her slim cut jeans. Christopher promised a casual night: dining at her favourite restaurant, The Keg, and a movie after.

After a quick check in the mirror to make sure she's put together, Amy realizes she's forgot to check out movie times earlier. She grabs her phone to quickly check what's showing. Amy stops at the top of the stairs and looks down into her foyer and living room. Cheryl finished these two rooms up late yesterday. These were the last rooms to be decorated. Amy still can't believe this is her home. She knows her mom would be proud of her home and the way it looks, it was something she had wanted Amy to finish and even mentioned it in her list to Amy.

"That reminds me, I need to check Item #5 off mom's list", Amy thinks with some excitement. The list thing might not be as hard as she thought it would be..

The rooms are gorgeous and make her feel like a princess as she comes down the spiral staircase. The front entrance is large enough to accommodate several people at the same time. Cheryl has hung an enormous crystal chandelier over a round oak table with a tall, formal floral arrangement. Large mirrors and pieces of art hang on various walls throughout the main and second floors. The soft moss coloured walls bring the marble and hardwood floors alive. The freshly painted white crown moulding throughout the entire house enhances the 12 foot ceiling. Cheryl has left the rest of the natural oak coloured wood trim throughout the house and it complements the darker, oak hardwood floors that are in all the rooms except the foyer, kitchen and bathrooms. The same moss colour flows into her formal living room and dining room.

Within a few days of the final closing of the purchase of this house Ann had organized a surprise from Amy's grandparents. Ann had learned that the executor of Jeff and Mary's parents' estates had put all of their furniture and large art collection into storage expecting Jeff and Mary to ship them out to Alberta when they settled down. For some reason, it was delayed for several months. Shortly after Amy's parents died, Ann learned about the furniture and had arranged for it to be stored until Amy and her brother had homes of their own.

The furniture had been divided into two lots, one for her brother Jake and this shipment for her. It was a wonderful surprise to receive an entire truck full of antique furniture and paintings that had belonged to her grandparents in Prince Edward Island. For months after the crates of furniture were delivered to the house, Amy had left them piled in the living room, too busy at the hospital to unpack them. It wasn't until Cheryl had started work on the house that together they opened all the crates and set out the furniture.

Her lot consisted of two complete bedroom suites of Queen Ann design. It contained a formal dining room table complete with six dining chairs and matching hutches, along with four Queen Ann side chairs. Amy was amazed at how similar her taste in furniture was to both of her grandmothers. She'd immediately fallen in love with every piece.

Cheryl had reupholstered all of the chairs in a variety of rich gold, peach and moss coloured fabrics. She'd painstakingly coordinated all the fabrics to bring both rooms alive in colour.

Amy fell in love with this house the first time she saw it. It was everything she wanted in a house. It felt like it belonged to her as soon as she opened the front door. While it was brand new, the builder had taken the time and expense to ensure the finishes and details resembled homes built in the late 18th century that lined both sides of her street. Rich hardwood floors, fabulous deep trims on the windows and floor boards, arched windows and entries to rooms, rounded corners, and amazing oak mantels on three fireplaces, one in the formal living room, one in the great room off the kitchen, and a third in the master suite. The elements of classic design mingled enchantingly together with the traditional, and all the modern conveniences, bells and whistles had been discretely provided. Amy fell in love with its simple elegance. The house was expensive, but was perfect. She loved that her house fit in with the homes in this established and elegant neighbourhood.

Cheryl had worked off and on for almost a year finishing all the rooms and the results were worth every minute and every penny. Every room is now completely finished and while the rooms could be featured in design magazines, each has Amy's personality designed into it. Amy seriously hopes that she'll be able to fall in love with someone as quickly and completely as she has for her dream home.

Now that it's finished, Amy rushes home to spend time enjoying her reading nooks and has plans to start hosting dinner parties for her friends and colleagues. Although Amy never really spends a lot of time on the phone with her friends, she remains close to a few from Riverside and her friends from both school and university, along with her cousins. She renewed her friendship with Sophie when Sophie returned to the city. It was a wonderful surprise to learn of her appointment to the hospital board and her job as CEO. They spend time together on their days off and enjoy lunches and breaks at the hospital.

Growing up with Ann and Ed, she couldn't t help but have friends. It's always been so much a part of her life, it's just second nature. She left these friends behind for so long, but over the past year, Amy's found these friendships as a great support to her. Since her mother's death she's come to appreciate her friends and their patience with her.

Amy's erratic and hectic hospital schedule has never left much time for a social life. However, in recent weeks, Amy's tried hard to reduce her time at the hospital so she can spend extra time with her dad. She's also trying to make a real effort to renew her relationships with her old friends. She realizes entertaining is Item #9 on her to do list. Amy's decided she should begin to work on her list not only to appease Jake but also because of this promise she made in her dreams. Hopefully she'll begin to understand why her mother spent so much time making these lists for her loved ones. Amy hopes she'll receive a great satisfaction when each of her tasks is completed and she can stroke it off the page.

Amy's thoughts are interrupted by the chiming of her door bell. She smoothes her hair one more time as she passes the foyer mirror. She checks her watch; Christopher's actually a few minutes early. He's certainly changed his old university ways, must be something to do with having to be on time for clients.

Christopher hands her a bouquet of flowers, "As I left my hotel, there was a shop with these just outside the door, I couldn't resist, I know how you like red roses."

"A rose by any other name," Amy smiles as she takes the bouquet. Amy has no idea where Christopher got the idea she likes red roses. Personally she's not a fan of red, favouring the pink shades instead. "Come in. I have to confess, I haven't spent any time researching movies. Maybe we should just choose once we get to the theatre."

Christopher follows her into the kitchen as she gets a vase for the flowers. "Your house is amazing, a real cry from that studio apartment you lived in when you were going to Yale."

"Would you like the full tour? Cheryl's finished and I am very proud of the final results. We probably have a few minutes before we have to leave for our reservations, right?"

As she tours Christopher upstairs and down, she proudly points out all the antique pieces she received from her grandparents. Christopher's impressed. He's now beginning to realize he may have a problem as he'd planned to convince Amy to come out to Toronto and see his place, intending to get her to move out there permanently. He has a large condo loft located right in the heart of downtown Toronto. It's a bachelor pad, but Christopher had hired a design team to fix it up. He likes the results, everything's very modern and sleek, nothing like this very traditional home that Amy has. Their tastes are really different, but he shrugs it off; he believes he'll be able to get Amy to move when the time's right.

"Maybe I can convince you to cook a meal here. You could invite Jake and Victoria and put your cooking skills to the test," Christopher smiles. "I remember the meals you used to prepare in that little studio. I was always amazed at what you could do with just a few ingredients, especially your omelettes. Those were the best after the late classes. I'd be starving and you always invited me to share your dinner."

Blushing, Amy agrees, "That's a great idea; let's plan something for later this week. If you can find out what night works best for you guys I'll see if I can get someone to cover me since I'm on call this week at the hospital."

"We should get going if we want to fit a movie in after dinner," Christopher moves to the door.

"I haven't seen a show in a long time and I must admit I've got no idea what movies are even showing, but I've got my phone so I can check on the way." Ann grabs her purse and jacket. Once outside, she sets the coded door and leaves.

"I see you have a remote security system. Good idea." Christopher looks around the neighbourhood. "This looks like a pretty secure area."

"Actually, there's a family across the street and their son's a police officer. I see the car there quite regularly. I've never met him, but his mom and dad are really nice people. They've welcomed me to the area. They brought over homemade stew the first night after the movers left. I really like them."

"Food is still a big winner in your life, I see." He jokes as he opens the door of his rental car for Amy to get in.

"If I offer to bring dessert when we have dinner with Jake and Victoria does that move me up a notch or two on your list? Christopher laughs at his attempt at a joke.

"Maybe" is Amy's reply.

Amy decides she'll call her mother's best friend Joyce for some dinner ideas either later in the evening or after she does her Sunday rounds at the hospital. She hopes it'll be quiet at the hospital since she has several items she wants to start work on.

Earlier in the year, at the financial board meeting, Amy had spoken to the board of the need to add another doctor to her team. With this addition finally in place, it's given Amy the luxury of having two days off in a week, something that she's never had since taking this job.

As Christopher backs out of the driveway, the neighbour's son drives up in his police cruiser. Amy thinks he looks familiar, they both wave.

"Well, at least you'll have a quick response if you ever need help," Christopher comments as he drives down the street towards the Keg.

Amy's amazed at how quickly the evening passes. Before long, they realize it's too late to go to a movie, so they sit back to slowly eat their dessert. It's been a great evening with both of them taking time to catch each other up on their latest happenings.

As they leave the Keg, Christopher's clearly not in too big of a hurry to let Amy go. "I hope you're not disappointed we missed the movie. We could still catch the later show if you like."

"No, I actually enjoy just talking; it's been such a long time since we sat and laughed and gossiped. Besides, I want to get to the hospital early and finish rounds. I've some yard work that I'd like to get done." They continue discussing the yard as Christopher drives Amy back to her house.

"If you're trying to impress me, you already have. I love the front of your house, those flowers and the pathway with the solar lights. It's so welcoming with the twinkle of the lights. My loft does not have a front yard like this, but I do have a roof garden with potted plants. Of course, I've a plant lady who makes sure they survive."

"Well, if you think the front is nice, come with me through to the back of the house. Dad's come by several times to help me get the garden set up in the back. After a lot of hard work, I'm finally almost finished there and I must admit his touches and advice have made a huge difference."

Arm and arm, they walk through the archway into the back. All of the solar lights are on and the entire yard feels alive. Amy feels pride in what she has achieved with lots of help from her father.

"Do I hear running water?" Christopher's amazed at how much work Amy's done in this huge back yard.

"Yes, actually that's our latest project. We finished it off just a few weeks ago. If you look to the back you'll see a series of small waterfalls. Once we cross this little bridge you can see the water plants. I actually put some fish in it, but they will probably die off this winter." Amy points out all the features of her yard.

As they turn to head back to the house Christopher stops in total amazement. Amy has an outside dining and living room, completely enclosed in a lattice that's encased in green vines, which runs the entire width of her house. Twinkle lights hang around the deck and are intertwined in the lattice work. Huge pots with large palm trees surrounded by cascading flowers of pinks, yellows and whites are situated along the deck and flank the stairway up onto the deck and house. He can see a massive barbecue with a kitchen on one side and tables and chairs in another grouping, with still another area featuring loveseats and comfortable chairs. She has flood lights to highlight several large trees that surround the yard. Off to one side he can see several apple trees with chaise lounge chairs under them.

"Where do you find time to work on such a massive yard?"

"Well, most of it has been created to be as maintenance free as possible. When I need help, Dad usually comes to my rescue." She laughs, "I try to spend time out here every evening. I find it helps me relax after a hectic day in the O.R. It's still warm out, would you like to sit out here under the stars and share a glass of wine?"

"That'd be great." Christopher makes his way to the loveseat and sits down.

Amy goes over to her small outdoor fridge and pulls out a bottle of white wine. She picks up two glasses and walks to the loveseat. She sets the glasses down and goes back to turn on her outdoor stereo unit. It comes alive with her mother's favourite songs.

"A couple of years ago, Jake and I bought mom an IPod and we chose all her and dad's favourite songs from the past. I kept a copy and I've found I actually enjoy the oldies," Amy explained.

"Hey, don't feel you have to apologize, I love these songs. Victoria shakes her head at me, but I can't get into the heavy metal music or those rap songs or Victoria's opera music." He reaches out and opens the wine for Amy, pouring them each a glass.

"I'll just have a small glass, since I see your neighbour's son's still visiting. The last thing I need is a DUI charge."

"So true, you've no idea of what I see come into emergency every day. If people who drink and drive had to spend time in our ER and trauma units I bet we could reduce offenses substantially."

She sits next to Christopher and they quietly enjoy the beauty of her yard and the collection of great songs.

Amy's phone rings out, breaking the mood. As she rises to answer it, Christopher checks his watch; he is amazed that they've been out in the yard for almost an hour.

"Jake says he's been trying to get in contact with you, Christopher. Have you shut off your phone?"

Amy hands her phone to Christopher. She only hears one end, but it appears Jake's been trying to reach him. It seems there is a problem with their transaction and he needs to get back to the office right away.

Christopher and Amy enter through her back door. They walk straight to the front door.

"I wish I could stay longer, but I better make quick time back to the office. It seems we have an emergency with my client. It amazes me; some of these guys never take a day off."

With that, he kisses Amy goodnight and sprints to his car. Amy waves goodbye. She notices her neighbours outside and she waves at them as well.

Amy cleans up the wine glasses and brings in the remaining wine. Pouring herself a glass, she picks up her IPad and sits down in front of her family room gas fireplace to start to review two new medical reports and a couple of journal studies she has downloaded from her office earlier. The flicker of the light adds to her mood of relaxation. As she goes to sit down she spots a penny on the floor. She picks it up and smiles. "*I love you too mom,*" she thinks to herself.

Before she finishes, she sends out a quick invitation to both Victoria and Jake to see if they're free on Thursday for dinner at her house. Both respond almost immediately that they'll be there.

Chapter Four

Amy's up early the next morning. She runs out the front door to pick up her paper. Grace is outside watering her flowers. Grace and Richard Henderson are her neighbours who live in the house directly across from Amy. Their house is a charming turn of the century two storey colonial style that's painted pale blue with white accents. It's surrounded by lovely old weeping willow trees and several flower beds containing a floral array of lilies, large peonies, baby's breath, and annuals such as begonias, bachelor's buttons, petunias and pansies. They have both recently retired and have welcomed Amy into the neighbourhood. Grace waves and wishes Amy good morning. Amy walks over to admire her flower beds.

"You sure have some lovely flower beds; I particularly love these deep purple lilies. I never knew lilies could be this colour." Amy bends down to smell the flowers. "Lilies are my favourite."

"You know, in the spring, I'm planning to split this plant, it's growing too big for its britches. Would you like half of it?" Grace smiles as she watches Amy. *Why can't Andy find a nice girl like this to settle down with?* She wonders to herself.

"Really, I'd love that. I usually steal plants from my father, but he doesn't have this shade of lily, only white and yellow ones." Amy replies.

"So you're off work today," Grace inquires.

"Sort of, I have to make my rounds at the hospital, but then I plan to take the afternoon off." Amy folds her paper in half.

"Well, you have a nice day." Grace's finished watering. "I'll put a note in my book to remind myself about the lily plant. Without lists I'd never get anything done."

Amy smiles, "My mother used to have lists all the time. In fact, before she died, she made me a list to follow after she was gone. Made my brother and father each their own lists too. Some of the things on my list make me laugh, like her Item #15 clean out the fridge before an onion spoils and smells up the whole kitchen. But some of them make me think, like Item #21 remember to colour coordinate the flowerbeds."

"Now that's a good idea; I might have to do that myself. My Richard is a good man, but I would shudder to think how he'd function without me cooking and cleaning for him." Grace bends down to pull a weed she spots in one of her meticulously groomed flower beds.

"Dad says Mom's list keeps him going. I think Mom felt the same as you." Amy smiles. It's still painful to talk about her mom and she hopes Grace doesn't notice.

Grace grins. She sees the bit of moisture form in the corners of Amy's eyes. "Well, unfortunately, we spoil our men folk a little too much. The girls today are smarter than we were back when we were first married, a woman's place in the kitchen and all that sort of thing. You girls have careers and great opportunities. I had a choice of a nurse or a teacher and since I fainted at the sight of blood, I figured teaching was the job for me. Richard and I met at university. He was getting his degree in dentistry. Now after forty five years it's time to focus on the plants. I wasn't sure about retirement, but Richard and I have found a way to enjoy ourselves. Of course, Andy drops by regularly; he thinks because we're retired we've become incapable of functioning for ourselves."

"Oh, Grace, I think you love it when your son drops by. You love to fuss. I bet you make his favourite pie just so he comes over," Amy winked.

"What is your favourite pie, that way I can get you to come visit and have tea one evening." Grace clearly wants a woman's company. "My daughters aren't close enough to drop by, Cindy lives in Vancouver and Joan is out in the middle of Saskatchewan. Cindy is a dental hygienist. Her husband is a police officer for the City of Vancouver and they have two little girls, Faith and Sherry. Now my other daughter Joan, she lives in Yorkton, Saskatchewan. She teaches and her husband's the city fire chief. They have no children yet, but Richard's hoping for a grandson. Andy's my baby. He's great to have around, but I sure miss my girls and our girl talks. It'd be nice to have company to talk about shopping and makeup."

"Well, I don't need pie to drop by for a visit. How about you come over later this afternoon and visit me. I have a chocolate cake I made the other night. I need help finishing it off. However since you asked about pies, I'm partial to apple pie."

Grace agrees to meet later and Amy turns and heads back to the house. She'll have to hurry or she'll never get back in time to get the pond cleaned out.

Amy's glad she's got such a light patient load today and she returns home quickly. Amy's just finishing all her tasks when the back gate opens and Grace announces herself.

Amy made her call to Joyce earlier to get some ideas for her dinner plans. Joyce gave her several good choices and promises to email the recipes. Without much thought to what she's doing, Amy's making her grocery list and another list to make sure she doesn't forget something. She's been sitting outside enjoying a tall glass of homemade iced tea.

She pours Grace a big glass of iced tea and cuts two pieces of chocolate cake with big dollops of vanilla ice cream. They sit and enjoy each other's company. Amy realizes how much she misses her mother's company and their talks. Grace misses her daughters. She tells her all about them and her two granddaughters. They have had such a good time; they decide they'll meet for lunch on Tuesday at the hospital. Amy gives Grace her card with her numbers so she can call when she gets to the hospital.

Chapter Five

Amy spends Wednesday night setting up her table and preparing her meal for Thursday. Jake and Victoria have agreed to come along with Christopher for dinner. She's decided to cook roast pork tenderloin, following Joyce's favourite recipe. She's made the fresh apple sauce and cole slaw, and cooks tender green beans with mushrooms in a cream sauce. Amy likes to have most of the work done so she can enjoy her guests, a little trick she learned from her mom.

Joyce gives her wonderful ideas for appetizers. Amy decides on a simple roll using soft red and white coloured tortilla shells. She spreads spinach dip over several soft white tortillas, inside she places either shrimp, slices of ham, or sweet red pepper strips. With the red shells, she spreads flavoured chip dip, preferring the dill flavour. In these she rolls shaved turkey breast. She rolls each shell up into a tight roll and covers each in a film of plastic wrap and puts them in the fridge. Tomorrow she'll slice them diagonally and place them on a white serving dish, with alternate rows of each type she has made. She'll add a bowl of salsa dip for added flavour. They are so easy to make and so attractive.

Not sure that Christopher will remember to bring dessert; Amy decides to make her mother's favourite, Pecan Ganache. Using crushed pecans as the base instead of pie crust, she only needs three ingredients so it's fast and incredible satisfying. It's the perfect dessert for the evening since Amy's able to make it the night before. Amy realizes there's one more item to strike off her mom's list: she has finally mastered her mother's favourite dessert without overcooking the chocolate.

Setting the dining room table is the most fun for Amy. She gets out her grandmother's fine china. Her grandmother had several sets of china. Amy guesses she must've inherited some from her mother as well as sets from her father's family. With choices of four complete sets of twelve place settings in each pattern, she chose the Royal Albert Val D'Or and Alberta Rose sets for herself. Jake had let Amy make her choices since he's really not fussy about dinnerware. He ends up with Old Country Rose and Royal Doulton Baroness Dinnerware for himself. Amy wonders if Jake has even unpacked the boxes of china, much less actually used them.

Grace has told Amy to pick a bouquet of her purple lilies so Amy decides to set up the white and gold of the Val D'Or and accent the table with shades of mauve and purples. She sets out her two formal crystal candleholders that her mother had bought her for one of her birthdays. She's found some mauve candles for them. She also found very nice pink and mauve linen napkins in the hospital gift shop.

Ready for the following evening, Amy decides to read a book that Grace had given her about handling lilies. She picks up a glass of milk and the last piece of chocolate cake and sits down in the living room to enjoy the remainder of the evening.

Amy settles down in front of the large bay window at the front of the house. As she finishes her last bite of cake, she notices Andy drive past in his own car. He flashes the lights as he sees her. She responds with a wave and a smile.

Later in the week Grace meets up with Amy for lunch at the hospital, she spends time talking about Andy. She's concerned he hasn't found a girlfriend. She sounds just like Amy's mom, and they joke about it.

Grace enjoys having lunch together with Amy. Amy has to admit, it's fun to meet someone outside the hospital for lunch. Once in a while, she meets up with Sophie for lunch, but normally she just grabs a sandwich and eats in her office while catching up on the endless supply of paperwork.

Grace confides how much she misses the action and bustle of the school. Amy suggests that Grace could consider volunteering at the hospital, maybe doing something with the children. Grace decides she'd like to work with the premature babies and young moms. Amy agrees that Grace would be great with new moms and that it might be the perfect place for her to spend some time. She gives her the name of the volunteer co-ordinator and suggests Grace give her a call.

Amy promises to think about other projects Grace might like to work with and they talk about it as they plan their next get together. Grace invites Amy over for lunch on Sunday after church.

Later that evening, Amy reflects on her time with Grace before she decides to sit back and read for a while. She remembers the printouts her father showed her and Amy puts away her book and decides to jot down some notes. She puts the ten steps she read from the study guide into her IPad and sets up a spreadsheet of all the steps. She then decides to put the dreams down on paper so she can start to dissect the dreams. With the information ready, she's set to begin work if she is lucky enough to have quiet time on the weekend.

Amy glances at her watch and decides to head off to bed for an early night since she knows tomorrow will be late by the time her guests leave and she cleans up.

Chapter Six

Amy rushes home from the hospital with less than an hour to put the finishing touches on her dinner and take a quick shower before her guests arrive. She completed her list last night before she went to bed and has everything ready so the evening will go smoothly. She is learning to rely on lists and is beginning to feel closer to her mother as she begins to understand the significance and ease of having lists. Even with her eidetic memory, she finds the lists help to ease the stress of missing something.

Amy puts the roast in the oven to cook. She gets the rest of the meal organized and ready to heat and serve. The salad and garnishes are dished up and she gets the bowls, platter and spoons ready to be set out. The wine and refreshments are chilling.

Amy runs upstairs and hops into the shower. She quickly dresses in the peach outfit she wore to her parents' 50th wedding anniversary. Tonight is the perfect evening to wear it again. Putting on her lipstick, she hears the bell on her stove signalling through her intercom system that it's time to add the sauce to her roast. She grabs one of her mother's aprons and puts on her matching heels. Moving down the stairs, she admires her table. She just has to dim the lights and light the candles.

Putting the final touches on the meal, Amy pours herself a glass of wine and puts on some music. As she takes a sip, the doorbell rings. She takes one last look in the kitchen to make sure it looks presentable to her guests.

Surprisingly, it's her brother and Victoria. Jake gives his sister a big hug and presents her with a bottle of his favourite wine. Victoria has brought a beautiful box containing her favourite Swiss chocolate bonbons.

"Wow, you finally finished the house," her brother looks around. "You better send Cheryl to see me; I need some work done on my place, although I'm not sure I want to wait as long as you have to get it finished."

"Jake, after mom died, I just had to take my time. I relied on mom's ideas and advice and it took me some time to get motivated into getting the job done. I'm grateful that it was Cheryl who pushed me to move forward and finally get the job finished."

Jake moves through the room and admires the art. "Grandma Green sure had great taste in art."

"She had even better taste in the furniture." Victoria admires the fine pieces she sees in the entry, living room and dining room. "This is exquisite."

"I have similar furniture, but mine is sitting in the spare bedroom in huge wooden crates. I'm waiting to decide whether I want to remodel my condo or find something already finished, maybe a house with a nice yard." Jake moves into the living room and plants himself in the chair by the window. "This chair is really very comfortable. Do I have one like this?"

"Actually, you should have two; they're probably in a really awful shade of green. Cheryl had these reupholstered." Amy brought them each a drink and set her plate of appetizers on the coffee table.

"Have you decided if you want to rent or buy?" Amy asked Victoria.

"Well, for the time being I'm still living out of a suitcase at the Westin. It's close to the office and I don't really have to do anything, but I have to admit I need to make a decision about my condo in Toronto. It doesn't make sense to keep it if I'm spending all my time here in Calgary. For now, I need to concentrate on this merger. Once it's finished, I'll take some time and decide which office I want to be located in."

"I'm going to do my best to convince her that Calgary has everything and more to offer." Jake winks at Victoria as he takes his drink from Amy.

"Don't bother sitting down, I see Christopher driving up now," Victoria announces as she picks up one of the shrimp rolls. "These are delicious." She pops a second one into her mouth.

Jake reaches for one for himself. "I better try one before you eat them all," he jokes with Victoria.

Victoria makes a face at him. Amy notices how much they enjoy each other. Jake reaches over and gives her a peck on the lips.

Amy opens the door before Christopher rings the bell.

"Wow, you're waiting for me, I feel so special," he drops a kiss on Amy's lips as he hands her a bottle of champagne. "I thought we might toast your new house. I have a small housewarming gift."

He hands Amy a long slender box. Amy looks at him inquisitively. "Nothing special, just a little something I'm told every home needs so I hope your house doesn't already have one."

Christopher takes the bottle into the kitchen and puts it into the fridge to stay cool. Amy follows with her little gift. She opens it and to her delight it contains a small silver candle snuffer.

"What the heck is that thing?" Jake picks it up.

"It puts out the flame of a candle, something I've been looking for but never seem to remember to pick up for myself." Amy takes it away from Jake.

"Why not just blow out the candle like I do?"

"Probably because she has her nice furniture and doesn't want candle wax blown all over it?" Victoria comes from behind to answer.

"Your taste in gifts has improved with age." Victoria picks up the candle snuffer to admire the delicate flower pattern embossed on its silver handle.

As Amy hands Christopher his favourite drink, Christopher walks towards the double glass doors. "Have you guys seen her back yard?"

With that, he hits the switch to turn on the outdoor lighting system that highlights all the features of Amy's back yard. He remembered Amy doing this the other night when he was over. Victoria and Jake both move to the window to admire the view.

"No wonder Dad spends so much time here," Jake teases. "I always hear him telling me about coming to your place. I had no idea what you two have been doing with all that time. Now I see. This is pretty amazing."

"You might need to rethink your idea of food preferences," Victoria taunts Jake. "Maybe you need to make some chocolate cake for your dad and offer some pizza and beer to his friends instead of golfing with them."

"It was Item 12 on Mom's list, keep dad busy with projects," Amy jokes, "Fountains, streams, running water, all things dad had to research and learn about. I think mom's had a couple of good laughs at the two of us struggling knee deep in mud and water."

Amy organizes dinner as her guests entertain themselves touring the yard and house. She's proud of her dinner and can't wait to have them try everything she's cooked. She notices that Christopher did forget to bring dessert and she's glad she made something that turned out so well.

Victoria returns to the kitchen and offers to help. With nothing left to do, they talk about the upcoming charity fashion show Victoria is volunteering with, handling ticket sales. It's for the local women's breast cancer foundation. "I'm glad Jake convinced me to work with this group. I'm meeting really nice people and having fun. It's something to do besides work."

Victoria convinces Amy to buy the last full table of eight that she has left. Amy decides she'll invite Grace and Sophie along with her mother's friends, Connie, Cheryl and Joyce. "It is really hard to decide who to invite, but I think my neighbour Grace would enjoy getting out and mom's friends have been so kind this would be a nice thank you for all they keep doing for dad. I'll probably ask a couple of other friends to come to fill up the table."

"That's a nice gesture," Victoria comments. "The nice part about being out here instead of in Toronto is having all these friends, I know more about your parents and their friends than of my own. I never really knew any of my mother's friends." She looks sad for a moment, but then perks back up. "I'm not sure about the fashions, but I know it'll be a fun event. I've worked with some of the folks who have organized the commercials on TV for the show. It was easier than I thought once I convinced one of Jake's hockey friends to introduce me to some TV people to put some advertisements on the air for me. We also have a couple of local comedians and some great music. Calgary's really full of some pretty amazing talent. We've only had to advertise twice and the tickets are pretty much sold out. Sure has made things easier for me. Last year I heard they still had tickets and empty seats that night. I'm glad I held a couple of tables back for late comers and friends."

Dinner's ready; Amy and Victoria carry the bowls and plates to the table. The men join them. After grace, Amy enjoys the camaraderie of her guests. She again notices how Victoria and Jake just seem to fit together. They laugh as they finish each other's sentences. She also realizes she doesn't have that same rapport with Christopher.

Christopher helps her carry the dirty dishes back into the kitchen. Amy pulls the Ganache pie and ice cream out of the freezer. "Oh my gosh! I forgot, I was supposed to bring dessert, why didn't you remind me?" Clearly embarrassed, Christopher grabs Amy's hand. "Please forgive me for being such an inconsiderate jerk."

"It's okay, I made this and decided if you didn't remember, we'd still have desert, and if you did remember, we'd have a snack for later. No big deal"

"Thanks, at least let me carry it back into the dining room for you." Christopher takes the tray and carries it out.

"You forgot the dessert, didn't you?" Victoria smugly grins. "You told me earlier in the week you were handling dessert; I wondered if I should remind you or let you forget.'

"Good thing for us, Amy plans for the unexpected." Jake picked up his dish. "Mom's favourite too. By the way, if there's any left, I'll store it in the fridge at my place."

"Actually tonight has allowed me to strike off two more items on mom's to-do list: first, mastering her famous dessert, and second, to start entertaining my family and friends." Amy is proud of her accomplishments.

Amy leaves Jake and Victoria discussing the left over dessert as she pours tea and coffee and everyone sits back to finish off the dessert.

"Amy, this was a great meal, Mom would've been proud of you." Jake smiled, "Here I thought you never paid much attention to domestic chores, Mom always did everything for us. When did you learn to cook?"

"Mom always let me help her, but to be honest, I called Joyce for some menu ideas."

As they retire to the living room with their cups of coffee and tea, they continue to talk about the events of the week. As often is the case, they discuss politics and science.

Amy's enjoying the evening when suddenly Victoria yawns. "Are we boring you, Sis?" Christopher asks.

"Sorry, I didn't get much sleep last night; I was busy preparing a brief for today. I'm so sorry Amy, but I'm exhausted. Do you mind if Jake takes me home?"

"Of course not, it's almost midnight and we all have to work in the morning." Amy's surprised at the time.

With that Victoria and Jake get their coats and say their goodbyes. "See you at the fashion show, if not before. And thank you for such a great evening. The food was great and the company was equally great." Victoria hugs Amy, Jake squeezes her arm.

"Do you want me to stay and help you tidy up?" Christopher asked.

"No, thanks for the offer, but Victoria and I tidied up the kitchen while you and Jake were discussing your clients," Amy answered.

"I'm so sorry about that, I didn't even notice."

"Not a problem, we enjoyed ourselves and it's not a lot of work."

Victoria's yawn has proven contagious and Amy now struggles to hide her own yawn. Christopher also admits he's tired. "It's late, I've got to get going as well, and we have a breakfast meeting at the office. I leave back for Toronto on Saturday morning; can we get together tomorrow night?"

"I wish I could, but I have a presentation to make to the board tomorrow night. How about I take you to the airport and we have breakfast before you leave?"

"Sounds great, I'll call you tomorrow to make arrangements." With that, Christopher gathered Amy in his arms. "This was a great evening. I love spending time with you." He kissed Amy.

As he leaves, Amy waves, and closes and locks the door behind him. She leans against the door and wonders if Christopher could be her soul mate. She goes back into the living room and picks up the cups and saucers. She tidies up the last few dishes and puts the kitchen and dining room back in order. All the time, she's thinks about Christopher's kiss. She wishes her mother was still here; Amy so badly needs to talk to her as she realizes she missed out on some serious dating talks that she should have had with her mother instead she was always busy dissecting frogs.

Amy shuts off the lights to the back yard and the kitchen. She walks through the dining room, hitting the switch to the chandelier that hangs over the table. The lights twinkle as they fade out. Amy's happy she can cross off a couple more items from her mom's list. She reminds herself to focus on a couple of other tasks on the list.

As she passes into the living room, she sees Andy's cruiser pass by. As usual, he flicks his lights and Amy waves back. She watches him drive away until he leaves the street. She walks up the stairs and at the top shuts off the lights to the living room and foyer. She must remember to tell Cheryl how much she appreciates the extra lighting she had the electrician install during the decorating. Checking her watch, she's shocked to see it is almost 1 o'clock in the morning; this is going to make getting up hard. She tells herself as she moves to the bedroom to get ready for bed.

Chapter Seven

The alarm clock wakes Amy out of a dead sleep. Jumping out of bed; she bounds straight to the shower, muttering to herself about how dark it is outside. Amy races down the stairs in record time. She hates being late for rounds, Friday's especially when most test results appear on the patient charts, which allow patients to go home for the weekends. She has several family conferences scheduled after rounds.

Not bothering to even make coffee, Amy grabs her coat, bag and keys to head out the door. As she opens the door, she sees an ambulance in front of Grace and Richard's house. Next to the ambulance is a police cruiser with lights flashing.

Forgetting about the time, Amy rushes over just as the EMTs are loading Richard into the back of the ambulance. She looks for Grace. Andy appears next to her.

"What's going on?"

"Dad collapsed this morning while Mom was getting her keys to take him to the hospital."

Before Amy has time to say another word, Andy grabs her arm and pulls her towards the police cruiser. Grace is already sitting in the back seat of the car, tears streaking down her checks. Amy climbs in and folds her arms around Grace. Andy shuts the door and jogs around to the driver's side. He hops in and follows the ambulance.

Amy struggles to locate the seat belt, pulling it around her. Grace is quietly praying, her face telling the story.

"Please Lord; do not let my precious Richard die." Grace prays, repeating the same prayer over and over.

Andy introduces himself and quickly explains to Amy that he received the call from his mother; she'd already called 911 for the ambulance. He was just heading to the precinct so he turned around and headed straight over. He'd just put his mother in the car when Amy arrived. By then the EMTs were loading his dad to head for the hospital. Apparently, his father had complained of severe headaches before he collapsed. Grace was getting him organized to drive to the hospital. She'd left him to walk to the garage to get into the car while she ran back upstairs to get her purse and keys. When she came down the stairs she found him collapsed on the floor in the hallway.

Amy's had just a quick look at Richard, but it's enough for her to know that he's not in good shape.

Amy pulls her phone out of her pocket and sends a quick text message to her assistant. *Julie, I'm heading to the ER, I'm going to be late for rounds.*

Andy adjusts his rear mirror and he meets Amy's eyes. Amy can see the pleading in his eyes. "It's okay Grace; I'm going to be right there with Richard as soon as we get to the hospital." She provides Grace with a reassuring hug.

"When we get to the hospital, Andy, could you please take your mom to the waiting area? I'll make sure someone will keep you informed on what's happening with your dad!"

Changing the subject Amy looks at Andy, "Have we met before, you look familiar to me?"

"Actually, I stopped you a while ago; you were in a hurry to get back to the hospital and pulled a u-turn in the middle of the street. I happened to be going over to visit the folks and thought you were some wild impaired driver."

"I remember that, I had a bad feeling about a patient and needed to get back to check on him. Thank you for not giving me a ticket." Amy smiles into the rear view mirror back at Andy.

They round the corner and Andy drives straight up to ER behind the ambulance. Amy's amazed at how quickly they've arrived. It seems like just a couple of minutes, she checks her watch and sees it's taken less than 6 minutes, good timing for emergency situations when time is critical. As soon as the cruiser stops, Amy opens the door; Andy's already at the door, surprised, Amy looks into his eyes. They're the most amazing colour, she thinks as she gazes into his face. For a second, it feels like time is standing still. Amy shakes herself back to reality. This is definitely not the time to be flirting; she's mad at herself for these unexplained feelings and shakes her head at herself in disgust.

"You go ahead, I'll bring Mom." Andy gently helps his mother out of the car. She's still quietly repeating her prayer to God.

Amy heads for the ER. The staff has been in constant communication with the ambulance. They're already reviewing the first EKG reports. They have equipment ready. Early indications suggest Richard's suffering from a brain aneurysm. They have the MRI ready and have called the neurologist to be on standby, ready to review the results. Dr. Robert McMullen, the head of neurology happens to be in the ER this morning. Amy checks in with him to see if he has any results. He's able to confirm that Richard has indeed suffered a leaking aneurysm. There already appears to be significant bleeding into the space closely surrounding the brain and they have alerted the OR and are now preparing a team for surgery. Dr. McMullen's preparing to meet with Grace and Andy to update them and arrange for the necessary paperwork authorizing surgery to be complete. Amy takes a minute to explain that she's a neighbour and friend to the Henderson's.

As they talk, Amy's pager goes off; there's a patient coming in that requires her immediate attention. "Please let Grace and Andy know that I'll check in with them as soon as I'm free." Amy hurries off to her patient.

Amy keeps her promise and as soon as she has finished her emergencies and rounds she heads back to meet Andy and Grace. It's been over three hours since Richard was brought in. Amy checks at the OR desk and discovers Richard's still in surgery.

Amy finds Grace and Andy sitting in a small waiting room near the OR, each with a cup of coffee in their hand. Grace sees Amy coming and rises to greet her.

"Have you heard anything?" she asks as she receives a quick hug from Amy.

"No, I just checked and they're still in surgery. But Richard's got one of the best surgeons in Canada working with him. The hospital's been very fortunate to attract some of the best talent, mostly because we have a great research centre for head trauma," Amy explains.

Grace tells Amy that Andy's called his two sisters. Cindy should be arriving from the airport in a few minutes and Joan and her husband are driving in from Yorkton. It's a seven hour drive, so Joan will not be at the hospital for several hours yet. She's been calling and texting every half hour to check on her father.

Andy gets Grace to talk to Amy about the two girls that Cindy has. Grace is such a proud grandmother she quickly starts telling stories about the girls. She gets her key chain photo album and shows off the two girls.

They are just starting grades one and two. Amy and Andy keep Grace occupied until a younger version of Grace appears around the corner. Grace sees her and immediately the two women embrace. Tears are rolling down Cindy's face as Grace welcomes her.

"I came as soon as I could," Cindy says as she wipes her face. "How's Dad?"

"We're still waiting for him to come out of surgery." Andy gets up and walks over to hug his older sister. "Sorry I didn't meet you at the airport."

"No, don't apologize; Mom needs you more right now." Cindy turns to see Amy.

"Hello Doctor, I'm Richard's oldest daughter, Cindy. How's my Dad?" she assumes Amy has come to report since she has her hospital ID on her white jacket.

"Cindy, this is my neighbour, Dr. Amy Murray. She lives across the street from us," Grace introduces her. "She saw the ambulance and came right over this morning."

"Nice to meet you, Dr. Murray." Cindy extended her hand and shook Amy's hand.

"Please call me Amy."

Amy starts to move towards the door to let Grace and her children talk. "No, please stay," said Andy. "I hate to have to explain all the medical terms by myself and I'm not sure if Mom's really been listening that clearly."

Dr. McMullen saves Amy from responding. He's just finished the surgery and has come to provide Grace with an update. "Mrs. Henderson, your husband has been taken to recovery. He'll be there for some time. Right now, he's stable. I've clamped two aneurysms. One had developed a slow leak and was bleeding into the brain. We've stopped the bleeding. The second aneurysm was smaller and we clamped it as well." He guides Grace over to the sofa and sits her down, taking a seat beside her.

"You need to know that the next twenty four to forty eight hours are critical as we monitor for hemorrhagic stroke and any brain damage. Once your husband has been moved into the ICU I'll check on him again. I have another surgery in just a few minutes, but someone will keep you informed."

With that, Dr. McMullen excuses himself. "Dr. Murray, I'll see you at the board meeting later today." Amy nods and smiles as he leaves.

"Perhaps you'd like to go down to the cafeteria for some lunch. You need to keep your strength up; the last thing Richard needs is for you to get sick on him." Amy reassures Grace, "I'll let the staff know they can find you downstairs if you like."

"Can I give you my cell number and they can call or text me if they need us?" Andy suggests.

"That's a good idea," Cindy says. "To be honest, I haven't had anything to eat and I'm starving. Mom, did you have breakfast this morning?"

Grace shakes her head, "I want to stay here. You can bring me something."

"Actually, Richard will probably be in recovery for at least an hour, maybe even longer, so you have lots of time to go down to the cafeteria. When you're finished you can go straight up to the third floor, to the Neurology ICU. There's a small waiting room, just inside the doors. That would be the perfect place to wait," Amy proposes. "There's nothing you can do sitting here right now."

"Well, since you put it like that, it seems we may as well go for some lunch. Would you like to join us?" Grace invites Amy to lunch.

"I wish I could, but I have a presentation to finish for a board meeting later today. I can meet you later though. Besides, Cindy just arrived and she needs to spend some time with you and Andy."

Together they walk to the elevator. Amy's office is on the second floor and she gets off after agreeing to meet up with them a little later.

Amy spends the next two hours in her office, catching up on reports and completing the work for her presentation at the board meeting. She's ordered a turkey sandwich from downstairs and eats at her desk as she works. With everything completed, Amy changes into her navy blue business suit, combs her hair and touches up her makeup. She still has an hour before the meeting, so she decides to pop down to see how Richard's doing.

Amy stops by the Nurses Station at the Neurology ICU. She works with the staff on a regular basis and knows most of them well. She finds out that Richard is back from recovery. They're monitoring him carefully.

As Amy's talking to one of the nurses, Andy comes out of the elevator. He's accompanied by another duplicate of Grace. This must be Joan.

"You sure look different when you're not wearing your hospital scrubs." Andy stares as he realizes how absolutely breathtaking Amy is.

"Why thank you kind sir." Amy smiles, "You must be Joan." Amy reaches out her hand to Joan.

"I look that much like my mom?" Joan grasps Amy's hand. "Mom's told me so much about you. You're much younger than I expected."

Andy changes the subject. "Are you going out on a date this evening?"

"No, actually I have to attend a budget meeting with the hospital board. I thought I'd drop by for a minute to see how your dad's doing."

"Which room is dad in? I'd really like to see him." Joan's anxious to see her father and exhausted from the drive.

"Of course, your father's just across from the nurse's station," Amy points.

"Only two can be in the room at a time, so I'll wait." Andy goes on, "You need to prepare yourself, he's got lots of swelling in the face." Joan nods as she heads to her father's room.

"Amy, please be honest, have you seen his chart? What should we expect?" Andy moves closer to Amy for a quiet conversation.

"I've not seen his chart, but his doctor's one of the best and I've got total confidence in Dr. McMullen. I expect he's taken time to fully brief your mom and you about the risks," Amy replies.

"He mentioned possibility of a stroke and infections," Andy acknowledges, "but I guess I just needed to hear it again."

"If there's any indication of stroke or heart problems I'll probably be called, but your dad's strong and so I'm praying for God's will. My mother always tried to drill it into my head that doctors are not God but only earthly creatures and not ever in control. As much as we'd like to think different, she's right in that regard."

Grace appears in the doorway and immediately moves towards Amy, who wraps her arms around Grace and gives her a hug.

"It's so good to see you." Grace releases Amy. "I thought I'd let Cindy and Joan have a few minutes together with their father."

"Are you OK?" Amy's concerned and Grace already looks exhausted. She knows even with no complications Richard's facing a long recovery.

"I'm fine. Cindy and I went down for a bite to eat awhile ago, but Andy has not taken time to eat anything." Grace turns to Andy. "You've been here all day, I feel like I've abandoned you."

Andy chuckles, "Mom, I'm a big boy. When I get hungry, believe me, I eat. However, now that you mention it, I could use a snack. Would you like to come downstairs with me?" He asks his mother.

"No, I'm going into the waiting room to spend some quiet time. But why don't you and Amy grab something. I'm willing to bet that she's not eaten lately." Grace looks towards Amy.

"Well, actually, I was going to grab a sandwich on the way to my meeting." Amy confesses.

"Then it's decided, Andy will take you down for a bite to eat. I hate to eat alone and I know you feel the same, so now you've got company." Without waiting for a response from either of them, Grace moves towards the waiting room that's located right next to Richard's room.

"Let me just check with the nurse on one of my patients. Do you want to meet me by the elevator? I'll just be a minute." Amy wants to check with the nurses before she leaves the floor.

With a smile on her face, Amy turns to the Nurses Station where Edith, the head shift nurse, has been watching.

"That police officer sure is easy on the eyes," jokes Edith, "If I wasn't married and was ten years younger you'd have some competition."

"Competition – what are you talking about?" Amy absently questions as she reviews the chart of a patient Dr. McMullen's asked her to keep an eye on.

"Oh come on, don't you see how he looks at you? Why don't you come back after your meeting and check this patient then? I'll call if we need you. I'd hate to keep such a good looking man waiting."

Amy gets to the elevator just as the door opens. "Perfect timing," she grins up at Andy, "Thanks for waiting."

He's tall, Amy notices, not realizing earlier that Andy is well over 6 feet. She smiles, "Actually, I had a sandwich sent to my office after rounds so I'm not starving, but I do want to grab something to eat. I never go to a meeting on an empty stomach; bad for nerves."

"I thought that might be the case. Mom tells me you have a busy schedule and don't eat properly."

"Why do mothers always worry about the food intake of their children?" Amy jokes.

With that, Andy takes her arm, "Lead the way and we can fill our tummies. I know my mother and she's smiling to herself about how smart she is. She's constantly playing matchmaker on me. This time I have to agree, she has great taste in choosing a wonderful, talented and beautiful friend."

Together they head for the cafeteria. Dinner rush hasn't started yet, so it's relatively quiet. They each fill their trays and find a place to sit.

"Thank you for buying me dinner, I can pay my own way, you know."

"I know, but I have a vested interest in keeping you healthy." Andy smiles and it takes Amy by surprise.

"You have the most amazing smile, it lights up your face." Amy puts another fork full of potatoes and gravy into her mouth. "I knew I was hungry, but this food actually tastes good, so I must be really famished."

Both Andy and Amy are used to eating quickly, and in short order their plates are empty. They sit back and share their work with each other. Amy's amazed at how easy Andy is to talk to and it feels like she's known him all her life. She finds she has shared more of her life with him than anyone she can remember and in such a short time. Andy has also easily shared his life with her.

Amy's pager goes off and reminds her that she has to head to the board room for her meeting.

Reluctantly, Amy realizes she has to leave. "I guess I'd better get to my meeting. I'd hate to be late to the finance meeting when I'm looking for more funds for my department." Amy's enjoyed herself and would love to have had more time to spend with Andy.

"Don't forget, I brought you here this morning. Just drop by Dad's room when you're ready to leave and I'll drive you home," Andy reminds Amy.

"Wow, I completely forgot that, it's been a long day. But I'll just grab a cab to go home."

"No way, I'll drive you home, no ifs, ands or buts on this one. I'll wait in Dad's room until you come."

As they walk down the hall, Amy concedes, "OK, I'll come to the room when I'm finished, I want to check in on him as well as another patient. Thank you again for dinner."

Amy checks her pocket; she has her memory stick ready for the meeting. Fortunately Amy does not use notes once she has prepared her presentation. Her photographic memory serves her well in these situations.

"Good luck on your presentation," Andy turns to head back to his father's room.

As Amy heads to the meeting, she realizes she has a smile on her face. *I can't believe, I'm actually looking forward to a ride home with a policeman.* She chuckles to herself before she heads towards the board room ready to face the board members.

Before she enters the room, Amy stops, adjusts her jacket, smoothes her hair, and takes a deep breath. Even though she's completely prepared for the meeting, she finds entering the board room intimidating.

As she stands by the door, her friend and Hospital CEO Sophie comes up behind her. "Who's that gorgeous hunk of man you were eating with in the cafeteria? Every woman in the room was drooling. You're the most envied woman in this place. It was all I could do to keep myself from running over to your table to meet him."

"Oh Sophie, quit being so dramatic. Sometimes you amaze me." Amy hates to hear that people gossip like this.

"I'm just teasing, I've never seen you look more beautiful and he's such a handsome man, you make a striking couple." Sophie smiles as she witnesses the different shades of pink cross her friend's face.

Sophie changes the subject to get back to business as she sees other board members approaching. "So are you ready for the budget meeting? Everyone loves your reports, no rustle of paper, you can answer all the questions without having to refer to notes and you aren't boring."

"I still get nervous. You know I practised on Mom and Dad and Jake for my first presentation. I saw their eyes glaze over as soon as I started. Mom suggested perhaps it was because they weren't medical professionals and didn't understand the technical details of my talk. That's when I realized that most of the board members aren't medical professionals, but elected politicians. So I changed my presentation to ensure it would apply to everyone." Amy still has sweaty hands and is looking for a wipe from her pocket as she speaks.

"That makes sense; perhaps I should suggest that to the rest of my presenters." Sophie thought about it. "Well those that are worthy of funding," She clarified. "Also helps when you look into their faces and smile."

"Well, it does help with quick recall. I still follow Mr. Hatfield's directions on memory capture to this day. I really do miss him; I loved him as a teacher and a mentor during high school and university. My eyes still mist when I think about him." Amy walks with Sophie into the large board room.

The room fills up quickly with men and women carrying huge briefs of financials and reports. Amy feels a bit light as she takes her seat after passing her memory stick to Edna, the secretary responsible for the paperwork for the board. "All my reports and financials are here for you." She smiles as she receives a grateful acknowledgement from Edna who appreciates not having to scan or type all the notes and scribble she usually gets from doctors. "Can you set up my presentation for the screen?"

"No problem," Edna replies, "Here's the remote for the projector."

Sophie calls the meeting to order and the presentations begin.

Chapter Eight

Amy's finished her presentation and she's satisfied with her performance; she's been able to answer all the board questions and has seen several board members nodding in agreement as she speaks.

As she sits down, she finds a penny on the seat of her chair. She picks it up with a smile and pops it into her pocket. She knows she did a great job and believes her mom would be proud of how comfortable she has become around her peers. Dr. Church begins her report on her maternity department. Each doctor's expected to stay as the other departments do their reports, so the board room is full.

Suddenly, her pager goes off, along with Dr. McMullen's pager. 911 for both of them; they both quickly excuse themselves from the meeting and head upstairs to the Neurology Unit.

Dr. McMullen checks and learns it's Richard Henderson; he's in full cardiac arrest. They hurry to the unit and find a team working on him. They both spend the next hour trying to stabilize his heart but are not successful. They clock his time of death and Amy takes the responsibility to tell his family who have been moved to a private waiting room.

Amy stops outside the closed door of the waiting room to say a prayer asking God to help her choose the right words. Still feeling very raw from her own mother's death, Amy knows this will be very difficult, especially since she has so many feelings for Grace and now, she's discovered, for Andy as well.

As Amy enters the room, Grace knows by the expression on her face that she's not bringing good news and rushes to Amy in tears. Amy hugs Grace as she explains that they did everything possible to save Richard but they weren't able to save him. It was his time and God has called him home.

The hospital Chaplin arrives and they spend time together in the room before they leave for home. Grace goes home with Cindy, Joan and her husband. Andy takes Amy home.

It's been a long day for Amy and she's totally exhausted. Not only did she have the stress of the board meeting, but now another death and her own pain has resurfaced.

Andy and Amy don't talk much on the way home, both deep in their own thoughts and pain. As Andy drives up to Amy's house, Amy feels she needs to say something.

"I'm so sorry I couldn't save your dad. We tried everything medically possible. We just couldn't keep him stabilized," Amy explains.

"I just had a feeling when I was alone with dad earlier; I actually said my goodbyes to him. I think he knew his time was near. We had a good last conversation, which I'll remember all my life." Andy looks over and gives Amy a quick smile.

"You're lucky, I was in surgery when mom's heart stopped and didn't even have my pager with me to hear it go off. I know there was nothing I could have done to save her, but I never got to really say goodbye," Amy confesses.

Andy reaches over and holds Amy's hand. "It's nice to at least share the pain with someone who understands."

As they continue to sit in Andy's patrol car in front of Amy's house, Andy asks about how she's been able to handle losing her mother. She confides in him that the pain's still very fresh and she doubts she'll ever lose the pain, but rather she's learning to live with it, one day at a time. She tells him about the letter and the to-do list her Mom left her. She manages to joke about the humorous items on her list like the reminder to help her Dad clean out the cupboard under the sink in the bathroom and to make sure he has food in the fridge.

Amy tells him what she'd been taught by her mother. "Remember the poem *Footprints*? My Mom had it framed and hung on the wall in her kitchen. I saw it every day and I never really paid that much attention to it until after she died. God and my brother and father, I lean on all of them at different times to get me through the sad days. It's the most painful thing I've had to go through in my life. But I know as a doctor that everyone must die eventually, we just never get an appointed time so we can fully prepare our family. Death does indeed come like a thief in the night."

"I appreciate your honesty. I could see in your eyes today with Mom that this has brought back a lot of pain for you as well."

"If you ever want someone to talk to, you know where I live." Amy opens the door before Andy can get out of the car.

"I'll take you up on that," Andy promises.

They wish each other good night and Andy spins a U-turn and parks in front of his parent's house to help his family prepare for the final farewell of his father. As Amy walks towards the house she finds penny on her front step. She picks it up and blows a kiss to the sky. She takes the penny inside and places it in a jar in the kitchen where she has started saving all the pennies she continues to find. She truly believes each penny is a message of love from her mom.

Chapter Nine

Amy checks her messages. She has several messages that she needs to deal with. Christopher has called to confirm he'll meet in the morning at 7AM for breakfast before he leaves back to Toronto. She sends him a quick text that she'll meet him in the lobby of the hotel at the airport.

It's still early in the evening, but even though it's been a long day Amy's not ready to go to bed. She heads out into the kitchen to check her fridge for ingredients to make a pot of stew. Luckily, she finds onions, celery, carrots, and potatoes, and she pulls out a big round steak from the freezer. She turns on her stereo and finds comfort in cooking. She reflects on her parents as she busies herself with her stew. She's surprised when she realizes she's made a huge roaster full of stew. She'll take some of the stew over to Grace tomorrow. She sees there are several cars parked in the driveway and down the street. Richard was a well known dentist and both he and Grace have so many friends.

When she finishes putting the stew together, Amy decides to make some cookies. She calls her Dad to see if he plans on driving in this weekend. She teases him with some raisin oatmeal cookies and he decides to come in after church on Sunday for dinner with her. She phones Jake to see if he wants to join them.

Amy's up bright and early the next morning to meet Christopher. They've agreed to meet at the Airport Hotel Restaurant. He has to drop off his rental car and this works great for both of them.

Amy spends the next two hours listening to Christopher before he heads back home to Toronto. He's got several meetings there and will be heading back again to Calgary to continue to work on his current transaction. Christopher's excited about a new client, again a large oil and gas acquisition. It seems their reputation as successful lawyers in the field of acquisitions and transactions has spread and they're becoming very busy. Amy has no idea how successful her brother has become. Christopher's so excited about this new opportunity that he doesn't notice Amy's quiet. She's still upset about the events that have taken place over the past twenty four hours. She shares her pain from yesterday and she's surprised and disappointed by Christopher's lack of understanding. He fails to comprehend the struggle to keep a patient alive and the sting of losing one. For Amy, the time doesn't pass fast enough as she feels he just doesn't care about her feelings. Christopher tells her he'll be back in a couple of weeks and they agree to get together when he returns. He asks if she would consider coming out to Toronto to spend some time meeting his friends and seeing the sites.

Christopher wants to take some holidays and spend time showing Amy off to his friends and co-workers. He also wants to arrange dinner with an old family friend to see if Amy will consider a job change. Knowing Amy, Christopher's aware he needs to tread lightly, but he hopes he can push with just the right motivators to get her to budge and move to Toronto.

Amy promises she'll check to see what she has for holidays. Maybe it would be fun to take a week off and go out to Toronto Even though she is not fond of the city it's still time away. She hasn't taken any time off since Jake and her father took her with them on a cruise last Christmas. She hadn't wanted to go then, but when she got home she realized how refreshed she was. In the end, she was glad she went. Amy promises she'll have some information when he calls later.

Heading to the hospital to make her Saturday morning rounds, Amy makes a mental list of things she plans to do today. She has a few things in the yard that she wants to get finished before the snow falls. They've had a fabulous fall, but the end of October is close. She also wants to carve a couple of pumpkins while her dad's there to help, so she needs to stop to pick up the pumpkins and treats for the kids.

Later in the afternoon, Amy takes her pot of stew over to Grace. She's watched for a quiet time between visitors. Joan answers the door and welcomes her inside. Grace is looking through picture albums with her granddaughters. Cindy's busy in the kitchen. She comes out and takes the roaster of stew.

"Thank you so much, we have so many fruit and vegetable platters, but this hot stew will be perfect. I was just starting to look through the fridge to see what I could make for dinner. I'll just make a few biscuits, a quick salad, and we'll have dinner ready. You're really thoughtful."

Grace introduces Joan's husband Philip and Cindy's husband George to Amy. They spend a few minutes discussing the weather and Halloween.

As Amy hears car doors, she realizes Grace has more company. Joan walks her to the door and tells Amy the funeral for her father will be on Tuesday at 2:00 PM at the Baptist church around the corner from the hospital. Amy says if they need anything else, just call.

Back at her house, Amy gets started on her fall work in the back yard. She finds it very relaxing to work in the dirt and talk to her fish in the fish pond. She's concentrating on her work and doesn't hear the gate open. She's startled when Andy starts talking.

"Were you just talking to your fish?" Andy asks.

Before she can answer he continues. "Wow, this yard is something else. Mom said it was pretty amazing, but this is beyond amazing." Andy's taken back by the yard.

"You startled me. I wasn't expecting anyone." Amy rises from her flower garden, wiping the sweat off her brow.

"Sorry, I didn't mean to frighten you; I needed to get away from the insanity over at the folks' house and took a chance you'd be home." Andy grinned. "Looks like you could take a break; you've worked up quite a sweat."

"I guess I have, would you like to have a glass of lemonade. I was just thinking to myself it must time to stop for something cool to drink. It's such a beautiful day; I didn't want to waste it inside." Amy moved towards her back deck.

"Well, if you can afford the time to take the break, it sure would be nice to just sit and talk." Andy followed Amy. "Did you do this by yourself?"

"Actually Dad and I worked up a design, he's come in several times to help me get it from our rough sketches into what you see here. I did most of the digging myself. Since the house was a new construction, the back yard hadn't been packed down, so the digging for the most part went fairly fast and was relatively easy.

For the next couple of hours, Amy and Andy sit back and just enjoy each other's company. They talk about their jobs. Amy's surprised to learn that Andy has both a criminal justice degree and law degree.

"Once I got my law degree, I decided to join the City Police Department. I thought there were enough lawyers to defend the criminals and a shortage of those who pursue and arrest them. I applied for the City Police because I didn't want to be transferred around the country like some of my friends who joined the Royal Canadian Mounted Police. Actually, I start a new job at the beginning of January working with the white collar crime unit. It's a new unit set up to handle more professional crimes, like computer and internet fraud and thefts, and insider trading at the security houses."

"Your parents must be so proud." Amy refreshed both glasses with lemonade.

"Well maybe now, but when I first decided to become a member of the force my parents were furious with me. Not using my education, and all. So, actually, I never told them about the recent promotion. I was going to surprise them this weekend with a celebratory dinner, but plans have changed." Andy frowned. "I guess I should've told them."

"I understand, there were so many things I now wish I'd told my mother, but at the time I thought I needed to spend all my time making sure she didn't worry about me. I think that may have caused her to worry more." Amy paused, "But, maybe not. I think my mother liked to worry; she kept lists to keep herself organized so she had more time to worry."

"Well, that would explain all the lists my mother keeps." Andy lightened the mood. "Dad called her lists his "honey do" lists. He would put them off until Mom would get mad and then he'd spend a whole day doing nothing but the things on the list."

Amy switches the discussion back to Andy's job. She's fascinated by his work and loves to see his face light up as he talks about what he'll be doing.

They truly enjoy each other's company and are shocked when the automatic lights in the back yard start to flicker on as dusk approaches.

Andy is startled and checks his watch. "Wow, look at the time! I've kept you from finishing your task."

"Actually, I'm pretty much finished for now. I need Dad's help to take down the vines; it's a two person job. These vines are wonderful during the summer. They keep the heat out of the house and it's really nice to sit out here in the shade, but in the fall when the leaves die off it's a lot of work to get them down." Amy's disappointed that Andy's leaving.

"Well, why didn't you say something, let's get it done right now. I've some time and I need to keep myself busy." Andy jumps up and is ready to get to work.

"Are you sure? It's not something I was going to work on today. I was hoping to con Dad into helping me when he comes for dinner." Amy's feeling uncomfortable about taking advantage of Andy's offer.

"Where's your ladder?" Andy's determined to get started. "If we hurry, we can have this done before it gets really dark."

Amy goes off to get the ladder and gloves. "Be careful those vines can issue a nasty bite on bare hands," Amy warns.

Together, they make short order of the job and in no time they're finished. Andy's putting the last of the leaves and branches into the recycle bins when his phone rings. It's his sister, Joan, wondering where he is and why he's missed dinner. He explains he's helping a friend and forgot the time. He'll return later in the evening. Amy notices he doesn't tell his sister where he's at.

"Well, since you missed your dinner, looks like I should at least feed you," Amy teases. "Do you happen to like Chinese?"

"Are you kidding, it's my favourite food. I love Chinese, I know this great place and it delivers. Not that I'm starving or anything," He quickly adds. He pulls out his cell phone and scrolls down until he not only finds the restaurant, but also its menu.

They quickly decide on what they want and finish up ordering. Andy and Amy are both covered in dust so they decide to eat at the kitchen nook rather than on the good furniture. Amy had given Andy a tour of the house earlier. It seems Andy owns a house about 15 minutes away, within walking distance to his precinct.

After dinner arrives, they talk about Andy's father and his funeral. Andy's giving the Eulogy and wants to reflect on his life. Amy talks about what she remembers from her mother's funeral and how she and Jake spoke about her. They talk through the meal and before long the plates are empty.

Amy learns a lot about Andy and his family. It seems, like her parents, Richard and Grace were wise with money and taught their children well. They took advantage of the good interest rates with some inheritance money and all three of the children were able to pay for their education with funds left over to purchase properties.

Amy tries to hide her yawns. After all the work in the yard she realizes she's really tired. Andy sees the yawn. "I better get home. I expect tomorrow will be busy with so many of dad's friends dropping by after church to see how mom's doing."

Amy walks Andy to the door. He leans over to remove a piece of vine out of her hair. Amy looks up and Andy very slowly moves forward and gently kisses her on the lips. Amy feels her entire body come alive from the tip of her toes to her lips. All too soon, the kiss is finished.

"Would you be interested in going to the movies or maybe bowling?" Andy hesitates, but hoping for a positive answer from Amy.

"I'd like that very much," Amy softly responds.

As Andy leaves, Amy stands at the door, watching. Andy turns and waves. Amy's sure she sees the curtains move over at Grace's house.

As has become a habit, Andy blinks the car lights as he leaves the street and Amy waves. Amy heads upstairs, dusty and tired. She wishes her mother were still around to talk to. Maybe tomorrow she'll ask her father how he knew when he had found the right person.

She grabs a quick shower and as she gets ready for bed she finds yet another penny on the floor in her bathroom. *Mom, I sure hope you're telling me you like him too,* Amy talks to her mother. She heads off to bed and falls asleep almost as soon as her head hits the pillow.

Chapter Ten

Sunday and Monday pass quickly and it's Tuesday, the day of Richard's funeral. Amy takes the day off as she knows the emotions she feels aren't just for Grace and her family. Her own feelings are still raw.

Amy's asked her dad to come with her to the service. Ed had already planned to offer to go with Amy, knowing how difficult this will be for her. Ed has a feeling Amy wants to talk to him about something, but he's never been good at knowing how to start, so he decides he'll do what he always does and wait for her to ask. Hopefully, after the funeral, they'll have some time to just talk. Ed's right when Amy suggests they have some coffee after the funeral luncheon is finished.

The waitress has taken their order, and Ed slips his coffee. "Richard was a pretty amazing man. I think I would've liked him; we could've been friends," Ed comments.

"Dad, everyone you meet is your friend, that's the kind of guy you are." Amy smiles.

Dad, I'm sorry I put you in such a difficult situation, but I'm really grateful you came with me. It was harder than I thought it would be." Amy dips her tea bag in her pot before she pours her cup full. "I saw you talking to Grace."

"I gave her a few bits of advice I have learned. I told her it doesn't get easier and the pain doesn't go away, you just learn to live with it." Ed still mists over as he speaks. "No sense telling her something that's just not true. I had enough of that at your mother's funeral."

"I'm sure she appreciated your honesty." Amy squeezes his hand. Her father's never been known for his diplomacy when sharing his thoughts.

"I sure like her son Andy, I think he likes you, you know, not like a brother, but maybe something more serious." Ed leaned over and teased, "You're blushing." He laughed out loud.

"Dad, really," Amy looked down. *Now is the perfect time to ask the question*, she thought to herself. "Dad, seriously, how did you know mom was the one for you?"

Ed's face lights up. "The moment I laid eyes on her, I just knew, but the first time I kissed her, my soul came alive. I felt like I was awakened from a deep sleep. I could hardly wait to see her again and I thought about her every waking moment. I'm amazed I finished college."

"Did Mom feel the same way?"

"She always told me she did. She said I made her body tingle from her toes to her nose. It was our little joke." Ed starts to reminisce.

Amy lets her father talk. It gives her time to sit back and listen to the stories. She has heard them all before, but now she's listening to see if something in the stories will trigger some answers to the questions Amy has. She wishes she'd had the opportunity to ask her mother these questions. Amy has never felt the emotions and feelings she has right now and she's confused about how to move forward.

Ed doesn't ask any questions. He can see that Amy has some decisions to make and he knows if she needs his advice she'll ask. He just hopes somewhere in his lists that Ann has provided the answers he's supposed to give to Amy. He can't remember seeing it, but he'll read the lists and notes again just in case he missed something. She left him several envelopes he hadn't yet opened, one for when each of the kids gets married and another couple for the births of their first children. Ed figures he has enough to do just getting the stuff done in the current package.

Amy mentions that she bought a table for the fundraiser that Victoria's working with. She's invited Connie, Cheryl and Joyce along with Grace and her two daughters to join her table; she's also inviting Sophie.

Ed shares with Amy that Jake and Victoria have been out to see him on several occasions. He mentions that Jake seems pretty taken with Victoria.

Like his wife, Ed's hopeful both of his children will settle down soon so that he can play with grandchildren while he can still bend down.

Chapter Eleven

Having taken the previous day off, Amy's up bright and early back at the hospital to check up on her patients and check her messages. After her rounds she heads to her office and, as she works, hears a knock. Checking her watch she sees it's still early.

"Come in." Amy rises to move towards the door. She's surprised to see Sophie at the door.

"What a nice surprise, come in." Amy moves towards the chair and the couch, but Sophie takes a chair across from Amy's desk.

"We need to talk," Sophie comes right to the point. "I received a surprising call yesterday and I'm disappointed you wouldn't talk to me about your decision."

Amy is caught completely off guard. "What are you talking about?" she demands.

"I received an inquiry from the Department of Cardiology at Toronto General Hospital, seems you've applied for a position at the hospital and they called to set up a schedule to review your personnel records with me." Sophie's voice is very sharp and Amy can sense she's very angry.

"What are you talking about? I would never leave Calgary and apply for another position. I love my job here. Are you sure they meant me?" Amy's shocked by what she's hearing.

"Are you serious? You did NOT apply for the position?" Sophie moves forward. "I received a call yesterday afternoon to arrange a conference call with the head of their department and the hospital CEO. Are you sure you didn't suggest you might be looking? Even in a conversation?"

"I'm dead serious; I haven't applied for any job anywhere." Amy looks totally confused. "I love my job, I just finished my house, and I would never leave Dad to go somewhere else. Not now, not ever and I have NEVER spoken to anyone!"

"I was so hurt to think you'd do something like this without talking to me first." Sophie begins to relax. "I need to call Dr. Johansson and get some more details."

"Can I be there when you make the call? I'd like to know how this happened." Amy asks, "What time are you planning to call?"

"Let's do it right after my meeting. Come to my office at say 9:45 and we'll make the call together." Sophie gets up and moves towards Amy and hugs her. "Thank you for not leaving. I'd miss you so much, as a friend and colleague."

Amy returns the hug, "Like I told you, not a chance of me leaving."

Sophie leaves for her office and Amy puts on her hospital jacket to run down to the lab to check on some test results. She starts to think about who would've done such a thing. Her mind keeps going to Christopher, but she hopes he has more respect for her than that. Perhaps it's just a mix-up of some kind.

Amy finishes up at the lab and gets to Sophie's office just in time. Sophie's assistant offers Amy a cup of tea, advising Amy that Sophie's just finishing up a call and will be with her in just a few minutes.

Amy sits down and checks her messages. Nothing urgent - a reminder from Victoria for the charity event and a note from Christopher.

He arrived in Calgary last night with meetings scheduled for today. He wonders about meeting her for dinner. Amy sends a quick email message to Connie, Cheryl and Joyce to confirm meeting at her house. Amy has suggested the ladies pack an overnight bag and spend the night since it'll be late and she knows they hate driving in the dark. She also sends a message to her computer to call Grace and her daughters once she gets back to her office. She'll remind Sophie after their call. She's about to send a message to Christopher when Sophie opens her office door and invites Amy in.

"I hope you haven't been waiting for me." Sophie's always the professional. "Did Edna get you a cup of tea?"

Edna comes around the corner carrying a tray with a tea pot, two cups and some cookies. She carries it past Sophie and puts it onto the desk.

Amy follows Sophie into the office. "Can you please put the call through straight away?" Sophie asks Edna.

"No problem, I've confirmed the call and it should be ready now." Edna leaves to go back to her desk.

"Thanks Edna," Amy and Sophie speak in unison and both smile.

Sophie pours tea and they both sit across from each other in Sophie's spacious office. The phone rings and Sophie puts it onto the conference speaker system so Amy can participate.

"Hello Dr. Johansson. This is Dr. Sophie Charter. I'm calling with respect to your inquiry regarding Dr. Amy Murray". Sophie pauses for a response.

"It's a pleasure to speak with you Dr. Charter. I'm pleased you responded so quickly to my inquiry." Dr. Johansson has a strong South African accent.

"I also have Dr. Murray with me. I hope that's okay with you. We appear to have some confusion here that we'd like to sort out with you."

"Some confusion, I don't understand."

"Perhaps Dr. Murray will shed some light on it for us," Sophie invites Amy to speak.

"Hello Dr. Johansson, it's a pleasure to speak with you. I've heard many great things about you and your research," Amy begins. "I know you're very busy, so I will not take much of your time. I need to know how you received my resume."

"Actually, I received a very strong recommendation from a very good friend of mine, Christopher Laing. We both attended a dinner party last week and he suggested you'd be moving to Toronto soon and he wanted to help you find the perfect location. I promised him I'd see what I could do. The next day he forwarded your resume, which I must confess is extraordinary. You've had an amazing career already for someone so young." Dr. Johansson continues on, but Amy doesn't hear the rest of the conversation. She's fuming mad.

Sophie asks a couple of additional questions to allow Amy time to regain her control. Dr. Johansson explains his needs and the expertise he's looking for.

When he has finished, Amy speaks. "Actually Dr. Johansson, you have an amazing program and a great unit. However, I'm not sure where Christopher got the idea I'm planning to move to Toronto. It's simply not so. I'm very happy here at the Hospital in Calgary and have no intentions of relocating any time soon."

"That's strange since Christopher's so very excited about your upcoming nuptials and is expecting you'll be moving to Toronto after the wedding." Now it's Dr. Johansson's turn to sound confused. "Have I somehow misunderstood something?"

"There seems to be some confusion, thank you for your consideration, but I'd appreciate you withdrawing my application from your process." Amy tries to sound polite, but she's now become so angry she can hardly think.

"Of course, Dr. Murray, but please, remember my department if you should change your mind and ever consider locating to Toronto."

Sophie continues to speak with Dr. Johansson for a couple more minutes while Amy sits in total disbelief. *What was Christopher thinking? How dare he interfere with my life? I need to go and talk to him right now.*

When the conversation's concluded, Sophie sits back in her chair and takes a deep breath. "Amy, I had no idea your relationship with Christopher is so serious. You never mentioned it, other than a few words in passing."

"That's because I'm not serious about him. It's been a few dinners and movies over the past year when he comes out for business with Jake and Victoria. I never really thought about Christopher in terms of a husband. No, that's not quite true, I did wonder how I'd know when I found the man for me, but I've never done anything to give him the idea I'm serious. He helped me keep busy after Mom died, that's all."

"Well, he must be a whole lot more serious than you are; it appears he's been making plans for you." Sophie wonders if Amy, in her own naive way, misunderstood his intentions. "Could you have misunderstood him or sent him some kind of message to make him believe you want to move to Toronto to be with him?"

Amy's been thinking just that, running their conversations through her head. "No, I was pretty straight with him last time we spoke. He asked if I'd like to come out to Toronto and I told him I'd consider it for a holiday, but I'd never leave Calgary."

"Well you need to have a conversation with him and settle this." Sophie's concerned for her friend. "Perhaps you want to meet up with him tonight."

"No, I want to meet up with him right away. Do you mind if I leave for a couple of hours? I don't want to wait, who knows what else he's done." Amy's growing more annoyed as she thinks about what Christopher's done to her life.

"Yes, you might want to talk to him before he puts your house up for sale." Sophie tries to humour Amy, but without success. In fact, her comments bring an icy look from Amy.

"I'll be back later." Amy hugs Sophie. "Thank you for helping me clear things up with Dr. Johansson."

"Just take a few deep breaths and relax, you don't want to say anything you'll regret." Sophie tries to calm her friend down as she sees the rage growing in Amy's face. "At least take a cab so you're not driving when you're this upset. The last thing we need is for you to have an accident."

"That makes sense," Amy agrees, "I'll catch a cab, I hate driving downtown and a cab will be faster."

"Are you sure you don't want to wait? Maybe think about what you want to say? What if Christopher's tied up in a meeting?" Sophie tries to stall Amy in order to calm her down.

Amy hugs Sophie a second time and leaves her office. Sophie says a little prayer for Amy.

As Amy waits for the elevator, she sends a quick message to Christopher to see if he's available. Unaware of what has just happened, Christopher suggests she meet at the office and they go for a quick lunch.

Amy grabs her jacket and purse and lets her assistant know she'll be back in a couple of hours. Dr. Kowalski's at the hospital and Amy sends a message for him to cover for her which is received with enthusiasm since Amy never asks such things of her staff and Dr. Kowalski's excited to take on the responsibility even for a couple of hours. Amy trusts his instincts and knows he'll not get in over his head in an emergency.

There's always a taxi cab waiting at the front of the hospital and today's no exception. Amy has no trouble getting a cab for downtown. As she sits back, she begins to regain her composure. She moves through a conversation in her head. She still can't believe Christopher would do such a thing and wants to believe there is some sort of reasonable explanation, but she can't think of one.

In no time, the cab pulls up in front of a very tall glass building; Jake's offices are on the 20th floor of a relatively new building overlooking the river. Heading straight for the elevators and up to the offices, Amy takes several deep breaths and asks God to give her patience and strength as she knows this is going to be an emotionally meeting.

Victoria and Jake are standing at the elevators and are surprised to see Amy. Jake takes a step back when he sees his sister's face. She's really upset about something, he thinks.

"Hey, this is a nice surprise," says Victoria, who didn't expect to see Amy. "If you came for the tickets, they are already at your office. I sent them over yesterday."

"No, I came to talk to your brother," Amy sharply tells them, "He's expecting me, I believe."

Surprised, Victoria answers, "Really, he never mentioned anything when we spoke earlier today."

"It's a spur of the moment thing," Amy replies. "Had an interesting meeting this morning and thought he might like to hear personally how it went."

Jake looks astonished. It's not like his sister to come to his offices. In fact, he's not sure when she was there last. "His office is the last door on the left." Jake points down the hall.

With that, Amy turns and walks down the hall.

"Okay, she must be really mad about something," Jake confides to Victoria, "She hasn't walked with that kind of determination in a long time. In fact, I can't remember when I've seen her like this."

"Should we delay lunch?" Victoria's concerned. "Something must be wrong."

"Might not be a bad idea, let's go back to my office and we can watch for her to leave." She does seem pretty upset. Jake decides he might need to help his sister out. He's not sure what has happened to get her so irate, but whatever it is, he decides he needs to be around.

Completely unaware, Christopher's excited that Amy's decided to meet him for lunch at his office. In a whole year, Amy's never met him downtown at the office. He sees her coming down the hallway and moves to greet her.

"Wow, it's so good to see you, I'm so glad you didn't want to wait until after work to get together." He tries to put his arms around her. She pushes him away.

"We need to talk NOW!" Amy spits out, "In your office, unless you want the whole world to know what an idiot you are."

Amy doesn't wait; she's already in his office. As he walks in, she slams the door shut.

"Hey, what's wrong with you?" Christopher's not sure what's going on, but he doesn't appreciate how he's being treated.

"How dare you make up my resume without my knowledge?" Amy's not just mad, by now she's furious and the cab ride here hasn't helped her mood any.

"What are you talking about?" Christopher responds.

"Don't you dare lie to me! I spoke with Dr. Johansson this morning. Why would you embarrass me like this? I have absolutely no intentions of moving and you know that. We spoke about that when you asked me when we met at the airport before you flew back to Toronto."

"No, you said you'd love to come for a holiday." Christopher tries to regain his composure.

"Yes, for holiday, but not to live there. You know I would never leave my job here; I love it at the hospital. I love my house, but most importantly you know I would never leave my father alone." Amy tries hard not to raise her voice, but finds it very difficult to try to control her emotions.

"Amy, you have to give me a chance. I did it because I love you. I want to marry you." Christopher fumbles in his pocket. "I bought this to give you tonight." He opens the ring box and sitting front and centre is an enormous, ugly, diamond solitaire ring that sparkles vibrantly in the bright lights of the office.

"No, you did it because you're trying to manipulate me into doing something I'll always regret." Amy pushes the ring back at Christopher. "I don't love you and will never love you, not the way my mom and dad loved each other. My dad would never have hurt my mom like this."

Amy moves toward the door to leave. "I never want to see you again."

Christopher grabs her arms, "Amy you don't mean that, you know it's the best thing for you to come back to Toronto with me."

Amy twists around and pulls Christopher's arm into his back. He cries out in pain. As she lets him go, she turns to face him, "Don't ever come near me again, do you understand."

Not waiting for an answer, she leaves Christopher as he nurses his arm.

Jake sees her leaving and catches up to her. "Amy, are you all right? Come with me, let's go downstairs and have a cup of tea. I can't let you leave like this."

Victoria stands in the hallway, she sees the pain on Christopher's face but she also sees the anger and rage in Amy's. "What have you done to hurt Amy?" Victoria turns to speak to her brother.

"I did what I did because I love her; she's too stupid to see that." Christopher moves back into his office. "Leave me alone."

Victoria turns to leave as she sees him lean over and take a bottle of Scotch out of his desk. "You are just like our father," She barks at him as she leaves. "All you care about is yourself!"

By now, Jake and Amy are in the elevator. Victoria decides to give them a few minutes before she joins them. She knows Jake will take Amy downstairs to the restaurant. It'll be crowded, but they have special privileges that the firm pays dearly for. It means there's always a table for them should they need to entertain a client without notice.

Jake and Amy ride down the elevator in silence. He needs to give Amy some space to calm down. Whatever it is, he knows Amy will talk to him if he allows her time.

The Maitre d' leads Jake to a table in a corner away from the crowds. He seats Amy and Jake orders tea for both of them.

Amy hates silence, but Jake's determined to let her speak first. Finally Amy starts, "Do you know what Christopher did?"

Jake quietly answers, "No but whatever it was, you're certainly upset, do you want to tell me about it?"

Amy takes a deep breath and starts to share with her brother the events leading up to her outburst at the office. When she's finished, she looks into his eyes. She has tears forming in hers but she refuses to let one tear fall.

"I'm not sure why Christopher would do such a thing, but I can see why you're so upset. Would you like some lunch before you go back to the hospital? Personally, I'm starving, but it's up to you."

"Do you have room for one more," Victoria hesitates as she arrives and wonders if she should've come.

"Please, join us," Amy extends the invitation.

"Whatever my idiot brother's done, please don't hold me responsible." Victoria holds Amy's hand. "I never want our relationship harmed."

"Oh Victoria, you've no idea, but I want you to know I'll never let my problems with Christopher come between our friendship and your relationship with Jake." Amy smiles as she looks first at Victoria and then at Jake. Jake seems to breathe a sigh of relief.

The waiter comes and they place their orders. Amy then recounts her story to Victoria. She finishes when their salads arrive. Having told the story a second time has helped to calm Amy down and she begins to regain her composure.

As they eat their meal, Amy finds herself relaxing and enjoying her company. She's still angry with what Christopher's done and knows she'll be angry for a long time, but she also knows that eventually she'll make peace with him, for no other reason than for the love she has for her brother and Victoria.

Victoria looks at her watch and jumps up. "I'm sorry, but I had no idea where the last hour went. I've got to get over to the banquet hall and start working with the rest of the volunteers. Amy, you're still coming tonight?"

"Of course, I have a table full of friends that are looking forward to a great meal and an abundance of entertainment. They've all seen the TV Ads and can't believe we're lucky enough to have tickets. Connie, Joyce and Cheryl are having a sleep over at my place. Grace and her two daughters are coming. Sophie's meeting me at the convention centre. We'll have a great time, I'm sure. I'm not going to let what happened with Christopher ruin tonight."

"Don't forget to bring your cheque book; we've got some fantastic silent auction items as well as the live auction." Victoria hugs Amy and rushes off.

With that, Amy gets up and Jake leads the way out of the restaurant and back to the elevators. He gives his sister a peck on the cheek as she leaves the building having spotted a taxi right outside. As she gets into the taxi she finds another penny on the floor of the car. She picks it up and quickly slips it into her pocket. As she plays with the penny in her pocket, Amy can feel a sense of calm come over her. Amy heads back to the hospital to finish her day before she goes home to get ready for the fundraiser. She has three scheduled surgeries for the afternoon and she checks her emotions at the door as she enters the operating room to start work.

Chapter Twelve

As Amy drives up to her house she sees a big blue van parked in front of the second stall of her two car garage. She smiles, recognizing the van from the days Cheryl hauled items back and forth during her renovations. She also notices several other vehicles on the block. *It has been busy for Grace*, she thinks to herself, as she drives into her driveway and into the garage.

She opens her garage entrance to her house to hear the ladies laughing and joking as Cheryl takes them on a tour of her favourite design job. Amy's so glad to have such a wonderful distraction since she's had over a dozen messages from Christopher on her cell phone. He sounds like he's been drinking and Amy isn't interested in any further conversations with him.

"Hello Honey, I'm home," shouts Amy as she follows the sounds of her guests.

Not missing a beat, Cheryl replies, "Did you have a good day at the office? Can I fix you something to drink?"

Laughing together, they hug. "I didn't realize how much I miss you guys, especially you Cheryl. Maybe I should try to find you a job with one of the neighbours so we can spend time together again."

"I've already assigned everyone their rooms and I have given them the grand tour." Cheryl continues to smile and joke. "It's like a college sleepover and I haven't had one for some time, so I plan to have some fun tonight."

"Bert put the seats in Cheryl's van so we can all go together. We figure with Grace living across the street maybe we'd be able to convince her son to drive us so we don't need to have a designated driver," Joyce announces. "I hear her son's a very handsome man, so it might be nice to have a chauffeur for the evening."

"I'll call Grace and see if I can find a driver for us." Amy dials the phone and speaks with Grace. Of course, Grace volunteers Andy without a moment's thought. She hollers to Andy in the background that he needs to change his poker plans for the night.

Everyone's looking forward to a fun night. Ed's told them about Grace's loss and they all have plans to help make it a fun night for Grace and her two daughters. They ask about the daughters. Amy fills them on what she knows about Cindy and Joan.

Amy checks the clock and realizes they're going to have to change quickly. They all scramble to their respective rooms to change. Amy changes into an elegant mock wrap dress with a side accent pin. The jersey fabric cascades gently over her trim body. The bright red is not a colour she would ever have picked for herself, but her mom had convinced her to try it on. It brought out the emerald colour of her eyes, she remembers her mother telling her. Amy pulls her hair back into low bun at the base of her neck. Her hair and the classic lines of the dress make for a very sophisticated look. She steps back to check the mirror and quickly slips her feet into a pair of black, classic, leather heals. She's satisfied she looks good; it's not evening wear, but not a boring business suit. On schedule, the front door bell rings. She rushes down the stairs.

She hears Joyce and Connie in the living room. Cheryl is right behind her. Together they answer the door to see Grace and her two daughters. Andy's standing back. Amy invites them in and makes the introductions. There's a light mood and everyone's looking forward to a fun evening of laughter and friendship. Amy stands back as the ladies grab their coats and head for the van. Andy teases as he guides his harem of beauties to their chariot. Amy leaves the inside lights on and locks the door. She hurries to catch up.

Andy helps everyone into the large van and drives towards the Telus Conference Centre where the Fashion with Compassion Charity Event is being held. The event is one of the highlights of the Fall season and the Breast Cancer Supportive Care Foundation of Calgary puts on an excellent event. Along with a terrific fashion show showcasing the latest designs by up and coming local designers, the organizers have brought in great performers and an outstanding array of entertainment. It's sold out and every woman is thrilled to attend.

The ladies in the van are all sharing their thoughts on the meal to come and Joyce focuses on discussing dessert with Grace. The two ladies have hit it off and Amy's glad. Grace needs the company and Joyce has spent the last year mourning the loss of her best friend. Connie, being much younger, has clicked with Joan and Cindy. Amy's sitting in the front with Andy. They've both noticed how well the women have already bonded. Andy concentrates on driving the large van.

"Sorry, I'm not much company for you here in the front; this van's likes driving a bus," Andy apologizes to Amy.

"That's okay, it's been one of those days, so I don't mind just sitting," Amy replies.

"Did you loss a patient?" Andy inquires.

"No, just had an unpleasant confrontation. I want to put it behind me for the evening, if you don't mind. Maybe we can talk about it tomorrow."

"Sounds like a plan to me," Andy responds as he manoeuvres the large van around the corner.

"Great, I think I'll just eavesdrop on the conversations going on in the back of the bus." Amy winks at Andy who smiles back.

Amy listens for a few minutes, but eventually sits back in her seat and enjoys the ride. Andy's quiet. She's comfortable with the silence between them. It feels right not to have to worry about entertaining him every minute of their time together. Remembering her parents, she recalls how they'd sit together and not say a word. Mom would knit and Dad would watch TV. It always felt good to be in a room with them, it was so tranquil. Amy experiences that same comfort now.

Andy breaks into her thoughts as he whispers, "A penny for your thoughts?"

Amy smiles. "My mom used to say that all the time when she thought I was quiet for too long."

"I guess I'm too much like your mom then," Andy jokes. "We're almost at our destination." Andy raises his voice so everyone can hear, "This is the last stop so please remember to take all your personal possessions. Anything left in the bus becomes the property of the driver."

Everyone laughs. Andy drives up to the passenger loading zone. He parks the van and comes around to open the front door for Amy and the sliding door for the rest. He helps each passenger out of the van. Each lady gives him a peck on the cheek.

"This is the best tip I've ever received. I might just take up driving van for a living," Andy jokes.

Andy makes arrangements to return in a few hours. Arm in arm, the ladies walk into the conference centre, good friends expecting to have a good time together.

Andy gets back in the van. He has a concern he wants to follow up on at the detachment office close by. He swings the van into the police parking lot. He leaves word at the front desk that he's left the van there and heads out to pick up his patrol car to check out the suspicious car parked on Amy's block. As they drove by earlier he was certain there was someone in the vehicle. With so many break and enter crimes in the city he wants to be sure one doesn't happen on Amy and Grace's street.

As he suspects, the vehicle's still there; it appears the driver's sleeping since he's huddled down into the driver's seat.

Andy pulls up behind the vehicle and puts on his lights. A quick check on the plates tells him everything he needs to know. He walks over to the vehicle. Christopher opens the window and Andy steps back; the car and its occupant reek of alcohol.

Slurring his words, Christopher asks the police officer what his problem is.

"Actually sir, I need to see your registration and drivers license." Andy flashes his flashlight into the car.

Blinking from the bright lights, Christopher tells Andy he has every right to be in the car.

In a drunken rage, he slurs as he tells his story.

"I'm waiting for the woman I want to marry to get home. She went out with friends. Today, when I gave her this ring," which he pulls out to show Andy, "she tells me she'll never leave her job and that I'm wrong because I got her the most sought after job in Toronto. She never wants to see me again. She threw this ring at me, right in my office. I've got to talk some sense into her. So go away and leave me alone." Christopher holds up the ring and then drops it into his car. He starts to fumble to find the ring.

"Sir, have you been drinking?" Andy's careful since he's already run a check on the rental and the driver registered with the rental agency. He'd quickly reviewed the driver history the car computer quickly provides on the driver and it appears Christopher has a reputation of being a bully to law enforcement and court personnel. Andy also knows his car recorder runs automatically when the lights are engaged, with systems monitor just in case of problems. "Sir, I need you to step out of the car."

Christopher staggers out of the car, grabbing the door to catch himself. He falls forward. "Do you know who I am?" He pushes his finger into Andy's face.

"No sir, which would be why I've asked for your driver's licence and registration." Andy shows great patience. "Do you have your documents for me to look at?"

Christopher pushes Andy away as he stumbles back towards his car.

"Sir, I can't let you get back into your vehicle and drive in the condition you're in. You need to come with me. I want you to provide a couple of sobriety tests for me."

Christopher refuses. At that moment, a second police car drives up.

"Hey, Andy, do you need a hand here? I was driving by and saw your lights." Constable Calvin Carter speaks to Andy through the open window on the passenger side of his cruiser. Calvin's met Andy several times before and is surprised to see him in a cruiser since he knows he's been promoted to a new unit.

"Thanks Calvin, but I think we should be fine," Andy responds to Calvin.

"I've had enough with your local yokels, get out of my way, I'm leaving!" shouts Christopher. He lunges forward as he takes a swing at Andy. Calvin's out of his vehicle and moves quickly to secure Christopher. Andy's taken by surprise as Christopher's fist connects with Andy's jaw.

Christopher quickly finds himself on the ground, arms behind his back and in handcuffs. He struggles in an attempt to regain himself without success.

Andy rubs his jaw, "Man I did not see that coming, especially from a lawyer."

"For as drunk as he appears, he sure can move. I expected him to fall, not to actually connect."

Calvin and Andy pick Christopher up off the ground and put him into the back seat of Calvin's patrol car.

"How do you want to handle this, sir?" Calvin brushes his hands together and leans against the cruiser.

"Well we have several choices here. The guy's a hot shot lawyer from Toronto, not a big deal since we have lots of grounds for charges." Andy rubs his jaw as a reminder of the sucker punch he just received. "But the guy just had his girlfriend throw his 2 carat diamond ring back in his face. I've never had that happen to me, but it's got to be pretty humiliating. He wasn't driving, the car was stopped. He's waiting for this woman to come home. I think he was actually sleeping with the seat all the way back when I pulled up. I initially checked the vehicle because of the recent rash of burglaries we have seen in the neighbourhoods further west. I thought he might be casing the neighbourhood so I decided to check it out. I'm thinking we can either put him in the cooler overnight, or drive him back to his hotel and tell him to go back to Toronto in the morning. Or we can throw the book at him."

"You know, it's just about the end of my shift and I was heading back to the office to work on a couple of other files. I don't need any more work tonight, especially from this hot shot. He'll probably throw up in the car. I'm really not in a mood to clean my car again tonight – did it twice already." Calvin's a good constable, but he knows he already has a desk full of work and a pile of reports that need his attention. He lets Andy take the lead on this one.

Andy opens the door. "Okay then, I'll secure his license for a 24 hour suspension and take him back to the hotel to sober up with instructions to go back to Toronto after he picks up his license tomorrow. I'll call the tow truck and have his vehicle towed to the impound unit. Now we really are showing this jerk how friendly the Calgary City Police are. I'll stop by and fill out the paperwork and hand in his license for the 24 hour suspension. You've been a great help and I appreciate it."

"I can take the license and do up that paperwork, if you like," Calvin replies. He knows that this detective will soon be in charge of a shift of men and women in the white colour crime division and hopes that someday he'll get his application considered to transfer up into this unit.

Andy shakes his head as he puts Christopher into the back seat of his car. Even though he's taking Christopher back to the hotel to sober up, he'll have to go down to the detachment office in the morning to get his driver's license. He's saved Christopher the embarrassment of arrest, booking, and a trial. Andy's not sure the guy will appreciate what he's just done, but maybe in the morning when he's thinking with a clear head he will.

Andy calls in for a tow truck and heads downtown to the hotel Christopher's staying in. He sees Carter in his rear mirror following just in case Andy needs some help with the drunk. He then heads back to the detachment to meet up with Calvin and files the report on Christopher for the 24 hour suspension and the vehicle now in the impound lot.

Back at his desk, Andy starts to write up his report. Andy does some checking into Christopher background and he's not happy with the results. Andy's concerned when he realizes it's the same person Amy's been speaking about. He's not sure Amy really knows this guy, nor whether she's aware of this man's reputation and business ethics. He may have been a good friend at one time, but his reputation in Toronto turns out to be questionable. Andy's also discovered that Amy's brother, Jake, left their partnership in Toronto because of some of Christopher's more questionable clients. He knows for sure that he'll need to be very careful with the relationship between Amy and Christopher. He was surprised when Christopher provided so much information. It was probably because Christopher was so drunk and drunks tend to be more talkative. Andy's also grateful for the internet, for his own computer skills, and to have found out so many details about this guy. He's surprised there can be so much information online. Without using any police resources, he found press released and stories about Christopher, his business and his education. It serves to remind Andy what his new job will be like when it starts at the first of the New Year.

He knew there was something on Amy's mind tonight, and that she'd either had a really bad day at the hospital or something else had happened. She wasn't her usually self. If what Christopher said was correct, and Andy believes he was aware of what he said even in his drunken state, then he has a good idea what's bothering Amy.

Andy's sure that Amy will tell him what happened the next time they're together. Andy's been surprised many times by how much they tell each other when they get together. He feels like he's known Amy all his life when they share memories and spend time together. He constantly relives his kiss to Amy and his body tingles with the feelings he's developing for her.

For Amy's sake he has to see to it that Christopher's encouraged to leave town quickly. He also realizes he has to tell Amy some of what has happened before Christopher does. He needs to be honest with Amy and he's pretty sure she will be upset if she finds out what happened before he's had a chance to tell his side of the story.

Closing the file, Andy checks his watch. He expects to receive a call shortly to pick up the group so he decides to drive over to the Conference Centre. He'll sit and have a pop in the Centre lounge. Maybe he can catch the final period of tonight's hockey game.

Arriving, Andy makes himself comfortable in a lounge chair in front of a big screen TV with a glass of orange juice. The room is full of men waiting for their women. Many have been there for some time and made friends with each other. It doesn't take much to become friends when watching a hockey game, especially when the home team's winning. As the winning goal is scored, Andy's phone goes off. He turns to answer the call and sees most of the men answering their phones. The charity event must be over.

The ladies decide they'll meet Andy in the lounge so he can finish up his drink and watch the finishing highlights of the hockey game.

The show's been a huge success and they're having such a good time, they don't want to end the evening. They each order a glass of wine and they share the evening with Andy. He's happy for the diversion since he knows he'll need to speak with Amy regarding the incident with Christopher.

Grace shows off the centerpiece that she's won. The combination of flowers is amazing and becomes the main topic of conversation. The newest floral designer to Calgary has outdone herself with her Fall celebration theme. The yellow snapdragons, orange gerberas, bronze cushion pompons, over sized yellow roses, red freesia and miniature pumpkins sitting in a large crystal bowl are accented perfectly by tall ivory candles. This donation of flowers is worth several thousand dollars for the entire event and every lady has taken a business card to ensure this new designer stays in business. Andy listens to the details of the arrangements, but to him they're just flowers.

Cindy declares the best part of the show is the networking opportunity it provides professional business women. Cindy works with several dentists and hygienists who are always looking for new promotional ideas for women. She wants to take the ideas she got tonight back to her office and perhaps do a similar event. Victoria offers to fly out to help Cindy with her new found contacts in the media to be able to sell out the show there as well. The Breast Cancer Foundation, as always, is the big winner tonight and a large amount of money has been made through the live and silent auctions.

Grace yawns and Amy notices. "Well, everyone, we should start for home, it's getting late and I, for one, will soon start wilting."

"Follow me, ladies; I'll escort you lovely ladies home. I know I'm the envy of the room to be sitting with such a fine group of ladies." Andy rises and helps his mother out of her chair.

Everyone says their goodbyes to Victoria and Sophie. Sophie's driving Victoria back to her hotel. They're getting together next week to start house hunting for Victoria with Sophie's friend who is a realtor. Victoria's decided she wants to move out to Calgary permanently and sell her condo in Toronto. With the difference in pricing she wants to buy a home near the Elbow River, although after speaking with the ladies tonight Victoria wants to look at the new condos with a view of the city and the river. Cheryl offers to assist with decoration and design, something that Victoria's excited to accept since she's very impressed with Amy's house.

Once they're all safely loaded, Andy carefully drives the van back towards Amy's house. Andy quietly asks Amy if she has time to meet for coffee in the morning. Amy leans forward and quietly whispers, "Is something wrong?"

"No, not exactly. I have something I want to tell you and now isn't the right time." Andy chooses his words carefully, "I can drive you to the hospital in the morning and we can stop for breakfast, but I know you have company tonight, so I thought coffee after your rounds might be more convenient for you."

"That sounds brilliant. We can meet in my office if you like." Amy's not sure what to expect since Andy seems as distracted and quiet as she was earlier.

"Hey, that's a great idea; I'll bring the coffee and snacks." Andy turns and smiles at her.

His smile is enough to melt away any concerns or thoughts she has and she smiles as she sits back into the van seat.

Grace suggests they all get together tomorrow night at her house for a farewell dinner for Cindy and Joan, who will be leaving for home on Saturday. With Halloween on Sunday they want to be home. The grandchildren have been away from their friends and school for almost two weeks, and Grace concedes they all need to get back into a regular routine even if it means that she'll be alone.

Amy convinces Cheryl, Connie and Joyce to stay over for another day and they agree to spend the day shopping, take Grace up on her invitation and then leave on Saturday. All the plans are finalized as Andy turns down the street to Amy and his mother's houses.

"Here we are ladies, delivered safe and sound." Andy pulls into Amy's drive way. He notices the street's clear of any unusual traffic.

Once again, he helps each lady out of the van and is rewarded with another peck on the cheek. He escorts Amy and her group to her door and turns to do the same for his mother and sisters.

All the goodnights are exchanged. He walks across the street with his family to deliver them safely to their door and then goes to get into his car to go home.

Cindy pulls Andy aside to whisper, "You need to get moving with Amy. I can see she adores you and you need to ask her out to dinner."

"Hey, we've already spent several meals together this past couple of weeks and I'm meeting her for coffee tomorrow. Of course, I'm not sure if she'll talk to me after what happened earlier." Andy's starting to have doubts about how to explain his actions with Christopher.

"Ok, spit it out, what did you do this time, Mr. 'I'm a police officer.'" Cindy stops dead in her tracks.

"Are you guys okay?" asks Joan.

"We're fine, just need to give little brother some advice. You go ahead and go inside. I'll be in shortly," Cindy explains.

Joan and Grace go into the house while Andy and Cindy continue their discussions on the curb next to Andy's car.

"Like I said, give it up; what did you do?" Cindy starts the interrogation. Andy takes a quick minute and thinks *she really should've been a cop or a lawyer, she's good.*

"Well, I saw a car sitting on the street a few feet down from Amy's earlier tonight. There was a guy in when I came over here and he was still there when we left for the Centre. So, I went back to the office, picked up a marked car and came back. I ran the plate thinking maybe there was someone stalking the area for possible break-ins."

"And?" Cindy probes.

"As I was saying," Andy continues, "I found out the vehicle was a rental and that Christopher Laing was the driver. I also found out that he used to be a business partner of Amy's brother, and that her brother left the partnership because of Christopher's bad choice of clients and other business associates. I also know that he and Amy went to university together for a while. Amy left school immediately after she was badly beaten and left for dead."

"So you connect the lines and what? What are you saying?" Cindy puts her hands on her hips.

"I did what every good cop would do; I checked the car and found the guy drunk out of his mind. He claimed that he'd proposed to Amy, and said something about him trying to get her a great job in the best hospital in Toronto. She apparently threw the ring in his face and walked out. He wanted to wait to talk to her again and in the meantime decided booze was his best friend. He took a swing at me when I was talking to Constable Calvin Carter. He happened to provide me with back up. Christopher connected my jaw with a decent hit considering he was probably seeing two of me. Anyway, he could've been charged with assaulting a police officer, impaired driving, resisting arrest and possible stalking. Instead, I took him back to his hotel room, impounded his car and told him if he's smart he'll get out of Dodge."

"Now you're going to have to tell Amy about this, you know that right?" Cindy's seeing the problem Andy may have. She may not have known Amy for a long time, but she knows how every woman responds when men do stupid things.

"Any ideas?" Andy asks hoping his sister can give him some advice. "I like her a lot and want to be honest with her, but I'm not sure how she's going to handle this when I tell her."

"Well you're right about honesty; it's the only way relationships survive. I'm guessing she may get pretty angry, but you have to be frank with her about concerns over burglaries in the area."

"I'm planning to be honest. I'm just not sure how far out on the limb I want to travel. I'm guessing that Christopher may try to get in touch with her as well. The sooner I can talk to her the better. That's why I've made arrangements for coffee in the morning." Andy stands with his hands in his pockets.

"Well, good luck with that." Cindy hugs her brother, "I like Amy a lot too and I think you'll make a great couple, so I'll be praying for you tomorrow. I hope you find the right words and that Amy will have an open heart. Let me know if you need anything else from me."

"Good night sis, see you in the morning." With that, Andy heads for his car and home. "Hey," he adds, "let's not worry Mom about any of this, please."

"My lips are sealed," Cindy promises as she turns to head inside. She knows she'll have to tell Joan, but she'll give her mother some story. What story, exactly, she's not sure, but something.

Chapter Thirteen

While Amy's in the shower the next morning she's surprised to see several ugly bruises on her wrists and forearms. She realizes they're from her confrontation with Christopher yesterday. It already seems like ancient history. She had so much fun last night with her friends and was hoping it would ease the pain of the incident in his office. Now, she realizes it's still as fresh as the bruises are and she'll probably have some more encounters before she's finished. She puts on a long sleeve top to hide the marks.

Leaving her friends to sleep in, Amy tiptoes out of her house and heads off to the hospital. She looks around as she drives off to see if there are any cars around. She wonders if one of the cars on the street last night was Christopher. She expects he'll try to do something stupid even though she's told him to leave her alone. She'll ask Jake and Victoria to speak to him about giving her the space she needs. For now, she'll wait and see what happens.

Amy arrives at her office to find an enormous bouquet of three dozen red roses. Reading the card, she shakes her head; how little Christopher really knows her. In her opinion, red roses are greatly overrated. She's even expressed her dislike for red roses on several occasions. She throws the *Forgive Me* card in the garbage, picks up the bouquet and takes it down the hall to Sophie's assistant, Edna.

"Good morning Edna, how are you?" Amy inquires.

"Just fine Dr. Murray. What a beautiful bouquet. A special occasion?" Edna queries.

"I thought it might be something you'd like. I received them and they're just not something I want to keep in my office. I think they'll look beautiful sitting on the corner of your desk." Amy sets the flowers on the corner of Edna's desk and steps back.

"Why, thank you very much Dr. Murray. You're so kind to think of me." Edna stands up and leans over to smell the flowers. "I love red roses, they are so elegant," she declares.

"Thank you for taking them off my hands. I'm off to do my rounds. I've got several pacemaker surgeries scheduled today." Amy smiled and leaves quickly to avoid any more questions from Edna. One more thing off her hands this morning.

Her rounds pass without incident. Amy makes it back to her office in time to meet Andy coming off the elevator. He has his hands full with Tim Horton's coffees and donuts.

Andy sees her smile. "That happy to see me?" he inquires.

Amy blushes, "Actually, I was thinking about police officers and their donuts."

Andy makes a face, "You need to watch out, otherwise I'll eat them all myself."

"Right, and then wonder why you have to work so hard to get ready for your annual physical endurance tests," she jokes. Amy opens the door for Andy to enter her office and plucks the little box of donuts off the coffee holder where Andy has them balanced.

Andy almost spills his coffee and they both laugh as they move to the seating area. Andy's glad things are starting on such a good note. He just hopes Amy can laugh – heck even smile – when he tells her about yesterday.

Andy's been practising what he'll say since his conversation with Cindy last night. Every scenario he runs through his mind he believes will make Amy angry, so he's not sure how to even start. They sit back and enjoy the giant sized, maple flavoured fritters.

"We should make this a habit," Amy tells him. "This is a great break, I have several pacemaker surgeries scheduled starting at lunch time. This is breakfast and lunch all in one."

"That's a good idea; I'd love to be a regular here at the hospital." Andy wipes the sugar crumbs off his face.

"Actually, I had a reason to come and I've got something I need to tell you. Before I do, you have to promise that no matter what, you'll understand I really do like you and want to spend more time with you." Andy gets serious as he sets down his coffee.

"Now you have my attention. What could you have ever done to think I'd be upset with you?" Amy smiles at him.

Andy leans forward and takes her hands. As he does, her sleeves slip up exposing the bruises on her wrists. "Amy, what happened here, who did this to you?" Andy gently moves his hands up her sleeves to reveal additional marks on her forearms as well.

Andy looks into Amy's eyes. She can feel the tears form. Andy takes hold of both hands as she quietly starts to tell Andy what had happened. She promised herself she wouldn't tell anyone other than her brother and Victoria, but she can't keep herself from confiding in Andy.

By the time Amy finishes she's shaking. Andy slips onto the couch beside her and wraps his arms around her and holds her until she stops trembling. Amy continues to share everything with him, including the delivery and disposal of the red roses.

Andy makes a mental note about the colour of the roses, remembering from touring her garden that pink are her favourites and also that she loves lilies. Andy's surprised to hear how determined Christopher appears to be. He then begins to tell Amy the reason for meeting her today. Andy continues to hold Amy and feels her stiffen at several points as he describes his encounter with Christopher.

Amy pulls away and looks Andy straight in the eyes. "Are you telling me you didn't know that it was Christopher's car on my street when you started?"

"Yes that's the truth; I didn't know it was your Christopher when I went back. I found that out as I ran a check on the plates." Andy's pleased Amy's asking questions and doesn't appear to be overly upset with him.

"Amy, I'll answer any question you have; I honestly thought I had a possible burglary suspect or stalker. I was surprised that it was the same Christopher Laing you talk about." Andy sits up straight as he answers her.

"But just for the record, he is not my Christopher. I really never want to see him again. You're not thinking he'd ever hurt me, are you?" Amy asks. "I've known him since we were kids; he'd never hurt me."

"Really? he did a pretty good number on your arms." Andy looks at her arms and Amy follows his eyes to her arms as well.

Feeling very self conscious, Amy pulls her sleeves back down to cover the bruises.

"Look, Amy, people change and sometimes you never really know someone until they're forced into a corner. Is he dangerous? I'm not sure if he'd hurt you or not, but I'd rather you didn't take a chance." Andy doesn't want to frighten Amy, but he isn't sure what Christopher is capable of doing.

"I just want to make my own decisions. I told him I'm not interested in moving or changing jobs. Why can't he just leave me alone?" Amy spoke with frustration in her voice.

"Sweetheart, you need to be careful. Christopher's exhibiting all the symptoms I usually see in domestic abuse; he could possibly be an abuser. Not many will just go away. They're bullies. I know you think you can defend yourself, but until we can get him out of your life you need to stay on the alert. I'd love to pick you up in the morning and take you home at night for my own peace of mind, if you'll allow me." Andy thinks this is a good start since he knows he'll never be able to concentrate at work unless he knows Amy's safe. He's pretty sure she'll be fine here at the hospital.

"I have to admit I'm a little shaken right now. I didn't want to involve a lot of people in my personal affairs." Amy likes the endearment Andy uses. "I don't want to put anyone else at risk. Maybe I should talk to Jake about this."

Just then her beeper goes off, reminding her she needs to head down to the OR for her scheduled afternoon surgeries. She checks her watch and is surprised to see how quickly the time has passed.

"I've got to go prep for surgery. I'll be safe and will check in with you before I leave the hospital. I hate to lose my independence and I'll think about what you've asked." Amy doesn't like the situation she finds herself in, but again, the prospect of spending more time with Andy is not such a bad thing.

Andy leans over and kisses her lightly on the lips. "Just be safe."

Together, they leave the office and head for the elevator. Amy gets off on the OR floor and Andy heads down to the main floor. He decides he'll stop at the Security office and just alert the hospital security to be aware of a possible security issue. He takes a few minutes to meet with security and is pleasantly surprised to hear they'll input Christopher's picture into their facial recognition computer to be alerted if he shows up at the hospital. Andy quickly has a picture sent over to their system.

Feeling much more comfortable about Amy's safety, he heads back downtown to the detachment office. He's got several files on his desk that he has to complete today. Back at his desk, Constable Carter drops by. He inquires as to how to proceed with Christopher's license from the 24 hour suspension. Andy decides he'll deliver it to Christopher at the law office; maybe he'll take the time to introduce himself to Jake. He's heard so much about Jake, and he wants to meet and perhaps discuss Amy's protection with him.

Motivated to get the files off his desk, Andy's surprised at how quickly he finishes up. Checking his watch, he sees he'll make it over to Jake's law office shortly before they typically finish for the day.

Chapter Fourteen

Andy leans on the top of the reception desk as he gossips with May, the firm's very friendly gal at reception. Obviously Jake and his partners are doing well since the firm has two floors in a very prestige building overlooking the Elbow River right in the heart of Calgary.

Seems May loves to gossip and she tells Andy all about Christopher. It appears he received a call from his secretary back in Toronto just after he and Jake had an argument earlier today. His girlfriend's been trying to reach him; she's gone into labour with their baby. Christopher left the office in a hurry and right after that Jake asked one of his assistants to pack up Christopher's office since he wouldn't be back anytime soon.

Andy sees a red head coming around the corner that bears a striking resemblance to Amy. He moves forward with an extended hand and says, "You must be Jake. I'm Andy Henderson."

"Good to meet you, Andy. I've heard a lot about you." Jake returns the handshake. "Let's go into the small board room. May, would you bring us both some fresh coffee?"

Andy follows Jake into a small meeting room. As Jake closes the door, he asks if Jake would be interested in a drink. "Coffee thanks, I'm still officially on duty. I also have to go back to the hospital to check on Amy."

May appears with a thermos of coffee. "Just made a fresh pot," she announces as she places the thermos and her tray with mugs, spoons, cream and sugar on the table in front of the gentlemen. They wait quietly until she leaves the room.

Jake makes sure the door's tightly closed. "The rooms are sound proof when the doors are shut tight," he comments as he returns to his chair.

"I understand you and my sister are good friends. Dad seems to like you and thinks your mother's a very special lady. I'm glad we finally get to meet." Jake sits back and removes his tie. "It's been a long day," he sighs.

"I agree." Andy sips the hot coffee. "I played chauffeur to your sister and her friends and my sisters and my mom last night. They sure seemed to have fun. In fact, they're all meeting up for dinner at my parents' place; I mean my mom's house," Andy corrected himself. He still feels very uncomfortable about how to describe things now that his father's gone.

"I know I have the same problem with my dad as you have - how to describe your parents when there's now only one without seeming disrespectful to the other." Jake picks up on Andy's comment quickly.

Jake checks his watch and Andy realizes time's moving quickly so he begins by telling him about why he has stopped in to speak with Jake. He tells him about the bruises on Amy's arm, and the numerous telephone calls and text messages she's received. He's careful with the information, since as a cop he can't disclose the incidents from last night when he picked up Christopher. Jake's aware of most details from the incident last night. It seems Christopher's already been into the office and didn't hold back on the events as he remembered them.

Jake brings Andy up to date with the fact that Christopher spent the greater part of yesterday afternoon drinking in his office until Jake sent him back to the hotel. Christopher was back at the office this morning still in a drunken stupor. He demanded Jake should support him in getting Amy to move out to Toronto. A very loud and verbal discussion followed.

In the middle of this, Christopher received a call from his secretary. His Toronto girlfriend was trying to reach him since she'd gone into labour with their child. When Jake heard that, he demanded Christopher leave immediately. He no longer wants to have Christopher involved with either himself or his sister. Christopher left directly to the airport on a flight his Toronto secretary organized. Arrangements have made to ship his files and personal belongings back. Of course Andy had heard most of this information from the very helpful May.

Andy and Jake discuss Christopher's character and whether Amy could be in any danger. Given the events that have taken place today, both believe Christopher won't cause any problems and Jake's convinced Christopher will stay away until he's invited back.

Chapter Fifteen

Amy arrives home to her house guests. She spoke to Andy earlier and promised she'd drive straight home carefully. Andy suggests they meet in the morning so he can bring her up to date on the events of the afternoon. Amy's curious, but with a house full of inquisitive women she doesn't want to discuss Christopher at all if possible lest they should over hear.

The ladies have been out shopping to get an early start to their Christmas lists. Amy checks out all the purchases. It seems to have been a very productive day for them. Grace and her daughters joined them at the mall for part of the day.

Joyce has her feet propped up. "My feet are killing me. I don't remember the Chinook Mall being so big." She grins as she takes a slip from her glass of wine.

"Well, we didn't have to check out every store, you know. We could've saved some for another day," Connie remarks.

"You know we all loved it. Amy, I wish you could've joined us. It would've been like the old days," Cheryl adds.

"Like the old days that were just a few weeks ago. I thought you'd be glad to have some free time now the house's finished." Amy hugs Cheryl. "But I agree I do miss our times together. It was fun."

"Let's choose a day next month and have a girl's day out," Joyce suggests. "We can wait until the malls are all decked out for the holidays. Christmas is my favourite time of the year."

"I agree, I remember how much you and mom love the holidays." Amy looks wistfully out the windows into the night. "I think this year I should decorate the house like mom always did. I always had so much fun helping her untangle the lights and listen to dad complain about all the decorations."

"Well, you're going to need to do lots of shopping. Your mother had decorations in every room of the house," reminisces Connie.

"I can use lots of help. Why don't we plan two special times, one day to shop for decorations and then another to help me put them all up over a weekend. I'd love it. That is, if you're all game to join me." Amy's enjoyed their company and wants to extend the invitation for more visits. These women play such a huge role in her life. They were her mom's best friends and were like furniture fixtures in her parent's house when she was growing up. With her mom gone spending time with these women is the next best thing to her mother being there. They're family.

"Let's do that," all three laugh, as they speak in unison.

"Why don't we invite Grace along? She's so much fun," Connie suggests. All agree that would be great as they check out the calendar to decide which days to get together.

With that done, they walk across the street for another wonderful evening with Grace and her family. Andy's late getting to the house, but he's pleased they've waited. He's pretty sure his mom will make her famous turkey dinner and he's eager to spend the last evening together before his sisters and their families head off to their homes and jobs.

Not to disappoint, Grace does in fact makes a complete turkey dinner. Everyone enjoys themselves for the evening.

Amy hugs Cindy, Joan and the girls. She's come to truly love the girls and is going to miss them. She promises she'll keep in contact and will be there for Grace. Amy knows how much Grace will miss having her family with her; she's seen how much Grace has relied on them these past days.

Chapter Sixteen

In Calgary, the seasons can change quickly. While October's been warm, November has come with a series of storms and snow. Spending the evenings at home has become a habit for Amy. To keep herself both mentally and physically in shape, Amy has always dedicated time every day for her martial arts. She holds her Tiger Chi and Chi Kung levels in Tai Chi. She's a black belt in Karate and also trains in Taekwondo. Each of these arts helps her keep her mind active and develop the strength, balance, flexibility and stamina she needs for her long hours in the surgery rooms. She learned these arts during her time at school. Martial art help to keep the mind sharp and works well for people with eidetic or photographic memories. She kept it up at university and continues to find relaxation in the techniques and routines she's worked out for herself over the years.

Andy's fascinated by Amy, watching as she works out in her exercise room in the basement. Her flexibility and strength astonishes him. She challenges him one night to a friendly competition and he quickly finds himself flat out on the mat. Andy wants Amy to train him to become more flexible, not to mention it provides yet another reason for them to spend time together.

Most evenings, Andy stops by after work to eat dinner with Amy and they spend time together. They have quickly formed a routine. Almost every night they either work at Tai Chi or Karate. Sometimes they take advantage of the space in the games room that Cheryl designed and put music on the stereo and dance.

One night Amy's alone because Andy has meetings at work. She decides to do some research on her IPad and comes across the work she had started doing to decipher her dreams. She decides to work on the ten steps. Remembering both her dreams and the steps hasn't been a problem. She answers all the questions in each step. Tonight she's relaxed and at ease; it's the perfect night, and she has a perfect mindset. Yes indeed, these first few steps are a piece of cake.

As Amy moves further into the process she begins to realize her first dream could have several meanings but she decides to move forward by looking at the obvious. She's in a warm protected environment, much like a fetus in her mother's womb. She starts typing out her thoughts as she moves through her memory of the dream. The heartbeat could actually be the mother's heart beat. A second heart beat could be the father lying close to the mother. Storms are exactly what they are, just thunder and rain. Maybe the parents are caught in a storm or the sounds of the storm are coming through a room. For some reason, she has always feared thunder storms, often seeking out the comfort of her parents when the storms would come. The sound of the train stops her. Maybe she's gone as far as she can with this first dream.

She reviews what she's written down about the second dream. Looking at it, she decides it's possible she's subconsciously put her guilt and pain together and wants to believe the message is from her mother. She still has the guilt and the pain, but both are easing up and she has started to move forward with Andy, family and friends. Maybe that's what her mother wanted her to do all along.

Reaching what she thinks is a dead end, Amy decides to spend some time going through her mom's lists, it's something she hasn't done in a while. An item pops up that she's surprised to see and can't remember having seen before.

Ann's written at the very bottom of the last space of the two page list, *Ed you need to find a replacement for Finnegan*. Amy realizes her mother intended this to go on her father's list. With his birthday coming soon, Amy decides it's the perfect gift for her father and she starts looking for the perfect companion birthday gift.

Reaching for her IPad, Amy pours herself another cup of tea and begins to search for Dalmatians. She finds a kennel on the outskirts of Calgary which would be very convenient. She calls and makes arrangements to stop by on Saturday morning on the way out to spend the day with her dad. Andy also has the same weekend off and Amy sends him a quick message He responds immediately and they decide it'll be fun to spend some time in Riverside. He's met Amy's dad on several occasions, but this will be the first time they've gone out to his place. Ed's birthday is actually mid week, but Amy wants to spend the day together with her two favourite people. She's amazed she feels this way about Andy, like Andy's somehow always been part of her life.

Amy sends an email to the owner of the kennel. Within a couple of minutes she gets a response; Sharon Talbert has owned the kennel and has bred Dalmatians for many years. Amy tells her about their family dog, Finnegan, and how she would like to find another dog to give her father as a birthday gift and replacement for their first dog.

Andy picks Amy up early Saturday morning and they drive out to the kennel to meet the owner and her puppies. Sharon's waiting to meet Amy to tell her that when she checked her records she was surprised to see that she had actually sold Finnegan to Amy's birth parents. Now Amy knows for sure that this is the best place to get a new puppy.

Amy sits on the floor of the kennel and is immediately surrounded by little puppies all eager to chew at her fingers and toes.

"Look at all these puppies. Now I understand the story of 101 Dalmatians. I feel like Anita sitting on the floor in her living room with all her babies," Amy laughs.

Andy gets his camera and starts to take pictures. He loves the sparkle in Amy's eyes and the joy she's expressing. His sweetheart is sitting right in front of him playing with her puppies. Andy realizes at that moment how much he loves Amy and decides he wants to capture these special moments on his camera.

One small puppy climbs up on Amy's lap and curls up. He is the runt of the pack. Amy picks him up and looks into his eyes. Tears form as she starts to cry.

"What's wrong?" Andy kneels down beside her.

"This little soul has the same eyes as my Finnegan. Is that even possible?" Amy looks into Andy's eyes. "This is the one; we need to take him with us."

Amy looks over at Sharon, "Can we take him home with us today?"

"Sure, if you like. He's a little small for his age, but with lots of care and love he'll grow quickly. He sure seems to fit into your arms just like he's already decided he wants to go home with you." Sharon's surprised since this little fellow has been a bit of a handful. He's so small and has never really made an effort to be seen and yet, here he is, cuddled up in Amy's arms like he belongs.

"Let's get the paperwork done and get some instructions for your dad. That is, if you're sure this is the one?" Amy's sure but she needs Andy to be sure.

"Are you kidding? Look at him. Doesn't he look like a Finnegan to you?" Amy laughs as she kisses the little puppy on the top of his head. "Isn't he the cutest thing you've ever seen?" She coos to him in his little floppy ear.

"I've never had the pleasure of meeting the first Finnegan, but I think we just found your dad his birthday present." Andy looks into Finnegan's little face, "So little one, do you want to go meet your new daddy?"

Andy and Amy get the paperwork completed and buy enough puppy food, vitamins, and toys to keep little Finnegan going for a while. They stop at the pet store nearby and buy a little bed, a new collar, a matching leash, and a kennel for him.

Fully outfitted, they head out to Riverside. Finnegan sleeps the whole trip. Sharon has him trained but warns he could have some accidents, especially if he gets excited.

Ed's outside shovelling the driveway as Amy and Andy drive up. He stops and waves. He smiles as he sees Andy. Amy's talked to him so often about Andy and he's pleased to see him again. Joyce, Connie and Cheryl have all told him about their great sleep over and the super time they had with Andy's family. Each have given their stamp of approval and are praying for the couple to realize how much they suit each other. Ed's convinced that Amy already knows that.

"Happy Birthday Dad," Amy greets her father. "I've found you the perfect gift for your birthday."

"You know I have everything I could possibly want and more. I just don't need anything." Ed grins. But he loves presents and Amy knows it.

Andy stands back and watches the two. He sees where Amy gets her love of life. Ed's grin as he looks at his daughter lights up the world. It's plain to see he adores his little girl.

Amy goes back to the car. Andy helps start to unload the back seat. Amy takes her little bundle of joy out of the car. Having slept for half an hour, the little puppy's ready to play and run. Amy sets him down out of sight of her father so he can have a little run.

Ed's curious as to what his daughter could be doing. Suddenly he hears a little whimper. He walks over to the side of the car. There on the ground is a miniature version of their beloved family pet who died shortly after the kids both left for university. He immediately gets on his hands and knees next to Amy. Little Finnegan runs straight over to Ed and licks his face.

Ed picks up the little pup and stands to hug his daughter.

"How did you know? I've been thinking about looking for a companion for a while now, but just wasn't sure." Ed's eyes quickly fill with tears.

"Mom left me a little note on my list; it was at the bottom of the page. For some reason, I don't remember ever seeing it until the other night. And guess what, this dog's actually related to Finnegan. Sharon Talbert sold Finnegan to Jeff and Mary. Can you believe it?"

Andy has his camera out and has already taken several pictures. He puts the camera aside and moves towards Ed. "Good to see you again, sir." Andy shakes Ed's hand.

"It's cold out here, let's go inside," says Ed, remembering his manners he invites Andy inside.

"Actually, sir, I have several packages I have to bring inside. Why don't you and Amy go in and I'll bring in the paraphernalia that goes along with a new puppy." Andy smiles as he brings up the rear with the first load. Amy has her hands full as well.

Along with all the puppy shopping, Amy's also brought a cake, ice cream and groceries for dinner.

Once inside, Ed looks through all the bags. "Wow, did you leave anything in the store?"

Amy teases him. "Puppies appear to be like babies; it seems they both need a lot of stuff."

Amy gets to work in the kitchen. She's made her father's favourite, beef stew, and she puts it into the oven to warm up. As she turns to open the fridge door, she spots another penny; she picks it up and blows a kiss into the air. Today she feels more alive than she has in a long time. She quickly puts together a salad and sets the table.

"You must be hungry," Ed watches her as he and Andy sit at the kitchen table. He's poured them all coffee. The whole time Ed has not put Finnegan down.

They spend the afternoon and evening together. Andy's amazed at how he seems to fit right in with Ed and Amy in the family home. It's like he's known Ed all his life.

After an early dinner, Ed's neighbours join in for birthday cake. Andy gets a chance to meet the men since he'd met all the ladies last week. It's quite late when Andy and Amy get ready to leave.

"You know you can stay over and leave in the morning. I've got lots of room. Amy you can stay in your room. Andy can have either the guest room or Jake's room." Ed's not anxious for them to leave.

"I'll go with whatever Amy decides, but I happen to know she brought an overnight bag." Andy grins at Amy.

"Yes and so did you." She answers back.

With that, they decide to stay over and leave in the morning.

Chapter Seventeen

After a very relaxing weekend Amy faces a busy week. With all the cold weather she has several new heart attack and stroke patients to deal with along with her scheduled surgeries.

Andy brings his mother's homemade clam chowder and buns over on Monday night. Under his arm, he has a package that he sets on the dining room table. After they eat the chowder and buns, they move to the family room where Andy brings the package to Amy for her to open.

"It's not my birthday." Amy eyes the package with a smile.

"No, this is something very special." Andy winks at her.

Amy opens the package; there in the box is a small 4x6 silver picture frame. Amy turns it over; there's one of the pictures Andy took of her and Finnegan at Sharon Talbert's kennels. Amy's sitting on the floor surrounded by puppies. She's holding Finnegan up to her cheek and looking straight into the camera.

Amy's a bit puzzled especially by the excitement in Andy's face. "This is a good picture of Finnegan, but I didn't expect to have my picture taken. I have very little makeup on and look at my hair, I'm a mess!"

"Amy, this is a special picture for me. It's the first time I realized how much I love you." Andy put his arm around Amy. "When I looked into your eyes through the camera lens I knew beyond a shadow of a doubt that I've fallen totally and completely in love with you. I want you to put this picture on your night stand so the last thing you see at night and the first thing in the morning is the picture of the exact moment I recognized my love for you."

Amy puts her arms around Andy's neck and kisses him with all her heart and soul. "I love you so much," she admits softly as she buries her face into his neck.

Later that evening after Andy's gone home; Amy closes her eyes to think about her mom. She wishes with all her heart that she could phone her mom and share this with her. She's finally beginning to understand the love her parents had for one another.

Amy decides to go to bed. As she picks up the picture Andy has given her, she looks down and sees a penny on the floor. She bends down and picks it up. *Mom, I'm going to believe this is from you as a sign that you approve of Andy.* Tears roll down her cheeks as she heads to bed. She's full of emotions – happiness, joy and love for Andy mixed with sorrow and loss for her mom and their missing opportunities together.

Chapter Eighteen

The next night Andy appears with another home cooked meal from his mom.

Amy lectures him about leaving Grace at home alone. "Your mom's alone all day, why isn't she here with us instead of sending the dinner and eating by herself."

"Are you kidding? She wants me to get to you through your stomach." Andy laughs as he kisses Amy after setting down the casserole dish.

Amy lifts the lid of the casserole dish. "Wow, this smells great. Chicken pot pie, this is one of my favourites. I'm starving; help me set the table while I make a quick salad to go with this."

Quickly, dinner's ready and the table is set. They sit down together. Bowing their heads, Andy says grace.

They share their day's experiences with each other.

Andy's excited. He's got two tickets to the Policeman's Ball, known as the Festival of Trees Gala, for the last week in November. It's a huge fundraiser that the local City Police and Royal Canadian Mounted Police join forces to host. It's a black tie event. Normally Andy stays away from such events, but this year he couldn't wait to get his hands on two tickets. He's excited to show Amy off to his co-workers who have heard so much about her and can hardly wait to meet her. He and Amy enjoy dancing and have spent many evenings together perfecting their moves.

Andy's excitement is contagious and Amy's bubbling with the chance to spend a dress up night with Andy.

She's excited about actually going to the Gala Ball. She's discussed the Festival with Grace and the ladies from home. They have plans to go to the day events and had commented on how they wished they could see the decorations for the evening with the hall set up. They've organized Sunday afternoon, the first day of the Festival, to get together and tour the Centre. The ladies are having a sleep over at Grace's house and planning to go shopping and have dinner on Saturday. Amy and Andy are both pleased Grace has become friends with this special group of women, especially since so many of Grace's teacher friends still work.

The festival has been held for several years and each year it gets bigger as more and more designers and businesses donate fully decorated trees, wreaths and other elaborate Christmas decorations. They're displayed in the Calgary Roundup Centre in Stampede Park. During the week, the show features these beautiful creations with a silent auction. The items are sold and the buyers' names are announced at the Gala Ball. It generates good profits for the street programs that the police sponsor.

Andy and Amy discuss the event and how much they're both looking forward to going. Amy's been to the displays before and she shares her memories with Andy. Neither of them has attended the Gala Ball and they discuss the black tie dress code. Andy tells Amy he has a tuxedo that his parents made him purchase for his father's retirement party. Amy's looking forward to seeing him dressed up in a suit. She knows every woman at the Ball will be envious of her with Andy as her escort.

Almost half a million people go through the doors to admire the various displays and to get the latest ideas on tree and home decorating for the holidays. Amy and her friends are no exception. They discuss the event and have developed a list for Amy of the basic decorations she'll need. Once they finish the tour of the Festival of Trees they'll head home to create lists of items she'll need to bring her house to life for the holidays.

The next day, Amy shares her excitement with Sophie. Sophie's immediate concern is for Amy to have a suitable and fashionable evening gown for the event. That night after work, they drop in at Sophie's favourite store in Calgary's China Town district.

After several false starts Amy finds the perfect gown. It's a very elegant and regal black velvet gown with a sexy side slit exposing her leg. It features a sweetheart neckline with a twist. Nine straps of velvet adorned with crystals connect to a dazzling halter neckline. The small band of material hooks in the back. The surprise of this gown is its back, or rather lack thereof. It's a backless gown that shows off Amy's elegant and shapely back. Amy thinks it's too daring, but Sophie convinces her it's the perfect dress. A beautiful full length black velvet cape completes the outfit. Amy's surprised when she checks the price of the outfit. She still has funds available for a new pair of evening shoes in matching velvet and rhinestone detailing. The three inch heels mean Amy doesn't have to alter her gown. She can hardly wait to see the look on Andy's face when he sees her in this outfit.

Chapter Nineteen

With an outfit ready to go, Amy relaxes and enjoys her routine of working at the hospital and spending every spare minute of her time with Andy. They've gone out to spend time with her dad, taking Grace with them. Grace enjoys her visit with Ed as well as her new friends. Amy loves the changes in her life and looks forward to each and every day.

Late Sunday night, Amy receives a Skype message from her brother asking if she's forgotten about him. He asks if they can get together the following evening for dinner and for Amy to invite Andy. Jake confirms he'll be bringing Victoria.

The next night the couple find Jake and Victoria already seated at their favourite restaurant. Amy notices that Jake looks at Victoria the same way she looks at Andy. She's happy for her brother.

"It's great to be able to get together. We haven't seen each other for a couple of weeks, but it seems like it's been forever," Jake comments as they order their drinks and sit back to wait for their dinner to arrive. "By the way, great gift you bought Dad. He hardly has time to talk on the phone these days. Seems Finnegan Jr. has really filled up his life."

"I know, we're so busy with our own lives that it seems the days go by so quickly," Andy agrees.

"Did you know, for example, that I'm an aunt?" Victoria isn't sure if Amy knows much about what had happened after their confrontation at the law office. "I apologize for just blurting it out, but you know me, I've got no idea how to be tactful with certain things."

Amy laughs. "That's what's so special about you." She sees Jake and Andy watching her. "Victoria, it's okay, Andy told me about his visit to the office and even though we may not talk on the phone every day, Jake always keeps me updated on happenings in your lives by email or Skype. I'm more disappointed with myself for not realizing Christopher was using me."

"Amy, I think he was just trying to figure out his life. Don't forget, we didn't have the solid family lifestyle you and Jake were blessed with. Not that I'm making excuses."

"Victoria, I've got a great new life with someone I adore," she says, looking into Andy's eyes and smiling at him. "I hope Christopher will find the same happiness."

"Well, he's got a beautiful son. He's still uncertain about his relationship with Judith – that's the baby's mother – but they're moving forward one day at a time."

"I'm happy with the way things turned out for all of us." Jake raises his glass. "Let's make a toast to happiness and love."

"Here, here," Andy agrees as they bring their glasses together.

"Actually, I wanted to get together because Victoria and I have an announcement we want to share with you." Jake takes Victoria's hand. "I asked Victoria to marry me yesterday and I want you to help us celebrate."

Amy jumps out of her chair, runs around to other side of the table and hugs both her brother and future sister-in-law together. "I'm so happy for both of you. I knew there was something you were keeping from me."

"Well, this calls for a Champagne toast," Andy signals the waitress, "Can you bring a bottle of Champagne, please." Andy also gets up and stands next to Amy, he shakes Jake's hand. He hesitates not sure if he should hug Victoria.

Victoria makes the decision for him and quickly hugs him.

The waitress brings a bottle and pops the cork. As she pours the glasses, Amy asks, "Have you told dad yet?"

"Yes, I went out to see him on Friday after work to talk to him about Victoria. Dad's excited and happy for us. Victoria and I plan to spend this weekend with him."

"Have you set a date yet?" Andy questions.

"Well, my father's coming out to spend the holidays with me this year. It's the first year he's offered to be part of my Christmas holidays since before my mother died. He usually goes to Switzerland or somewhere skiing with his friends," Victoria shares.

Andy cringes; he can't image what life must have been like for Victoria. Amy's mentioned in the past bits and pieces of what she knows about Victoria and her childhood.

"So, are you spending the holidays at the hotel?" Amy asks.

"That's the other good news I want to share with you." Victoria smiles, "Thanks to Sophie's friend, who happens to be Jim's sister from the office, I – no we – found a perfect house and we put an offer on it."

"Wow, you really have been busy," Amy jokes.

"We take possession at the end of the December. It's a brand new show house, move in ready. We just need to wait until the builder finishes their latest show home to replace it."

"It's the first show house that was built before development was ready, so we bought it as is," Jake adds. "We not only love the house, but the colours, so we decided to just make things easy."

Their dinner arrives and while they eat, the conversation involves discussions on the location and design of the new house. The house is only about twenty minutes away from Amy's house. She's so happy for her brother and Victoria.

As they finish the discussions around the house, Jake turns to his sister. "Actually, Victoria and I have a favour to ask you."

"Really, you know I'll do anything for both of you." Amy grins, "What do you need someone to help pack your place up?"

"No problem," Andy jumps right in, "I can bring some friends for added muscle for the heavy lifting."

"No, that's not what we had in mind," Victoria chimes in.

"But we'll keep the offer open," Jake teases.

Andy and Amy look at each other and over at Jake and Victoria. "So what do you need?" Amy asks.

"Let me ask, Jake, please?" she moves forward on her chair. "We want to get married at your place during the Christmas holidays and we'd like you to be my maid of honour."

Jake adds, "Andy, I'd be honoured if you'd be the best man."

Andy and Amy look at each other, shocked.

"Of course, we'd be thrilled," Amy answers for both of them immediately.

Andy recovers from the shock. "But Jake, you must have lots of friends that you've known way longer than you've known me!"

Jake nods his head in agreement. "True, but here's the problem: I've got three best buds who are my partners in the law firm. If I choose one over the other, I'll have problems. I've got hockey friends, school friends, church friends, lots of friends, but the problem we've got is that we don't have a lot of room for a big wedding. We want to be married over the holidays and you're the most neutral friend I have. No one will get upset with me choosing you."

"So, it's because of my relationship with your sister?" Andy rubs his chin, "Not the best reason I've ever heard, but, why not? No, I'm teasing you, I'd be honoured that you consider me a friend worthy of such an important event."

"Thanks so much Andy, we didn't want to insult you or anything, but why create problems if it's not necessary and besides we want a small wedding with just our family and a couple of friends. We don't want to wait and we've not had any luck finding a place to have the wedding, so we thought you might help us out."

"Does Dad know? Maybe he wants you to get married in Riverside." Amy's concerned for her dad's feelings.

"Actually, it's his idea," Jake says, "Victoria and I spoke with him last night about it and I talked to him about the plans on Friday night."

"What day did you have in mind?" Andy wonders.

"That's up to Amy," Jake and Victoria both answer and then laugh.

"Christmas is on a Saturday this year, so what about New Year's Eve?" Amy suggests. "Whatever day works for you guys is okay with me."

"At least you'd be able to remember your anniversary date," Andy jokes.

"That sounds great for us, don't you think, Jake?" Victoria looks at Jake for confirmation.

"Any day works for me, I just want you to be my wife." Jake reaches over and gently kisses Victoria.

The waitress comes to take their dessert order. They order dessert, coffee and tea and spend the next two hours discussing plans for the upcoming wedding, the holidays and their jobs.

As they finish the evening, Victoria and Amy make plans to meet after work the next night at Amy's house. Clearly Victoria doesn't want a big wedding; she has very simple plans and is very willing to go with whatever Jake wants. Her plan only includes her father. She's not even sure she wants Christopher to be invited. For the next night's dinner plans Jake offers to bring pizza and Andy offers to bring some treats. As Andy drives Amy home, they discuss the events of the evening.

"Wow, I didn't see that one coming, did you?" Andy asks Amy.

"Well, I'm not surprised about the engagement, but I thought they'd want a big wedding," Amy answers. "I'd want my friends and cousins at my wedding."

"Does Victoria have any other family except her father?" Andy inquires, again making a mental note of Amy's comments about what she'd like for her own wedding.

"Not that I know about. She's only ever talked about her brother and parents. Her grandparents are both dead, like mine. That I know for sure. She's never talked much about her family or any extended family."

"The bit I have heard her say suggests she's lead a pretty lonely life." Andy shakes his head. "I can't imagine Christmas without my family, can you?"

"No, they spent two Christmas holidays with us while we were going to school together. Even when her mother was alive they never had traditional holidays like we did," Amy remembers. "I never thought much about it at the time; it was great having friends stay over for the holidays. I'll ask Dad more about it next time I talk to him."

Andy drives Amy to her house. "Looks like mom has gone to bed early tonight," he notices as they walk up the steps and into the house.

Once inside, he kisses Amy goodnight. Amy melts into his arms as she returns his kiss. Andy lingers outside and listens for her to lock the door and then heads home. He realizes why Jake doesn't want to wait to plan a big wedding. *Smart guy, I'm not sure I'd want to be planning a wedding for six months or a year.*

He was best man for two of his friends on the force and these guys were both in wedding mode for over a year. He saw the roller-coaster of emotions and the stress caused by flower arrangements and cake flavours. He'd been a best man for each of his sisters as well. He remembers spending time with his dad in the back yard while the women were in the kitchen pouring over bridal magazines. It was months before he could sit on a chair without first having to move some kind of wedding book or decoration.

All that work and the day went by as quickly as any other day, but with a flurry of emotions. *Nope, he can see Jake is one lucky man in more ways than one.*

Chapter Twenty

Amy's cell phone rings just as she finishes up her rounds the next morning. Her father would like to meet her for coffee downstairs in the cafeteria.

"Not much has changed in here," Ed comments as he hugs his daughter.

"Nope, the whole hospital's the same. Different patients, but the same old building and mostly the same staff." Amy hugs him back.

"Dad, what are you doing in the city, is everything alright?" Amy's immediately concerned since she knows her father hates to drive in the city.

"Well, I had this great idea, but I want to run it past you before I talk to Jake and Victoria." Ed clears his throat. "I don't want them to think I'm meddling in their wedding plans, so I want to talk to you to see what you think. Joyce offered to baby-sit Finnegan for me so I could make the trip."

"Sure, but you could've just called me. Why drive to the city?" Amy asks

"Well, if you like the idea, I'm going to see if I can catch up with Jake and Victoria for lunch or something. You know, I've never been to their law office downtown. It's something I should've done a long time ago, so I just felt adventurous today."

"That sounds logical. So what's the grand plan?"

"I ran into my friends George and Patricia from the Westview Golf and Country Club yesterday. I mentioned the kids wanting to get married over the holidays. One thing led to another and before I knew it, they offered to open up the Dining Room for any day between Boxing Day and New Year's Eve. Normally they close down for the entire week from the day before Christmas until after New Years. This year they wanted to try offering a New Years Dinner and Dance. So they'll have staff available if we let them know soon enough. We can have any date from Christmas Eve until the day before New Year's Eve. What do you think?"

"Dad, I think it's a great suggestion; Westview Golf and Country Club is beautiful. The Dining Room with all of those amazing floor to ceiling windows and massive fire place is just spectacular. The food's not bad either. Remember Joyce's niece was married there last winter? You're a genius." Amy reaches over and kisses him on the cheek.

"I don't want you to be upset or disappointed not having the wedding at your house."

"Actually, Dad, I've been really concerned about how to convert the living room and dining room to make enough space to properly set up the area to make it work."

"So, do you think Jake and Victoria will like the idea?" Ed's concerned and doesn't want to upset them.

"I think they'll love it, they don't seem to care about where they get married, they just want to have a small wedding and Victoria wants it to occur while her father's here." Amy checks her phone. "Sorry Dad got to go. Have something happening in ER that needs my attention.

"No problem, I need to get downtown anyway. I've got my GPS set so I should be good." Ed's very proud of himself. "Jake and Victoria bought it for me for my birthday, thought I'd test it out."

"Are you spending the day? We could meet up for dinner tonight," Amy inquires.

"I'd love that, why don't I stop over to say hello to Grace and wait for you to get home. Maybe we can get Jake and Victoria to join us. I'll invite Grace and Andy too."

"Super, I'll try not to be too late." Amy gives her father a hug as she leaves for the ER.

Ed returns the hug and heads out to the parking lot for his adventure into the center of the city.

Chapter Twenty One

The last week in November appears along with a Chinook. Temperatures rise and the huge snow piles start to melt away. It's perfect weather for the week of the Festival of Trees.

Andy's been busy the past several evenings, so Amy's been back and forth on her IPad with Cheryl and Joyce to develop a list of must have Christmas decorations. They've arranged a shopping day to handle the purchases.

Amy's excited that Jake and Victoria have decided on the Westview Golf and Country Club. It makes life so much easier for everyone. Plus, they've been able to increase the guest list to almost one hundred people. Jake and Victoria are now able to invite more of their friends and family members.

Victoria fell in love with the outfit Amy plans to wear for the Gala Ball and suggests she simply have it dry cleaned and wear it to the wedding. Amy's not sure she wants to wear it to the wedding; she thinks it's a little over the top for a wedding. Victoria is open to Amy finding another dress. Victoria's already bought her dress, a white velvet winter wedding dress that she found by herself. They've decided on Christmas plants, and red and black and white as the colour scheme.

By the time Saturday morning comes Amy's glad for the weekend off and for having nothing planned for the day. Cheryl and her group have kept Amy busy every night with online shopping and now there's a massive pile of boxes, bags and decorations sitting in the family room and garage waiting for next weekend, when Amy's scheduled the house decorating day with an evening filled with pizza and movies as the reward for the day.

Amy spends part of the morning organizing the purchases of the week. In the early afternoon she heads off to have her hair done. It's been a while so she's decided to get a cut before the hairdresser puts her hair into a fashionable upsweep. She's purchased a few crystal jewel combs for her hair.

Amy's looking forward to sitting back and relaxing, she's decided to go for the full deal, exactly what her dad used to tease her mom about. With her elegant heals, she realizes she needs a pedicure as well as her nails done. Amy has everything laid out and ready to put on so she can quickly get ready once she gets back home.

Cocktails are scheduled for 6:30 to 7:30 and Andy is picking her up between 5:30 and 6:00 so she wants to be organized and ready. She plans to stop over at Grace's so Grace can take a couple of pictures of her and Andy. She has two reasons, first because she wants pictures of them together in an elegant evening setting and second she's promised to send a picture to Victoria to make sure she'll be happy with their attire for the wedding next month.

Amy's very excited about this evening and is looking forward to dressing up. It's been a long time since she's gone anywhere formal.

Amy arrives back from the salon with lots of time to spare. She takes her time putting on fresh makeup. She's happy with the results and she feels as fantastic as she looks.

With her look complete, Amy takes one last look in the mirror. Satisfied, she decides to go downstairs to wait for Andy.

At the top of the stairs the chimes announce Andy's early.

"Wow!" is the only word Andy seems to be able to come up with. He stands at the door completely speechless.

"You look very handsome yourself." Amy pulls him inside. "Close your mouth, if it was summer you'd have it full of flies."

Andy can't believe his eyes. Amy knows she looks good, but again "Wow" seems to be the only word he can say.

Amy laughs as she realizes she forgot her cape and gloves. As she heads upstairs she hears Andy gasp. Smugly, she knows he's definitely seen the back of her dress.

With gloves, cape and hand bag in her hand, she comes back down the stairs. Andy's not moved and is still watching her, this time with a huge grin on his face.

"Got any more words?" Amy teases.

"Actually, yes, I've been practising all day." With that, Andy gets down on one knee. He takes Amy's hand.

"Amy, I've fallen totally and completely in love with you. I can't imagine spending my life with anyone else but you. I spoke with your father last night and he's given his blessings for me to ask you to marry me. Amy, will you be my wife?"

Andy opens a small box he has in the palm of his hand. Amy falls to her knees so she's eye level with Andy.

"I love you too and I want to wake up every morning next to you for the rest of my life." She leans forward and kisses him. Andy drops the box and wraps his arms around her and returns a very passionate kiss.

Suddenly Andy realizes he hasn't given her the ring. He pulls away and looks down in his lap for the small pink satin box. He carefully takes the ring out of the box and places it on Amy's ring finger.

Andy's chosen what he believes is the perfect ring for Amy. The presence of the ring on her ring finger is just right and it fits perfectly. Not too small and not too big and not too gaudy. The beautiful soft pale pink and white diamonds and the impeccable workmanship are breathtaking! At the center is an absolutely fabulous Old European Cut 1 carat soft pink diamond. While the diamond is large, it is set down into the band. There are three rows of four perfectly set princess cut diamonds on each side of the band for the perfect touch of sparkle and added 'wow' factor. The semi bezel setting of the pink diamond protects it beautifully and the results are no prongs or sharp edges to get caught on anything.

"Do you like this ring?" Andy asks, looking up into Amy's eyes, "I remembered you don't like solitaries so I had my friend make this ring especially for you."

"Andy, it's perfect in every way. I love it." Amy holds out her hand. "Just as you're perfect and I love you in every way." She leans over to kiss him one more time before they have to leave.

They're interrupted by the door chimes. It's Grace ready with her camera. "I can't remember if you're coming to me or me coming to you, but since you didn't come, I decided you must be waiting." She announces as she comes in.

"Sorry, we're running a couple of minutes late." Andy's face is red.

"Well, let's get the show on the road; stand over here by the fireplace." Grace is busy organizing her camera and misses the winks exchanged by this newly engaged couple.

They move in front of the fireplace where Grace is fussing about the perfect pose. "Amy, I absolutely love your outfit. You're going to be the envy of all the women tonight. And Andy, well, Amy you need to keep your hands on him all night."

"I've learned so much from my camera course; I want this picture for the final mark. It's got to be perfect. Now big smile for the perfect picture."

Amy and Andy humour Grace by continuing to follow her directions to pose and smile. Suddenly Grace notices Amy's ring. She puts the camera down and looks into Andy's face and then at Amy.

"Is that what I think it is?" She hesitates just slightly. With solid nods from both Amy and Andy, she moves forward with an oversized hug for both of them. Letting go, she looks at the ring.

"Isn't this the most beautiful ring you've ever seen?" Amy's gushing over the ring. "It's exactly what I imagined my engagement ring would be like."

Amy relives the moments leading up to the proposal and suddenly stopped mid sentence. She looked at Andy. "Hey did you say you went out to Riverside to ask my father for my hand last night. Dad's known for over 24 hours and never told me?"

"Yes, and you always say he can't keep a secret." Andy grinned.

"I hate to dampen such a wonderful time, but you guys are going to be late. Prince Charming, you need to take your beautiful Cinderella to the ball."

"I want to hear all the details in the morning. I'll have brunch ready for 10 tomorrow." Grace hugs both again as they leave for the ball.

As Andy helps Amy into his car Amy declares, "I would've been happy just staying at home with you!"

"I know, but we're all dressed up and I want to show off my new fiancée to the world." Andy winks at her as he reaches over and kisses her before he puts on his seat belt. "I'll need to protect you from all the men that will be swarming around you tonight. Did I tell you how absolutely incredibly beautiful you are?"

"You did, but a woman never tires of hearing compliments." Amy pulls off her glove and stares at her ring. "This ring is so special. My favourite colour and the design and style, you're an amazing man."

"Well, it's hard to not know you love pink. Just look in your garden all the pink and white flowers. Besides I've seen you buy flowers, they always have different shades of pink, light to dark. Your dad mentioned your mother's favourite colour was pink so I thought the ring would have special meaning to you."

"Andy, I think you're going to make me cry." Amy's eyes glisten. "And that'll wreck my makeup."

"Hey, it's a night for celebration. Let's see if you're going to get that tree you bid on, especially since I understand there's no tree or tree decorations in any of the collection of boxes you've got spread out all over your family room." Andy smiled.

"How did you know about that? Your mother?" Amy questions.

"Heck no, your dad told me. He knows everything it seems. Did you know he talks with my mom almost every day?"

"No! so we have spies in the mix."

"Well, she sure wasn't as excited as I thought; she must've already known something." Andy realizes.

"Maybe, but I think she must have something up her sleeve; she sure was in a hurry for us to leave. Should we be worried?"

"Nah, she just wanted to get back to all her old cronies. Don't forget they've been giving her the gears for years that I haven't found someone."

They decide to treat themselves and use Valet parking as they arrive at the centre. They walk into the most amazing sight; the decorations for the evening are spectacular. Amy and Andy walk around the room admiring the table decorations and the beautiful decor. There are twenty five decorated trees set up around the room. Each tree has a stand next to it with silent auction bids that had been completed over the course of the Festival open to the public. Along with the trees there are fake doors set up that host wreaths. There are also fake fire places set up with wreaths and mantel decorations. The front of the room hosts a stage with a stand shaped like a giant tree. Each wooden layer has tiny lights sculptured around it. The stand holds hundreds of potted Poinsettias. Standing back, it appears to be a giant red poinsettia tree with sparkling lights decorating it. Twinkle lights surround the room and the bottom of the stage.

On each beautifully set table, there's a Christmas centre piece with three candles. Red napkins with gold rings are placed in the center of each plate setting with sparkling silverware. Crystal wine and water glasses reflect the light. The event's been sold out with 500 people in attendance. Men in black tuxedos and the women beautifully attired in amazing gowns move around the room, admiring or bidding on the trees and decorations or networking with friends and acquaintances.

Amy very discretely takes out her phone and captures several pictures of the room to send off to the girls. With that promise kept, she shuts off her phone so she has no distractions.

Andy's surprised to see so many people he knows and he's equally amazed that Amy knows so many corporate big shots and politicians. They spend the next half hour moving around the room, speaking to friends and acquaintances. Andy's proud to introduce Amy to the people he works with. The first time he introduces Amy as his fiancée they both giggle. Fortunately the first person they speak with is an old police buddy and hockey team member who's there with his wife of ten years. They spend a few minutes with them. It doesn't take long before many others join their little group. Many recognize either Andy or Amy and are pleased to see them.

Amy's surprised to see what a tight knit community the City Police are. It doesn't take long before the news of their engagement has spread around the room. She is also shocked to see how many people she knows, either through patients or through the volunteer work she's done at the hospital.

Amy meets one of the hospital board members and is surprised to learn she's the MC for the evening. Vivian Burns is pleased to hear about Amy's engagement and is surprised when her husband realizes he knows Andy from a local youth organization they both volunteer with.

Andy hasn't seen the trees before and goes around with Amy to admire them. He instantly picks the tree that he's certain Amy's bid on. Sure enough her bid's still on top.

"How'd you know this is the one?" Amy's surprised again as she realizes how well Andy already seems to know her and her taste.

"Well, let's see," Andy teases, "The tree's a big green tree that looks so real you want to touch it, it's covered in pink, gold and white velvet ribbons and roses and lilies. That's my first guess."

"Actually, it's not white, its cream, but close enough. In your opinion, isn't it the prize winning tree?" Amy stands admiring the tree. It's an eight foot Douglas fir covered in tiny twinkle lights (1500 according to the notes by the design team); on top an angel adorns the tree in a gold outfit with tiny pink pearls on the hem of her dress. The floral decorations mimic tiny corsages of pink roses, gold ribbon and cream coloured lilies. The glass decorations are bountiful and each branch has something special on it. Tiny crystal angels fill in the spaces. Amy again checks her bid to make sure she's still on top.

"I want to check again just before dinner since the bidding closes when the cocktail hour's finished and the meal begins." Amy wants this tree. "I can either spend a whole day trying to find all the decorations to do my own tree or I can just buy this one. Besides, it's going to a great cause," Amy justifies.

"Hey, I'm with you honey, I'll run back over here just as we sit down to make sure no one else has the same idea," Andy volunteers. "Least I can do for the woman I love and plan to marry," he adds.

Amy smiles at him and squeezes his hand.

"I thought this dress might be too revealing, but I see lots of dresses with similar plunging backs," Amy comments.

Andy immediately responds, "Are you kidding, look at the plunging fronts on some of the dresses."

They're joined by the Chief of Police, Richard Richburg and his wife, Laurie. Andy starts to introduce them but quickly learns that Laurie volunteers at the hospital and knows Amy.

"Dear, I heard about your engagement from Vivian. Congratulations to both of you." She leans forward, "I hate to gossip but some women shouldn't wear plunging necklines."

"I better not have any costume malfunctions while the press are around," adds the Chief. Focusing on Amy he adds, "I hope we get a chance to talk later this evening. Laurie's told me so much about you, Amy, I feel like I know you already, and of course Andy here is one of my best men."

Andy turns red and is pleased to hear Vivian at the microphone asking everyone to take their places.

Andy starts to pull out their tickets so they can find their seats. "No need to look, you're at our table," Laurie informs him. "When I saw your name and Amy's name on the guest list I pulled a favour. I wanted to ask Amy for some direction on an idea I have at the hospital."

Andy relaxes as they head for the table when he sees four other detectives and their wives standing by the table. Amy again squeezes his hand. He hasn't realized he's tensed up. They smile at each other as Andy helps Amy to her chair.

As everyone's almost seated Andy quickly gets up and heads back to the pink tree to make sure Amy's name's still at the top of the bid list.

As Amy explains why he has suddenly left the table, Laurie leans over to Amy to say, "He remembers his promises. That's a great characteristic to have in a husband."

The spotlight is on Vivian as she welcomes everyone and introduced Father Dietrich, Chaplin from the RCMP K Division headquarters to say grace. With grace completed, everyone sits down and the first of four courses are served. Everyone at the table begins to relax after the initial shock of finding they're sitting with Chief Richburg and his wife. Laurie's an old pro at these events and in short order she has everyone laughing and joining in.

Once dessert is served, Vivian begins her program for the evening. While it's her first time to host the Festival of Trees, she's been involved in the program from its inception and is proud to have the job. She has arranged many activities and speakers. Throughout the program, the winning bids are announced. When the bid for the pink tree is introduced Andy takes Amy's hand under the table and holds it.

"The successful bid for the pink tree is a personal friend of mine. This bid also includes the fireplace decorations and door wreath. Dr. Amy Murphy, would you please stand up? There you are my dear. Amy dear, please have your handsome young man stand up as well."

Totally unprepared for what's about to happen, Amy looks to Andy as they both shyly stand up together. Amy's shocked that she also won the bids for the rest of the pink tree decorations since she didn't bid on them. Andy quickly grins at her and she realizes who entered the bids. She reaches over and squeezes his hand acknowledging that she knows it was him.

Vivian continues, "I want to congratulate both of you on your engagement to be married. Everyone, will you please rise your glasses as we toast this dynamic young couple on their engagement."

A big round of applause followed the toast and the couple quickly wave and sit down, both truly shocked and blushing.

Andy leans over and whispers in Amy's ear, "At least no tinkle of glasses, we can be grateful for that."

Amy nods in agreement. Vivian announces all the winners of the evening. She also provides a gift for each person in attendance. The tree of poinsettias at the front contains a plant for each guest. Also, she has each person check the bottom of their saucer for one person at each table wins the spectacular Christmas floral centre piece as well.

The traffic sergeant's wife, Marisa, is the winner for their table. As the meal and entertainment conclude the stage is mechanically moved to one side and the dance floor with a full orchestra is featured.

"This is my favourite part," Laurie explains, "Rick and I love ballroom dancing and we never get much practice. I'm hoping this year we can get a program for the youth to get them off the streets and into a space to learn to dance."

"That'd be great." Amy's excited by this. "I know several people that would love to be part of that kind of program, especially with all the dance contests on TV these days."

While tables clear people start to move around the room. The band starts to play and it appears everyone's waiting for someone to get on the floor to start dancing.

Chief Richburg rises and invites his men and their spouses to join him and his wife on the floor. Not wanting to appear to be disobeying an order, the dance floor's suddenly full.

The couple burns off the calories of the meal by dancing together and with others in attendance. Chief Richburg asks Amy to dance and as they guild around the room he asks if he can drop by her office sometime in the next week or so.

"Is everything alright?" Amy's concerned.

"Yes, but I happen to know you've captured the heart of my favourite detective," Chief Johansson reveals.

Amy smiles. "Actually, I should be reporting a theft; he's completed and totally stolen my heart."

The Chief laughs. "No wonder, you're a very funny lady, not to mention talented. I hear you're the head of the cardiology unit at Rock Valley General Hospital. Did you know Andy has already completed the preliminary application for a security check on you for marriage purposes?" He continues to swing her around the dance floor as they execute a perfect fox trot.

Amy smiles. "It seems Andy's been a busy little beaver. He actually had my engagement ring designed by a friend and then spoke to my dad before he asked me."

"Good thing you said yes." they share a laugh.

Amy starts to ask about the security clearance issues and is interrupted by the Chief. "Let's enjoy the music. Andy will bring the paperwork to you and we will go from there, but I know there'll be no problems with the department approving your marriage with Andy. I also need to talk to you about my mother who's going to be moving to Calgary and will need a cardiologist since she recently had bypass surgery out in Nova Scotia."

Amy agrees to meet with the Chief and his mother, and with that they finish their dance and return to the table. Many people are starting to leave and Amy's surprised when she checks the time and realizes it's well past midnight.

Amy and Andy collect their plants at the door. Each has been wrapped in plastic and placed in small boxes for transportation to their new home. The tree manager for the event collects payment for the winning bids and makes arrangements to deliver her decorations shortly after lunch the next day.

With that, they wait for their vehicle from the Valet, saying goodnight to others leaving at the same time.

Once in the car, they discuss the events of the evening. Amy's elated that she not only has a new tree but all the rest of the decorations that go with it. They discuss their plans for the next day. They also start to throw around ideas for setting a date for their wedding. Andy's pleased to hear Amy wants a spring wedding. They agree to talk in the morning before they have brunch with Andy's mom. Amy reminds him that she's decorating tomorrow and her friends from Riverside will be in by noon. Andy offers to help with the outside decorations after he finishes up at his mother's. She's already called dibs on his help.

Andy helps Amy into the house with both plants, declaring he'll just forget to water his and it'll die. Once inside they melt into each other's arms for a final goodnight.

As is his routine, Andy waits outside until Amy has locked the door. He notices his mother's curtain move. He smiles knowing Amy's safe and being watched over by someone who loves her almost as much as he does. He waves to the curtain and hops in the car. He unties his tie and unbuttons the top of his shirt. He's had a great night and is pleased his proposal plans to Amy went off as he'd planned. He sits back in the seat to drive home and wonders about the plans and how many arrangements his mother's already made that will have to be changed.

Chapter Twenty Two

Amy snuggles down in her big bed, closes her eyes and dreams she's wrapped up in Andy arms. The alarm wakes her up. She smiles and looks at her hand with the ring Andy put on her finger last night. *It was not a dream.* She looks over to the nightstand to see the picture of her smiling with Finnegan in her arms and remembers Andy telling her it's the first time he realized he loves her.

The phone rings. "Good morning beautiful, you need to get up. I'll be there in a couple of minutes with coffee and muffins," Andy speaks softly into the phone to Amy.

"I'm getting up now. I'll be ready in a few minutes; you know the code, so come on in if you get here before I'm ready. I love you." As she talks, she's already up and rummaging in her closet for something to wear.

"Be there in ten, I love you more." Andy hangs up. *Good thing it's cold out this morning*, he thinks to himself. However long they wait to be married, it'll be too long for Andy.

Amy quickly hops in the shower; she'd taken out all the pins from her hair last night, so she's in and out in a couple of minutes. She puts on her comfortable wine coloured lululemon jogging outfit. She looks great and it's the perfect outfit to wear to meet her future mother-in-law for breakfast and decorate the house for Christmas.

She hears Andy from the kitchen intercom announcing he's waiting. Quickly, she pulls her hair into her trusty pony tail, grabs her socks and sneakers and heads downstairs. At the bottom of the stairs, she finds another penny. As she picks it up, she realizes she can now cross off item #3 from her mom's list; she has in fact found her true love.

Andy's brought her favourite, Tim Horton's maple syrup muffins and coffee. He has poured the coffee into two mugs and put the muffins on plates. He turns around and takes a deep breath. Amy's fresh from the shower; her hair's still damp with a shiny makeup-free face. She's just as beautiful as she was last night. He sets down the coffee cup and gives her a lingering kiss.

Amy drops her sneakers and socks and returns Andy's embrace. With regret, Andy lets her go. "If we want to get any of our own plans started before we meet up with my mom we need to get busy."

Amy picks up her socks and puts them and her sneakers on. Andy finds the calendar on his phone. Together they start looking at dates.

"Is there any date that is really special to you?" Andy asks.

"Actually, my birth parents were married on May 21, the Saturday of the Victoria long weekend. I'd love that date – that is, if we can make it happen on such short notice," Amy replied as she bites into her muffin.

"That works for me, although it seems like an eternity till then." Andy takes a gulp of his coffee and burns his mouth. "Wow, this is still really hot."

Immediately, the doctor takes over. "Are you okay? Let me look."

Andy smiles at her, "Do you know how many times a day I burn myself on Tim Horton's coffee. You'd think I'd remember to give it a minute, but I'm not paying any attention today. I wonder why?"

"Back to business. Can we set this date?" Amy gets serious. "I've been a bridesmaid once already and I can tell you the bride spent months planning every detail. I'm not quite that focused right now, but we have a lot of work ahead of us, especially with all the details and ideas my aunts and mom's best friends will have for us."

"Hey, my mom's an expert; she's already married off two daughters," Andy responds.

They spend the next hour making plans for guest lists, places to try to book, and general plans. The phone rings and Grace wonders when they're coming over.

Laughing, they grab their coats. Amy pushes her phone and IPad into her pocket and they head across the street, holding hands as they go. Amy stops in the middle of the street when she recognizes her dad's truck in Grace's driveway.

"Looks like she called in some reinforcements," Andy jokes as he pulls Amy out of the street.

Grace is waiting at the door along with Ed. Ed hugs Amy as she comes through the door.

"What are you doing here?" she giggles as she hugs her dad.

"Well, I know that Andy asked me if he could marry you and I happened to hear," as he turns and smiles at Grace, "that he gave you a ring last night. I jumped at an invitation for brunch when Grace called, so here I am, along with my buddy, Finnegan."

Finnegan shares his well wishes with a big lick as Amy gets down greeting him with a hug. He bounces around the room with excitement.

"Speaking of brunch, I'm starved, how long till we eat?" Andy gives his mother a bear hug.

Amy shows her father her ring. "Isn't it the most beautiful ring you've ever seen?" she asks.

"Very nice indeed," Ed replies.

Grace announces she has everything to eat and they sit down to big plates full of pancakes, scrambled eggs, sausages, ham and bacon. She also has fresh fruit and cheese set out.

Together they hold hands as Ed says grace. Amy's surprised at how comfortable the four of them always are when they're together.

As they eat, Amy and Andy share their experiences from the previous night. They tell Grace and Ed about the gala ball and the engagement excitement from so many of their friends and acquaintances. Amy's excited about her Christmas tree and looks forward to getting the decorations up. She's glad she took a couple of minutes last night to send the pictures she'd taken to everyone. Seems everyone was impressed, judging from the responses she's been receiving on her phone.

They turn their attention to the engagement. Ed passes Amy an envelope. Amy recognizes her mom's handwriting. It reads *For Amy's Wedding*.

"Your mom asked that I give this to you to help plan your wedding. I'm guessing it's another to do list to help you along with your plans." Ed gently smiles. "You know how she loved weddings."

"Yes and I remember she had lots of ideas and opinions. I'll read it over tonight." Amy wants to be alone when she opens it. Amy stares at it for a couple of minutes.

Grace decides she needs to give Amy some space to deal with this, so she changes the subject by inquiring about dates.

"Do you have some dates in mind?" Grace asks.

Amy looks at Andy and he nods in agreement. "Actually, we're thinking about the long weekend in May."

Ed smiles. "Good choice, I know three other people who'll be very happy with that decision."

Andy explains to his mom, "It's the day Amy's birth parents were married."

"Well, we've got a date; next we need to plan where to have the wedding ceremony and the dinner." Grace pulls out her note book.

Amy has her IPad already beside her as well, and they smile at each other as they start making notes.

Ed suggests they speak with his friend Doug from the plant whose daughter, Sara, is the banquet coordinator at the newly renovated Greenwood Inn. It's easy to get to, has lots of parking, has accommodation for out of town guests and since we have an the coordinator, it could be the perfect place. The fact that they are just in the process of reopening after their major renovations could mean the place might be available.

Grace has volunteered to help Amy as much as possible since she has a lot of time on her hands and has already helped two daughters plan their weddings. She's careful not to overstep her relationship with Amy. Amy's grateful for the way Grace wants to work together. Ed wants to be available to help Jake with his wedding plans first. With the ability to invite more people, Jake and Victoria are going to need all the help they can get with a wedding happening in just a little over one month. Ed teases that within a few months he'll double the size of his family.

Amy's already decided who she wants to have in her bridal party. She plans to ask Cindy and Joan, Andy's sisters, and Victoria. Amy also wants to ask Sophie to be her maid of honour. Andy decides he will include Jake and his best friend Steve. He first met Steve at the police training academy and they have been friends ever since. Andy stood up with Steve last year when Steve got married. Andy also wants to include two of his best friends, Brian and Troy. They started grade one together, played hockey together, and Andy has been there for both of them as they've been there for Andy over the years.

They also discussed having Andy's two young nieces as junior bridesmaids since they are too old to be flower girls.

For the flower girl, Amy wants her cousin Zack's little girl, Jennifer. At three years old she's captured Amy's heart. Even as a baby, Jennifer would cuddle into Amy's arms. Now at three, she loves to call Amy and Amy loves to share all their chatty conversations. She's already envisioned Jennifer as her flower girl and is excited about the prospect of taking her shopping for a dress. Since Amy's cousin Carrie has twin boys almost the same age, she's considering the two boys each carrying a ring. As identical twins, in tuxedos that match Andy's, Amy sees the wedding party complete. Andy shares the vision and agrees. They make plans to speak with each wedding party person directly. They plan to have a dinner with the whole group over the holidays when everyone's hopefully available. Ed and Grace believe they've make good choices.

The rest of the morning passes quickly and everyone is happy with the plans that have started to formulate.

Andy and Amy head back over to her house as Ed takes Finnegan for a small walk, leaving Grace to start getting her decorations organized. Ed is going to help her with putting up her big tree. Ed has volunteered to help get the boxes out of the storage attic in the garage where Richard has them neatly labelled and organized. He's also agreed to help Andy with decorating the outside of both Grace's house and Amy's as well. It's a tall order to fill in just one afternoon.

Amy puts coffee on as Andy starts to open all the boxes in the family room. The doorbell rings and Joyce, Cheryl and Connie are there ready to start helping Amy with her decorations. They plan to stay overnight and have plans with Grace for the next day. They all hug Amy and Andy as they learn of the couple's engagement. The room is filled with excitement and noise.

Shortly after that, the tree manager from the Festival arrives to deliver Amy's tree and her decorations. Because Amy has double doors on the front of her house, they have left the tree decorated and wrapped in large pieces of plastic wrap. The tree's brought in and set up next to the fireplace waiting for its final home. The odd decoration has fallen off, but the delivery team places each in their proper location based on the detailed pictures that they have of each of the trees. They leave the detailed photos and the special storage bags. Amy's so pleased that Andy surprised her last night with the fireplace decorations and the matching wreath. Everyone's excited to get started on the decorating; especially now that the first tree is up and decorated.

Ed and Andy quickly find themselves organized and ready to handle the outside decorations. They set to work putting up the decorations for Grace. Richard had always put the decorations up and was meticulous in his handling of the various sets of lights and yard art. After every Christmas he'd sit down and lay out his plans for the following year, carefully keeping each year's plans in a rotation that kept the neighbours excited to see his set up. Last year had been no exception and Andy finds the plans carefully filed under the current year. They follow the plans to the letter. It makes the decorating very easy. Richard had purchased new decorations, replacement bulbs and cords during the after holidays sales.

It seems they're finished in no time, and after stopping for a mid afternoon snack they are ready to tackle Amy's decorations. Joyce and Amy have done both online and in store shopping earlier in the month and have all the outside decorations laid out in bags and boxes on the floor in the garage. It's not as easy this time since there are no plans to follow. Andy puts a reminder note into his phone to work with Amy on a plan as soon as the holidays are finished and before the decorations are taken down to make it easier for next year.

Without a plan and after several false starts the men complete the basic decorations and wait for an inspection by the ladies before they move forward. The decorations are simple in comparison to the elaborate display of decorations Andy's dad has. Andy reminds Amy that his dad had collected his decorations and made intricate plans for years. All in all, it's a productive afternoon. As dusk begins to fall, everyone starts to think about food, so they decide to order in Chinese food from the local restaurant that delivers.

Inside the house the living room's decked out with the gorgeous tree and the mantel that is decorated with two elegant stockings hanging in place. The first Poinsettia from the night before is on the foyer table with Amy's favourite nativity scene, a scene from the Thomas Kinkade's Star of Hope collection given to her by her mother. Amy has the second big Poinsettia plant sitting in her family room. Amy's staircase is decorated in garland with dozens of twinkle lights, roses and pink bows and gold ribbons. She's decided to continue to add decorations to each room as she's out and about during the holidays. Joyce has reminded her that her mother spent several years developing her inventory of Christmas decorations. Ed suggests maybe she should come out and look through all the boxes of stuff and pick out some decorations she'd like from his storage room. Amy agrees to do that on her next trip out.

Amy's mom had a favourite Christmas decoration theme which included several dozen nativity scenes. Over the years she'd bought and passed many of her favourites from her collection on to both Amy and her brother. As a result, Amy has several sets of nativity scenes including crystal sets, wooden sets, ceramic sets and porcelain sets. Amy's put them out throughout her house.

The dining room is set up with Christmas table runners of gold velvet with pink ribbon and tassels. Throughout the house, the colour theme of gold, cream and pink is followed.

At exactly 5 o'clock right on schedule the outside lights come on and the inside decorations turn on with the flick of the light switch. Amy's pleased with the results and she's had great fun with Joyce, Cheryl, Connie and Grace.

Dinner arrives and they sit together at the kitchen table enjoying their time together. The discussion turns to the two upcoming weddings. With Jake's wedding organized and ready to go, they take a few minutes to discuss some gift ideas. Since they're buying a new place and bringing their two households together the ideas for gifts are limited. Amy suggests a romantic cruise or holiday to some tropical island where the weather's warm. Ed reflects on the wonderful 25th anniversary first honeymoon that he and Ann took to Paris. Amy agrees that Paris is beautiful in the summer, but since both Victoria and Jake have been there it might be nice to consider someplace warm. She reminds him of the great time they had on their Christmas cruise last year.

The evening comes to an end early since everyone is exhausted. The ladies decide they're staying with Grace since they spent their last sleep over at Amy's. Amy admits that since tomorrow's a work day she will not be much fun, so they head off across the street. Amy tries to convince her dad to stay, but he wants to get Finnegan back home since he's had so much excitement. Finnegan's exhausted and has gone to sleep next to the Christmas tree.

"I don't want Finnegan to get too confused. All the attention and especially all the treats I saw everyone sneak him I just do not want any accidents here," Ed explains.

Amy laughs and hugs him. "I know Dad, and you were just as protective of Jake and me."

Ed wakes Finnegan up and together they head back to his truck and he honks the horn as he leaves. Everyone stands out in the street to wave before the group heads across to Grace's house.

Andy stays back in the doorway with Amy, his arm around her waist. They walk inside and Amy stands to admire the job they've worked hard to complete.

"You're amazing." Andy smiles down at Amy. "I've had so much fun with everyone here today, but next year, let's do the decorating by ourselves."

Amy agrees as she cuddles up to say goodnight. She yawns and covers her mouth. "I'm sorry, I'm a little tired. It's been some weekend, getting engaged, starting plans for a wedding and putting up the inside and outside Christmas decorations."

"You know when you say it like that, I feel a little tired too. It's been an incredible twenty eight hours." He kisses the end of her nose.

"You're counting the hours since we got engaged?" Amy reaches up and kisses his cheek. "That's so sweet."

"Actually, I've downloaded an app that calculates the days, hours and minutes until our wedding. Remind me to show you when my hands are not so full." Andy pulls Amy into his arms and holds her tight as he kisses her.

As per his ritual, Andy leaves and waits outside the door until Amy locks it. He then heads down the driveway to his car parked on the street. He waves across the street. He's not sure if anyone's watching, but just to say a last good night. Once in the car, he flicks the lights to Amy and heads off home.

Finally alone, Amy takes out the envelope her dad gave her earlier. Inside is a letter from Ann. In it, she tells Amy how proud she is that Amy has found her soul mate and tells Amy about how she handled her own wedding plans along with the plans she made for their 25th anniversary vow renewal. She also explains to Amy that she will come to realize that the love she feels for her future husband will grow as the years pass. Amy has tears running down her face. She can hear her mother's voice as she continues to read. Amy is surprised; there is no actual to do list included, just the story of how her mom went about planning her wedding. It appears Ann wants Amy to plan her own wedding based on what her and her fiancée want.

Chapter Twenty Three

December starts out busy as Amy wakes up to snow, mountains of snow. A major snow storm has moved in and everything is covered with 8 inches of snow. Having grown up in Riverside she's not concerned. Her Navigator has 4 wheel drive capacity and she loves the challenge of getting through the snow. History tells her the hospital will be very busy today so she hurries off to work.

As she drives to work, she remembers learning how to drive in the winter with her dad. The local ice rink fire hydrant was hit and the entire parking lot was flooded with water. The cold turned it into an enormous outdoor skating rink. She and Jake took turns in the family car learning how to drive on ice. It was scary back then but it gave her great confidence in the ice and snow. Now, stormy weather and icy roads don't scare her.

As Amy predicts, for the next twenty four hours she doesn't leave the hospital and catches a few hours sleep in her office between surgeries and ER work. Andy also puts in long hours since the snow covered roads have caused many accidents.

The snow puts people into the festive mood and between patients Amy receives several invitations to dinners and Christmas parties. She sends text messages back and forth with Andy, who also has several invitations, mostly from fellow officers who usually host Christmas parties. Rumours of their engagement are also causing some excitement and Amy's received several messages of congratulations from her many family and friends.

Chapter Twenty Four

As is typical in Calgary, the cold weather passes when a Chinook comes along bringing in warm temperatures. With Jake's wedding coming up, Amy spends time with Victoria helping her handle invitations and decoration ideas. She spends time with Andy in the evenings as they continue working on their own wedding arrangements. They visit the Greenwood Inn and meet Sara. She's an amazing coordinator with tons of wedding experience.

The banquet room is gorgeous, gold and teal blue, which will blend nicely with Amy's colours of pink, silver and grey. They're excited to learn the room is available for Saturday night of the May long weekend.

Now that they have a hall, they speak with Pastor Trevor at Andy's family church just a few blocks away from Amy's house. He's excited to be part of their wedding since he performed the ceremonies for both Cindy and Joan. It's been a really hard decision for Amy since she would've loved to have been married in her own church out in Riverside, but it just doesn't make sense to have their guests drive an hour out to Riverside and then back into the city for the dinner and dance. Andy suggests perhaps she'd like to invite the church pastor to participate, but Amy has met Pastor Trevor and likes him and feels comfortable in Andy's church. After all, it will become their family church once they're married and have their own children.

With the dining room and food taken care of and now the church and Pastor Trevor in place they start to work on the rest of the guest list.

That night, before Amy goes to bed she realizes she needs to get busy finding her dress. This makes her sad, since every daughter wants to share this joyous time with her mother. Amy goes to bed with a heavy heart. After a restless sleep, Amy struggles to get ready for work. As she rushes down the stairs, she's overcome with her grief and exhaustion. She sits on the stairs and starts to cry; it's the first time in a long while that she feels such sadness.

Suddenly she feels a breeze across her face; her prayers for her mother have brought her some comfort. She goes back upstairs and splashes her face with water. As she comes back downstairs, Amy finds a shiny new penny on the floor. Smiling and blowing her mother a kiss into the air, she hops into her car to head to work.

As Amy drives to work, she calls her dad to see if he'll come into town later in the week and spend an evening helping her find the perfect wedding dress. He's delighted to hear from her and loves the idea of spending time with his daughter. He's already realized it's going to be hard on the two of them without Ann there. They decide to get together the very next night right after work. Later in the morning Amy makes an appointment at the Bridal Centre. She decides to call Grace and see if she'd like to join her and her dad. Grace is thrilled and honoured to be included in such a very private and personal outing and immediately agrees. She decides she'll grab a taxi over to the hospital so they can all meet together.

Amy's already planned for her wedding party to go dress shopping when they're all together over the Christmas Holidays, but she really wants a quiet time shopping for her own dress with just her dad and Grace. Their opinions are important to her and she values the quiet times she has with each of them. She also realizes it's going to be very emotional for her and she wants to have Grace with her to help both her and her father get through one of the toughest parts of the wedding planning.

Chapter Twenty Five

Andy picks Amy up the next morning so she doesn't have to play musical vehicles. Her dad's made arrangements to pick her up after work. Grace is meeting them at the hospital and together they'll head out to the Bridal Centre to find her wedding dress. Her dad plans to stay overnight at her house since they'll go for a late dinner. Amy is excited; she looks forward to spending time with her dad and Grace together by herself. Not only has she never gone shopping with her dad and Grace together, she's never gone wedding dress shopping for herself.

She has an appointment with the Bridal Centre owner who happens to be an old neighbour from Riverside. Josie used to live in the house directly behind her parents before she divorced her husband and moved to the city where eventually she became the owner of the store. It's now considered the biggest and best in Calgary. Amy has not spent any time looking at dresses, so she has no idea what kind of dress she should be looking at. She wistfully remembers the conversations about weddings she had with her mom after attending the weddings for her various cousins. Her mom definitely had opinions for better or worse.

She smiles as she remembers her mother's voice telling her how she'd like Amy's wedding after one wedding they had both attended many years earlier.

As the day moves on, Amy starts to do something she seldom does; she keeps checking her watch for the time. Finally the end of the day arrives. Her dad pops into her office just as she's closing her system for the day. "So are we ready to shop?" Amy comes around her desk and hugs her dad.

"I've got to admit, I'm excited." Amy grabs her coat. "Grace just called; she should be waiting at the entrance in a few minutes. Did you leave Finnegan with Joyce?"

"Yes, he's spent a fair amount of time over there playing with Joyce and Al. Just like you and Jake, he considers it his second home. If he gets out on me, I know where to go first to look." Arm and arm they walk together to the elevator. As the elevator opens, Grace greets them. Together they leave for the Bridal Centre.

Josie greets them at the door. She's known Amy since she was a little girl and is excited to show her some gowns. She already has some ideas for Amy. She quickly checks out Amy's exquisite engagement ring. "Amy, your ring's spectacular. I see hundreds of rings, but this is the most unique and most elegant thing I've ever seen. It looks custom made."

"It is. Andy had it specially made for me." Amy proudly holds out her hand to let Josie see the ring. The light from the chandelier makes the ring sparkle even brighter.

The small group head upstairs to the private viewing area that Josie's booked for them. She's already pulled several dresses for Amy to start trying on. Amy shares with Josie some of her memories of the discussions she remembers having with Ann after each family wedding they attended.

Josie smiles. She remembers discussions with Ann as well. "Actually, it was all the talks your mom and I had when I was having so many problems with my ex-husband that made me decide to come to work here and later buy the business. Your mother should've been a wedding planner; she'd come up with some pretty incredible ideas over the years. I've actually incorporated many of them into this place."

"Well, it looks like we came to the right place," Grace announces as she makes herself comfortable in one of the luxurious chairs arranged around a platform. "Ed, I've never met Ann, but I sure get the feeling we'd have gotten along nicely."

Ed smiles, "I never paid much attention to the gossip Ann always had with her friends after weddings. She spent hours planning Amy and Jake's weddings."

Tears form in the corners of Amy's eyes. "I sure remember, and I've promised Mom that I'll try my best to make sure I incorporate all the ideas I remember. Josie, do you think you have an idea of what Mom might have wanted for me to wear?"

"I think so. I've pulled several gowns, including a new one that just came into the centre this morning and no one has tried on," Josie replies. "Amy, let's get started, shall we?"

Without waiting, Amy follows Josie into the change room. Once in the change room, Josie shows Amy several dresses and Amy chooses the first dress.

"This is beautiful. I had no idea these dresses could be so detailed. Look at the bead work on this dress."

The first dress is a high sheen satin and silk blend ball gown. It has a sweetheart neckline that accentuates a bodice of ornamental lace and beading that drops in the back into a low V and has long fitted sleeves of lace. The skirt has ornamental lace and bead trim in the front and back. The cathedral train is beautiful and elegant. It's completely detachable and is about 10 feet in length. The lace trim surrounds the bottom of the dress and trims the entire train. An exquisite lace cut-out has been set into the centre of the train. Beading of pearls, rhinestones and Swarovski crystals have been intricately sewn into the lace.

Amy steps into this gown and Josie zips up the back. She attaches the train. Amy puts on the white satin shoes she'd recently purchased. Amy looks into the mirrors and lets out a gasp. Tears start running down her face; she suddenly realizes how perfect this dress is. The reality of the fact she's about to become a bride hits her.

"Look at me in this dress. I feel like a princess. Does a bride usually fall in love with the first dress she tries on?" Amy can't believe how much she loves this dress. It fits her perfectly. Josie hands her a Kleenex and she mops up her tears.

"I wonder if Mom would've liked this dress," Amy wonders out loud.

"Well, let's see what your father and future mother-in law think, shall we?" Josie opens the door and moves to the side so Amy can pass through.

Amy's shocked to see the expression on her father's face. She sees tears falling down his face. She looks over at Grace and is surprised to see the same reaction.

"Do the tears mean you like this dress?" Amy inquires, "Because I love it." She swings to the side and gasps again. She hasn't seen the train until now; she finds herself surrounded on three sides with floor to ceiling mirrors.

She turns to Grace and her father. "Am I nuts because I'm not trying on anything else? I want this dress."

Josie has left the viewing room and now returns with a veil and tiara head piece to put onto Amy's head. Amy shakes her head. "Sorry, Josie, but I want to wear the head piece Mom wore when she was married. She wore it on her 25th anniversary and I thought it was amazing."

"Amy, darling, can I make one small suggestion?" Grace carefully asks.

"Of course, that's why I brought you and Dad." Amy turns to face Grace.

"Well, I wonder if it's possible to add a few pink crystals to match your wedding ring onto the bodice and trim?" she suggests. "It's only a thought."

"I like the idea." Amy turns to Josie, "Do you think it's possible to have a few pink stones added just around the front of the dress?"

"Of course, and I think it's a great idea."

Amy walks around the room. "I'm surprised the dress is not as heavy as it looks. Can we take the train off to see how it feels by itself?"

Josie shows Grace how easily the train detaches. Once again Amy swings around in her dress. Clearly this is the dress.

Several other sales women come over to see the dress, they agree it's a spectacular dress and it definitely suits Amy perfectly.

Amy turns to Josie. "Can I buy this dress or do I have to order one?"

"Normally the display gowns have been tried on by so many people I always recommend that we order a new dress, but since this is a brand new gown, never before tried on, I can sell it to you if you like. I've got to be honest; I've not even priced the dress. It was unpacked earlier today and I set it aside for you just before you arrived. Let me go check on a few details. I'll be right back." With that, Josie heads to the office to check the invoices. Even she has to admit the dress is made for Amy.

While Josie is gone, Amy and Grace put the train back on the dress. "Do you want me to take some pictures?" Grace asks.

"I'm not sure. I want it to be a surprise and I'm afraid if I have pictures I won't be able to wait and I'll end up showing the pictures to Andy," Amy confesses. "He already knows I hate to keep secrets."

Grace laughs. "I guess you're right there."

Ed adds, "He's a quick judge of character, that's what makes him so good at his job."

Josie returns. "I'm so shocked, I very seldom have a dress come in that a bride steps into and fits perfectly. It's the right length for the shoes you have picked and the shoulders and length of the sleeve also fit. If you like, you can have this dress. I can store it here until closer to your wedding."

It's decided that Amy will get this dress and Josie will store it for her. As they head to the office, Ed pulls Amy aside. "I want to buy this dress for you.

Actually, your mom and I had put money aside for your wedding, but the dress is my special gift to you."

Amy hugs her dad. "Are you sure, I've got my own money dad, I can pay for my dress."

"No, this is something I want to do." He hugs her and turns to Grace. "Now that Amy has her dress why don't you two head down to the other stuff we saw as we came in. I'll take care of this bill and meet you down there. I wonder if buying the other outfits is going to be as easy."

"Dad, I saw the men's section on the other side, maybe you want to look at a new tux for yourself while we're here." Amy winks at him. "Just in case your old one has shrunk."

"Let me handle this and then we'll see how much time we have left," Ed replies. He follows Josie over to the cash register while Grace and Amy head over to check out the little girl dresses.

A beautiful red velvet gown catches Amy's eye. Next to it is the identical dress in emerald green. She grabs her phone and sends a couple of pictures to Victoria. Amy's had several conversations with Victoria regarding the black evening gown she wore to the Gala. Amy feels she would like to wear something different.

Victoria loves the dress. It's a simple cherry red fitted gown with a scalloped sweetheart neckline. The hemline gracefully flares at the bottom and gently pools at the back. The long slender sleeve has the same scalloped trim as the neckline. Amy decides she should try both dresses on and they both fit perfectly. She sends two pictures, one of herself in each dress, to Victoria and Victoria decides the red dress is what she'd like Amy to wear. Amy, with Victoria's approval, purchases the dress. She decides she can use her black shoes, gloves and cape from her gala outfit.

They spend the rest of the time looking at the dresses and tuxedos. Ed decides he should get a new tuxedo since not one but both of his children are getting married. He's had the same tuxedo since he married Ann, so it may be time for something new. Together Grace and Amy help him with his decisions.

Having finished their purchases for the evening, Amy calls to see if Andy would like to join them for a late dinner.

They meet at the Chinese Restaurant around the corner from Amy's house. Amy is very happy with her shopping and Ed is pleased he has a new tuxedo. Grace has seen a couple of dresses she'll consider as well. It's late so everyone's ready to finish dinner and go home to bed.

Later that night when Amy's in bed she thinks about her wedding. Finding the perfect wedding dress on the first try was amazing and she envisions herself in her dress walking down the aisle with Andy standing at the front of the church waiting for her.

As she finishes her nightly prayers Amy believes her mom is smiling down at her and she peacefully falls into a wonderful sleep.

Chapter Twenty Six

The days pass quickly and Amy keeps busy by helping Victoria and Jake finalize their wedding plans. Amy and Andy make their Christmas lists and enjoy shopping together for their family and friends.

Amy has spent some time searching for the perfect Christmas gift for Andy. She finds several good gift ideas, but finally, while shopping with Victoria, she finds a white gold Pharaoh chain necklace and a guardian angel. On the back she engraves a message to Andy – "All my heart and soul, love Amy"

Amy decides to book two weeks of holidays. She figures with Christmas and Jake's wedding she'll want to have time for not only the wedding, but for herself, and more importantly for Andy and her family. With a strong staff now in place in her department, Amy's granted the time, agreeing that she'll make herself available if necessary. Her department assistant is a very capable man and she's been successful in finding another new doctor to join the team who recently moved to Calgary from Ireland. Dr. Vincent Giles is eager to prove himself and promises he'll do his best to help make sure the unit keeps running while she takes time off.

Andy has several weeks of holidays available that he's carried over from the prior year and decides to take the time off as well. He's excited to be able to spend time with Amy and not have to hurry to and from work. He also recognizes that he needs to be refreshed to start with his new department right after the holidays.

Excited to have so much time, Amy books her holidays from December 22 through to January 5. She still has one week from last year and another four from this year. She'll save those for her wedding, although she'll have more holiday time for next year. She's already made several lists to help her get as much work done as possible on her own wedding plans on the days following Jake's wedding.

This year, the holidays are full of energy and life. She and Andy plan to spend Christmas Eve alone together to exchange their gifts. Christmas Day they'll spend with Andy's family. Both his sisters and their families will be home so it'll be a hectic day. Boxing Day will be spent with Amy's aunts and their families.

Since all of the people from their wedding party will be around for the holidays, Amy and Andy have planned to have an evening together with everyone on December 27. Amy's planned the meal and prepared all the lists for groceries and discussions of plans. She has created a jumbo white board with all the plans outlined. Joan, Cindy, Sophie, Victoria and the girls have a day booked at the Bridal Centre with Josie to find the bridesmaid and flower girl outfits. They'll also pick up the tuxedos for the two ring bearers. Little Jennifer is excited about shopping with the big girls and shares her ideas with Amy on a very regular basis.

Amy's left the day before and the day of Jake and Victoria's wedding open to help with any last minute plans.

The last few days of work before Amy's scheduled holiday pass quickly and before she knows it it's the morning of her first day off. She enjoys her toast and tea while reading the paper. By the end of her first day off, Amy's finally completes all her shopping and gift wrapping. She sits to reflect on the changes in her life from this time last year. She barely remembers last year; she'd spent so many days after her mom's funeral feeling numb.

Andy's been busy on his first day off, picking up his sister Cindy and her husband George, and his two nieces Faith and Sherry from the airport. Cindy hugs her little brother and congratulates him on his engagement to Amy. The girls are excited about spending time with Amy again. They rush in to greet their grandmother when they get to the house, excited by the presents they have brought and happy to be back with their grandmother. Grace loves the girls and continues to spoil them terribly.

Grace's house is full of noise and laughter again and she's happy to have the distraction of a wedding and family since the holidays can be a lonely time for those who have lost family. It's her first year without Richard and in her quiet time she morns her loss, not for him because she knows he's in a better place, but for her and the loneliness she feels.

Everyone's mindful of Grace's struggle and shower her with their love and affection. They share their stories and adventures together while making cookies and Christmas baking for the upcoming holiday meals.

That night, Amy and Andy pile everyone into their vehicles and they drive around the city to admire the decorations. Fortunately the weather continues to cooperate with very reasonable temperatures.

Joan, Cindy and the girls spend time on Christmas Eve morning with Amy getting ready for her dinner party on Monday night. They have a great time baking and cooking. Amy's trying to recreate many of her mother's favourite holiday dishes. She has finally mastered the perfect sized cabbage rolls and they are neatly lined up in the roaster and placed in the freezer until Monday morning.

Later in the evening, Amy and Andy share a quiet dinner together, the only dinner they'll have alone during their entire holidays. They leave for Church for the Christmas Cantata early because they know the church will be full.

Every year the church opens its doors on Christmas Eve for a celebration of holiday music. There are so many talented singers and musicians it's become a very popular event and many people come from surrounding churches. Andy and Amy meet up with their families who have arrived early and saved them seats. The evening's amazing. The enactment of the birth of Christ is played out in song and music. The two hour concert passes quickly.

After the concert the couple return to Amy's house where they exchange their special gifts with each other. Amy makes Andy open her gift to him first.

Andy is over the moon with the beautiful necklace and guardian angel pennant Amy has given him. He's never owned anything like it and immediately puts it on. Inside the Christmas card Amy has written *Love looks not with the eyes, but with the heart and soul. This angel is to keep you safe, but she will remind you how much I love you, with all my heart and soul."* Amy kisses Andy after taking time to admire it on him.

Andy gives Amy her huge and very heavy box. She opens the box only to discover another gift wrapped inside with two heavy Sears catalogues at the bottom. She giggles as she tears open the second box only to discover yet another box inside it. This time she finds two cans of tomato soup inside along with another beautifully decorated box. Each box contains something for weight until finally, after opening six boxes; she reaches the last box and inside is a tiny pink velvet jewellery box. She opens the box to find a delicate pair of white gold earrings. They are tiny hearts with the bottom of the heart curved into a small circle before making its way up to the top of the heart. Inside the small circle is a small pink diamond that matches the stone in Amy's wedding ring. The centre of the heart has a small pearl held in place by another small circle. A row of tiny white diamonds forms an arch across the top of the heart. Inside the lid of the jewellery box is a small inscription. Andy carefully wrote '*You hold my heart and soul*'.

Amy puts the earrings on and goes to the hall mirror to admire them. Andy stands back and watches.

"These are the most beautiful earrings I've ever seen. Where did you find them?" she turns and asks.

"My friend designs several pieces for a local jewellery store with the theme 'love and soul.' He made this set for me when he came across another set of pink diamonds that were the perfect match to the stone in your ring," Andy confesses. "Frank called me and asked me to stop by, I knew as soon as I saw them that he was right; they're perfect for you."

Amy puts her arms around Andy and whispers in his ear, "Merry Christmas darling. I love you with all my heart and soul." Andy returns his love for her.

For Amy, the rest of the evening follows a tradition her mother had; they sit together in the family room and watch several Christmas movies including Bing Crosby's White Christmas and the Miracle on 34th Street, while nibbling on the cookies and treats Amy and the girls made earlier in the day.

It's well after midnight when Andy leaves for home. He'll be back early in the morning. Amy's dad, Jake and Victoria have been included for Christmas Day with Andy's family. They're all meeting for breakfast at Amy's place.

Chapter Twenty Seven

Amy awakes to a phone call from Andy wishing her a Merry Christmas and reminding her they have 147 more days to go. She laughs as she hops out of bed after checking the clock. She knows her father and her brother and Victoria will arrive shortly.

Spending a little longer on herself, Amy dresses for Christmas Day. It is something her mom always liked to do. Amy decides she likes that tradition and will carry it on. She's found a beautiful outfit while out shopping and decided it's too perfect not to have. The black pants are a perfect fit and she found a lovely white and silver threaded blouse along with a red leather jacket. She finishes off the look with the new earrings Andy gave her last night. Feeling very festive and knowing she looks good, Amy heads to the kitchen to put her Christmas morning breakfast in the oven, another tradition from her mom. She's also put together some overnight buns and has them baking when the doorbell rings.

Her dad, along with his sidekick Finnegan, and Andy arrive at the same time. She hugs both of them and takes the brightly coloured packages her dad has in his hands. She makes a fuss over Finnegan's Christmas necktie, which apparently Santa brought for him. After depositing the gifts under the tree, they all head to the kitchen for Christmas tea and Holiday coffee. While pouring the cups, Jake and Victoria arrive. Victoria's excited; they plan to pick up her father at the airport later this afternoon. With the bad weather in Europe his flight was delayed overnight, but he sent her a text message just before the plane left the runway saying that he's finally on his way.

It's great fun opening the gifts with two new members of the family. Victoria and Andy have added so much love and joy to this very special holiday. Once the gifts are exchanged, they all head out to the kitchen where Amy already has the table set up and the breakfast's ready to eat. The aromas of freshly baked buns and speciality coffees are almost too much to handle and no one needs to be called twice to come to the table.

As is their Christmas Tradition, Ed says grace and Jake recites the Christmas story. Amy has provided Victoria with her first Christmas decoration; a hand crafted Nativity Scene, which Jake uses as he recites the story.

Once breakfast is done and the kitchen's tidied up, they head across the street to Grace's place where the girls are eagerly waiting to open the rest of their presents. They've opened the gifts in their stockings and the gifts from Santa and their parents earlier. Breakfast's been finished and their mother, aunt and grandmother are busy in the kitchen getting ready for their Christmas dinner. The girls set the table with Grandma's china. They love this job and take great pride in knowing how to properly set the table, something they've learned from their many family functions with their grandparents. Grace loves a formal table and has taught the girls to enjoy the task.

Now, finally, presents can be opened. Everyone takes a seat as Andy takes over the honour that used to be his father's and begins to hand each person a gift to open. Each takes their turn opening the gift, and Andy starts the process again. Victoria and Jake are surprised to receive gifts as well. Grace found Victoria the perfect bridal book. Jake's received a pair of champagne glasses and a bottle of champagne. Joan and Cindy didn't forget the couple either, giving them gifts for their new home together.

With the dinner in the oven, Grace and the girls spend time going over their to-do lists in preparation for Victoria and Jake's wedding. With two weddings coming up, it's hard not to talk and share experiences and stories.

Jake and Victoria have hand delivered most all the invitations to their friends and family members. The house they have purchased is ready for them to move into next week as well. Victoria's condo in Toronto has sold very quickly and she has a moving company hired to pack and move her possessions. Since she'd packed up most of her stuff on her last trip out to Toronto, the condo was ready for the final stages of packing and moving. She also had the Salvation Army bring a big truck to take things that she didn't want to move. Most of Jake's possessions have also been packed up and ready to go.

After the gift opening, the men spend time in the living room watching TV. Christmas movies are the order of the day. The men talk golf and hockey, since they're all active hockey players.

Amy's surprised how quickly and comfortably the two families fit together. It doesn't seem long before dinner's ready. Again, a fabulous meal is served at Grace's table. Everyone holds hands as Andy once again takes his father's role by saying grace. For Grace, it's a bitter sweet day; she loves her family but truly misses Richard. Christmas was his favourite time of the year and every place she has turned and every decoration she's unpacked is a reminder of his absence. Amy has worked hard to ensure Grace and her family have a good time and she remembers her pain last year without her mother. She shared those feelings with Andy last night and spent a quiet time together in remembrance.

After the meal, the men take control of the kitchen as they clean up the dishes. The girls go into the living room to discuss plans to go shopping for the bridesmaids' outfits on Monday. They're excited when they hear Amy's story of finding her perfect dress. They discuss the colour scheme for the wedding. Grace and Amy regale their adventures at the Bridal Centre, telling the women all about the beautiful dresses in the store. Everyone's looking forward to spending the day together with Amy and Victoria. Victoria's shy about discussing her dress with everyone; she wants them to be surprised next Friday when she walks down the aisle.

Earlier, at her house, Amy has shown Victoria the dress she bought. Victoria loves it and is excited and happy because she knows Amy's dress will complement her own dress perfectly.

Finishing in the kitchen just in time to head off for the airport, Jake and Victoria get their coats on to leave. Giving hugs and Christmas wishes they take off. Not wanting to drive in the dark, Ed and Finnegan leave shortly after as well.

"I've never seen Finnegan with his head hung so low, his eyes look like he's ready for bed," Andy teases.

"He's definitely not going to be much company on the way home, that's for sure. He's had a great time with the girls and I'm pretty sure his stomach is very full with all the food he has managed to sneak." Ed laughs. "It's been a great couple of days and I'm really pleased to see that he behaved himself at every place we've been."

"I would expect nothing less, Dad." Amy adds, "After all he's been trained by the best. Look at how he picks up his own leash after you."

With more hugs, Ed and Finnegan head out.

Everyone retires back to the living room where the conversation turns to pictures. Grace decides to download her pictures from the past couple of days onto her laptop. She leaves the room and returns with a huge stack of picture albums. They spend the next few hours laughing and studying pictures of the girls and Andy as they grew up. It seems Grace, like Amy's mom, loves to take pictures and there are pictures from every period of their lives, from Grace's wedding forward. She shows them the picture of Amy and Andy that she used as her final picture for her camera course. She received a perfect grade for the picture and is very proud of it.

Amy checks her watch some time later and is surprised at how late it is. "Wow, it's been a full day; I can't believe what time it is."

"Yeah, and you get to do this all over again tomorrow," Andy reminds her.

"Another full Christmas dinner. And I know my two aunts will overdo it this year since they have new people to impress." Amy laughs. "You better make sure you bring a jogging suit to change into. They won't be happy until you're groaning in agony."

"Works for me. I'll just have to spend time with you in the gym." Andy hugs her. "To be honest, the martial arts have come in handy during the combat training the Chief has us do to prove we can still handle the bad guys. I hate to brag, but I'm probably one of the few cops in our precinct that didn't have to hit the gym hard in order to pass."

"Maybe you should start a training centre," Phil teases, "It kills me when I go to prepare to do my annual physicals."

"Come on over anytime, I'll teach you some techniques that might be helpful," Amy invites. "I usually work out at least every other night, so feel free."

Amy hugs everyone goodnight and Andy helps her home with her gifts. It's been a long day and Amy has to admit she's tired. Andy jokes with her as he reminds her they have 147 nights until their wedding. The outside lights on all the houses on the street are lit up and Amy admires the neighbourhood. Andy and her dad did an amazing job on her house and Andy already has ideas for next year. They've spent a bit of time working on a new app they each downloaded that has allowed them to start a plan for next year and even provides a complete list of lights they'll need to buy after the holidays when they're on sale.

Amy opens her door and gets a whiff of her Poinsettias. She must remember to water them again in the morning to keep the blooms until at least after the holidays.

Andy unloads everything by the hall table and gathers Amy in his arms. "I've wanted to do this all day. You look absolutely positively divine."

"Why thank you kind sir, you look extremely handsome yourself." With that, Amy reaches up and kisses his nose. "Have I told you how much I love you?"

"Probably, but I never tire of hearing those magical words."

As has become their habit, Andy stands outside the door until he hears the door lock latch and Amy stands by the window to wave goodbye as he drives out of the driveway and down the street.

On his way home Andy thinks about how his life has changed in the last few months. Anyone who says there's no such thing as love at first sight has never encountered his beautiful fiancée. Andy realizes his love for Amy grows stronger every day. He can only begin to imagine how he'll feel in fifty years. He's envious of Jake with only five more days until his wedding, while he faces his own 147 day wait.

Chapter Twenty Eight

Boxing Day has turned out to be as hectic as Christmas Day. In fact, with so many little ones, it's downright noisy. Amy's Aunt Katherine has a huge house and it's full of children. Zack and his wife Anita have three children; Logan's 7, Benjamin's 5, and Jennifer's 3. Alex and his wife Emma have two children, a boy Justin age 4 and a girl Jasmine age 6. Carrie and her husband Brett have two sets of twins, boys and girls. The girls, Vanessa and Virginia, are almost 8 years old and the boys, Jordan and James, have just turned 3.

The kids are all downstairs with the men when Andy and Amy arrive, but within minutes of coming through the door Jennifer has pushed her way to Amy, hugging her legs and causing Amy to almost lose her balance. Andy catches her and steadies her. Laughing Amy picks Jennifer up and gives her a big bear hug.

Amy's warned Andy that the house is very busy, but Andy is not expecting so many small children and so many distractions and so much noise! There are kids coming at them from everywhere and all Andy can do is stand there as he watches Amy down on her knees engaging the kids with hugs and tickles.

Katherine comes to the door with her apron on and shoos the little ones away so Amy and Andy can get their coats and boots off. "Merry Christmas and welcome!" She hugs both of them.

"Congratulations on your engagement," she says, giving them another set of hugs. Katherine's so excited for them.

Amy shows off her ring to her aunt. Suddenly, the men lumber up the stairs and shake hands with Andy. Andy has not met any of Amy's cousins and is surprised at how easily they make him feel welcome. In no time, he heads downstairs with them to watch a hockey game. Amy heads off to the family room to greet the women.

Again, Amy receives hugs and exclamations of joy for her engagement. Of course, the conversations turn immediately to Jake and Victoria's upcoming wedding. Everyone's excited to get together later in the week for a wedding, especially Jake's.

Chaos continues as there always seems to be at least one child crying for some reason or another. Each mother handles the crisis quickly and effectively with complete calm. Amy hopes she can handle motherhood as well as her cousins and their wives.

The door bell interrupts the wedding discussions and the whole greeting routine starts again. This time, her dad arrives alone, leaving Finnegan with Bert and Cheryl for the day. Jake and Victoria are right behind him along with Victoria's father. Amy sits back with little Jennifer in her lap as everyone greets the bride and groom. Poor Victoria, she has no idea of the circus she's about to join and her father stands in shock at what he sees as total confusion.

It's not long before her dad and Jake escort Howard downstairs with the men. Sara and Owen arrive a few minutes later. Their arms are full with gifts and food and Owen makes a couple of trips to the car before the men even realize he's there. Trevor and his wife Heather are right behind them with their four very grown up children, Diana who's 16, Todd who's 18 and a senior in high school, Samuel who's 19 and in his first year of university and his sister Hannah, who's 22 in her third year. Samuel and Hannah are both following in their parents' footsteps as architects. Trevor and his family flew in from Arkansas to spend the holidays with his parents and to attend his cousin Jake's wedding.

With everyone present, Katherine, with the help of the others, puts the finishing touches on dinner. The adults all gather in the dining room and the children sit at the kitchen table and their own small children's table. It's a great meal and everyone enjoys the feast that Katherine's spent a lot of time preparing. Amy's concerns for how Andy, Victoria and her father Howard would respond have been quickly put to rest. Andy seems to fit right in, a hockey player and all. Apparently even Howard played hockey as a teenager and appears to be having fun. Victoria remembers the cousins from childhood, having spent many holidays and weekends with Amy and Jake.

After dinner and the cleanup, everyone retires to the living room for gift opening. With such a big group, they have a gift exchange that involves everyone buying a gift they really want to keep for a price set this year at $25.00. Each gift is wrapped and then placed in black garbage bags. This way no one knows their own gift. Everyone draws a number out of a bowl. The kids have their own gifts that they have bought and wrapped and also participate. The kids' gifts are separated out, but the teens are included in the adult group. The kids go first and everyone has great fun watching them open their gifts.

The gifts are handed out according to the number drawn. The first person gets to open the first gift. The second person can take the first gift or open a new one. Each gift can be passed three times before the final holder of the gift gets to keep it. It's great fun and everyone works to take gifts back and forth. Andy draws the first number and takes his time picking a gift. He slowly opens the gift and finds a golf scope in a handy little case that confirms the distance from the ball to the hole. There are several avid golfers in the group and the gift is taken from Andy and makes the rounds three times before it's taken out of play and finds itself in Howard's hands, he claims to have been looking for this for some time. Andy's second gift is a small black velvet evening bag. Victoria decides it's something she needs and takes it from him. With much laughter, the next number is drawn. Eventually Amy gets a turn; her gift is a garden tool bag complete with kneeling pads, and something she wants to keep. Everyone has fun and burn off some of the dinner with all the laughing and joking around.

After gift opening, dessert and coffee are served. It's been a lot of fun and Amy's happy to see that Andy fits in well with her family. Jake's also pleased that both Victoria and Howard appear to be enjoying themselves.

After dessert, Jake wonders where Howard's gone. He's surprised to see Howard sitting on the floor. Jennifer and Emma are combing his hair and Vanessa is painting his finger nails. He quietly pulls Victoria over to watch.

"You know, I remember him doing that with me when I was just little. I wish we could've kept that relationship as I grew older," Victoria whispers.

"Maybe he'll have that relationship with you again, especially after we have our own children." Jake grins at her.

"That would be so special for me." Victoria returns his smile.

"Let's get back to the kitchen and leave the girls to have their fun." Jake pulls her back into the kitchen.

With small children, the party ends early. Amy's glad; she has a lot of work to get ready for tomorrow and is excited to go shopping with the girls. Jennifer has invited herself to have a sleep over with Amy. Anita gives Amy a bag with Jennifer's pyjamas and a change of clothes. Amy's surprised at how organized Anita is. Anita explains they sometimes stay late and it's easier if the kids are in their pyjamas since they usually fall asleep on the way home.

Jennifer keeps Andy and Amy entertained on the way back to Amy's place. They have great plans for what to do when they get to the house. Unfortunately for Jennifer, the hectic day finally takes its toll. Just a couple of blocks from Amy's house, Jennifer falls fast to sleep. Andy carries her up to Amy's bed; Amy takes off her coat and tucks her into bed. They can carry out their plans tomorrow.

Amy and Andy head downstairs and sit down to reflect on the events of the day, relaxing with cups of hot chocolate. They spend some time going over the plans for tomorrow for their wedding party. Amy and the girls are going dress shopping in the morning and they'll all meet back at the house in the late afternoon for an early dinner.

Andy decides he will put the finishing touches on the meal and ensure both the ham and roast are put into the oven at the correct times. Amy has everything listed for the meal and Andy's excited to be able to show Amy he can handle her list. Amy has the table set and has already prepared the desserts.

Sometime later, Andy leaves for home to catch up on some much needed sleep. Amy heads upstairs and crawls into bed next to Jennifer. Jennifer's fast asleep and hasn't stirred. Amy's absolutely exhausted and falls asleep as soon as her head hits the pillow.

Chapter Twenty Nine

Jennifer wakes Amy early and they get dressed and head downstairs for breakfast. Grace, Joan and Cindy, along with Faith and Sherry, come over a short time later. Victoria and Sophie arrive at the same time as Andy. Andy is taking his cooking responsibility seriously and decides he wants to be sure the food's all completely cooked and the meal's ready on time.

Anita and Carrie plan to meet at the bridal store with the twins to get their outfits and determine their sizing. Once Jennifer finds her dress and gets sized, Anita will take her home.

Everyone heads over to the Bridal Centre to meet up with Josie. Amy's struggling to decide whether to try on her dress again for the girls to see. She thought she wanted everyone to be surprised, but she always wants their approval.

Josie has the two ring bearers try on their grey tuxedos first. They'll pick out the vest and bow tie colours to match once the dresses have been chosen. With that completed, their focus turns to Jennifer. There are so many choices to make, but Amy finds a little dress that has the same scalloped neckline and shape in the same material as her dress. Jennifer has great fun putting on the dress and dances around the room for everyone's entertainment. As with all three year olds, the decisions are made quickly and Anita and Carrie take the children back home.

The rest start to look at the gowns. Amy would like the colours to stay in the range of pink shades that she and Andy agreed upon, with accents of grey and black. There are so many shades and styles, and Amy wants to let each party member pick a style that best suits each body type. Everyone has gone into the main area to pick a style; colour can be ordered in, so Josie has suggested they look at style first.

To everyone's amazement, they have all chosen an extremely similar style and Amy's further surprised to see how similar the style is to her own wedding dress, even though no one has seen or been told about Amy's dress. Amy decides to show them her dress once they finish trying on theirs to see how they all look together before the dresses are ordered.

The full length evening gowns all have deep v necks and sleeveless tops with rouche bodices and full skirts from the waists. Each has a crinoline underneath and the hem line has a lace overlay trim similar to Amy's wedding dress. The dresses each have the scallop trim outlining the v neck. Sophie picks the identical dress but with a short sleeve. They all try on their dresses and each dress suits and fits nicely. They decide on a soft pink colour, very similar to the pink crystals that are going into Amy's dress.

Amy asks Josie if she can try her dress on for her friends to see. She wants to be sure the style of the dresses will work together.

The girls stand by waiting for Amy to change into her dress. There are "Wows" aplenty as Amy walks out of the dressing room. As they stand together Amy is moved to tears as she realizes how much she loves her dress and how well they all work together.

They leave their measurements for Josie as she organizes the ordering of the dresses. Amy's already made payment arrangements and the girls are shocked when they discover their dresses have been paid for.

"Amy, you can't pay for my dress," Sophie argues.

The others all chime in with the same opinion.

"Please, let me do this. You're all choosing dresses you'll probably never wear again to make me happy, so the least I can do is pay for them. Besides, I have the money that I set aside for my dress and Dad insisted on paying for it, so this is budgeted money," Amy insists.

Reluctantly, not wanting to make a scene, the girls allow Amy the opportunity to pay for their dresses.

"Just so you know, we're not going to forget this," Sophie threatens with a smile.

With the dresses handled, everyone heads back to Amy's place. The women spend the afternoon enjoying each other's company and putting some finishing touches on suggestions and ideas for both Amy and Victoria as they head towards their weddings.

Andy's been busy in the kitchen and refuses to let anyone in to offer assistance. Jake has arrived and he's allowed in the kitchen. Andy's brothers-in-law wander over from across the street; Phil and George have spent the afternoon moving snow from the sidewalks and back yard for Grace. Andy's best friend Steve arrives with his wife Donna.

"There sure is a lot of laughing coming out of the kitchen," Joan comments.

A loud crash followed by another bang indicates pots and possibly glass has fallen.

"Nothing to worry about," Andy shouts, "We've got everything under control."

Amy sits back down just as the smoke detector in the kitchen sounds. Again, Andy shouts that he's got things under control.

Victoria and Amy look at each other as the women laugh, "Just so you know, one of the reasons I like to do the cooking is because I let Phil clean up the kitchen," Joan confides.

"I'm not sure how long we'll be in the kitchen to clean up tonight... it might be worth remembering that in the future *we* should cook and *they* should clean," Cindy adds.

Andy announces dinner is served and the women join them in the dining room. "Just so you know the potatoes are a little scorched, the pot boiled dry on me," Andy warns.

"And the pot with the peas fell, so we aren't having two vegetables, just corn." Jake informs them.

The men each carry a dish proudly. They have made ham, roast pork, Amy's cabbage rolls, potatoes and corn.

"Did you get the salad from the fridge?" Amy asks. "And the tray of pickles and cheese? What about Maureen's ham sauce?"

"Nope, didn't see that. Let me get it out." Andy trots back to the kitchen and returns balancing more dishes, which Amy quickly rescues before there are more accidents.

"You guys have to try the ham sauce; it's the best I've ever tasted." Andy pours it on like gravy.

"That is, if there's any left," Jake comments.

"Not a problem, I made a double patch. Andy loves this. It's a recipe from one of mom's friends from the church," Amy informs the group.

"Yep, Ann made this every week for us. I put it on everything. Amy always makes a big jar for me." Ed smiles at his daughter.

"Yes Dad, there's a big jar of it in the back of the fridge for you to take home!" Amy teases.

Dinner is a fun event, with lots of laughter and jokes. It's great to see how everyone has come together.

It's much later when everyone leaves and Andy finally finds himself alone with Amy. They spend the rest of the evening exchanging stories regarding the day's events.

Tomorrow's a quiet day and Andy and Amy decide to drive out to Banff to spend the day in the mountains by themselves. It's really the first day they have to spend together in several weeks and they look forward to the quiet time.

Chapter Thirty

Before they know it, Friday has arrived, the day of Jake and Victoria's wedding. Victoria and Amy spend the morning at the hairdresser spa for the "full deal". The Westview Golf and Country Club have handled all the arrangements with respect to the dinner and dance. Katherine has, with Carrie's help, done up the floral arrangements and decorations. It's their gift to Victoria and Jake that they presented at a small surprise bridal shower Katherine hosted a couple of weeks earlier. They've made arrangements to meet Victoria and Amy at the church with the bouquets along with the church arrangements and boutonnieres.

Once finished at the hairdresser and spa they head out to Riverside to get dressed for the day. Since Jake and Andy are at the house with Amy's dad and Victoria's dad, the girls head across the street to Al and Joyce's place to get ready. Joyce is thrilled to host the girls. They'll be married at the family church and Pastor James is pleased to officiate since he's known Jake and his family since the day he took over the small church from Pastor Ron.

Joyce is eager to help the girls change, but first she has a snack for them.

"It's a long time until dinner will be served, so you'll need a little something to just tide you over," she explains.

"A little snack, good, but you've got enough food here for a dozen people, Joyce, as usual, you've outdone yourself." Amy hugs her.

"Well what's left will be eaten by Al, so not to worry." Joyce grins. "I love weddings and what with my kids all married off...I'm really happy for your mom, God bless her. The hours we spent when you kids were young, planning parties," she dabs her eyes, "Well, it was just plain fun."

Victoria and Amy both put their arms around Joyce. "No tears, we don't want to ruin our makeup."

Quickly changing the subject, the girls start to dish up plates. Neither realizes how hungry they are.

"I wonder if Jake and Andy are having something for lunch", Victoria wonders as she fills her mouth with Joyce's amazing potato salad.

"Not to worry, I handled that. They have the same lunch as you girls are having here, just a little more of it, being men and all," explains Joyce as she chuckles at her little joke.

Amy laughs. "I should've known. What would we do without you?"

"Well, I don't know about that," Joyce turns red, "I just know the men will be starving and, as men are, they'll probably eat something stupid."

The door bell rings and the photographer, Stewart, arrives right on time. Everyone quickly finishes eating, but not before Joyce invites him to share a bit of lunch with them.

After lunch, Victoria and Amy start to get dressed. Amy's gown is perfect and Victoria has fallen in love with it. They are both pleased with how great the colour works with the rest of their plans.

Victoria takes her dress out of the bag; Amy hasn't seen it yet and immediately realizes it's perfect for Victoria. The dress is a simple A line style. It's a beautiful white velvet gown with a wide satin trim around the bottom of the skirt and train. The bodice is embellished with satin embroidery work and pearls, silver beads, and crystals. Amy helps Victoria into her dress. The photographer starts to take pictures once the dress is zipped up. The dress has a full length white velvet coat with a white fur collar.

With both girls dressed, they turn their attention to the small blue satin box Victoria's dad gave her earlier in the week. Set inside is a beautiful tiara with a short veil, the tiara consists of a single row of tiny silver flowers set between little crystal stones, each flower contains a small pearl. Howard had the veil cleaned before he brought it with him. The veil is trimmed in a small row of tiny pearls with silver beading. The veil is just about the same length as Victoria's hair. She'd previously decided to leave her long auburn hair down with gentle curls on the bottom. She sits down for Joyce and Amy to help put the headpiece in place. Stewart's busy clicking pictures as they finish up.

With all the finishing touches in place, Victoria puts on the coat so Stewart can take more pictures outside in the yard.

Joyce has been watching out the window for the men to leave. "Coast is clear." She advises just as the limo drives up to her driveway.

"Perfect timing," she tells the girls.

Amy gets her cape on to keep her warm. Joyce puts her coat on as well. Again Stewart takes a few pictures of them in the yard. Al had moved snow so they get outdoor pictures without getting their feet cold and wet. They get into the limo and head for the church. They arrive at the church a couple of minutes past the hour. Everyone's been seated in the main sanctuary which is up a flight of massively wide stairs. Amy's amazed, there are red poinsettia plants lining the stairs, with tiny twinkle lights and white and red satin ribbons and bows covering the stair case railings. Victoria's thrilled to see the decorations and appreciates the work Katherine and her family did in providing this wonderful gift to her and Jake.

"This is amazing; I wonder what we'll see inside?" Victoria whispers to Amy.

Katherine brings the bouquets to the girls. "I hope you'll like what we've done in the main sanctuary." She says as she passes the flowers to the girls. Victoria's bouquet consists of red roses, white lilies, holly, evergreen bows, hypericum berries and mistletoe. Amy's bouquet is a miniature version of Victoria's. The fragrance from the bouquets is marvellous.

Victoria's dad comes out from the other room and stops dead in his tracks. "Victoria. Look at my little girl." He moves forward to hug her. Tears have formed in his eyes. "You look just like your mother, she would've been so happy and so proud, you've grown into such a beautiful and amazing woman."

"Daddy, don't make me cry," Victoria warns, "I can't walk down the aisle with streaking mascara."

He laughs and looks over at Amy. "You look stunning as well, Amy. I keep forgetting you are grown up women; to me you're still giggling little girls."

He turns more serious and pulls Victoria to one side. "You know your brother did decide to make an appearance, along with his wife and small son. I hope this isn't going to cause any problems."

"Let me just give Amy a heads up so she's okay with it. He's my brother; I've spoken to Jake about it. We sort of expected him to show up, even though he said he wasn't coming when we invited him. Thanks for letting me know.' She kisses her dad and then goes to speak with Amy.

Just then, Joyce appears. "I'm being signalled, they're ready for you folks. Give me a minute to get back up the stairs and let the pianist know you're ready to go."

Amy gives Victoria a quick hug and starts up the stairs. She enters the main sanctuary and stops; Katherine and her helpers have done an unbelievable job. The entire center aisle is lined with poinsettia plants, as are the stairs. There are twinkle lights and Christmas trees lining the entire front of the church. More flowers of red and white are interchanged with the Poinsettia plants on the four steps leading up to the platform at the front of the church. On the altar at the front, one dramatic floral arrangement of pure white sits front and center next to the candles with Ann's Bible carefully set off to one side. In the program there's a note at the bottom of the page that reminds all those in attendance that this arrangement is in memory of those who aren't present. It's a family tradition that Ann started at her 25th wedding anniversary as a tribute to her own parents and for her friends, Jake and Amy's parents.

Joyce whispers to Amy and she starts walking again. This time her eyes focus on Andy, who is standing next to a very nervous Jake. He gives her a reassuring smile as she continues to move forward. Amy takes two steps up towards the platform and stops and turns as the music changes and Victoria enters through the doors. Everyone rises as Victoria and her father make their way to the front of the church.

Amy sees Christopher sitting in the front pew; he's sitting with a very attractive blonde who is holding a small baby. He smiles at her but she doesn't change her expression. She focuses in on Andy for his strength as she moves forward to her designated spot. Amy keeps her eyes on Andy for the entire ceremony and has no recollection of anything until Andy's eyes breaks away as he hands Jake the rings. She's embarrassed as she realizes she's been thinking about her own wedding and not paying attention to Jake's service.

The ceremony is completed and after greetings in the receiving line, the bridal party go off with Stewart to get the wedding pictures taken inside the church and outside in several locations. The weather is warm enough and the sun is shining bright so it's not too cold for the shots.

Slowly everyone heads over to the Westview Golf and Country Club to enjoy the evening and its festivities. The club house is equally as decorated with lights, trees and poinsettias. The table center pieces include flowers similar to Victoria's bouquet. Right after the ceremony Katherine and her team quickly moved all the flowers and trees to the banquet hall. The entire club house is alive with flowers and lights by the time the guests start arriving for cocktails.

Victoria's dad has arranged the wedding cake through a local bakery in Calgary. They've done a spectacular job. The cake consists of three separate cakes, each on its own tower pedestal surrounded by rose petals. The cakes are three sizes; the first one, the largest, is an 18inch square German chocolate cake with chocolate liquor mousse filling. The second is a 14 inch square red velvet cake with alternate layers of chocolate mousse and vanilla strawberry cream. The smallest is a 10 inch square white vanilla cake with mango and orange mousse. Each of the cakes is identical in design and style, with white fondant shaped into tiny pleats covering the sides and top. The centre of each cake has a edible bouquet of red coloured chocolate shaped poinsettia flowers with tiny green chocolate ivy leaves falling down the side. A small fan made from white chocolate completes the center of each cake. The cakes are front and center and everyone looks forward to sampling them since the bakery's been featured in several major magazines and on several home and garden television shows.

Once the bridal party returns for cocktails, Amy and Andy realize they're going to eventually come face to face with Christopher. Andy gets them each a glass of wine and they decide to speak with Christopher who's sitting with his wife and the baby. Howard sees Amy and Andy heading towards them and decides it's best if he lets them handle whatever it is that needs to be handled. Ed also sees this happen and moves towards Howard. They're both prepared to step in should the situation warrant it.

Christopher rises as he sees Amy coming towards them. "Hello Amy," he says as he clears his throat.

"I thought you'd come to your sister's wedding," She replies.

Andy moves next to Amy. "Hi Christopher, it's good to see you again." Andy extends his hand and they shake hands.

"I'd like to introduce you to my wife, Judith, and our son, Christopher Howard the third," he makes the introductions. "Judith this is a long time friend, Amy. We went to school together."

Judith doesn't seem to be aware of the tension, obviously not understanding the dynamics of the relationships. "Hi Amy, it's a pleasure. I love your outfit; it's perfect for a winter wedding. Andy, nice to meet you as well."

Andy and Amy both take turns shaking hands with Judith. "Is this your first time to Alberta?" Andy asks, making small talk.

"No, actually I was out a couple of years ago; I have an aunt and uncle who live in Edmonton. I was hoping we could spend some time with them, but maybe another trip." She grins.

Judith has short blonde hair and a perky appearance. She moves the baby back into his portable bed.

Judith notices Amy's engagement ring. "Wow, what a beautiful ring. It's very unusual. Is it an engagement ring?"

"Actually, yes, it is, Andy and I are planning a spring wedding." Amy holds out her ring and smiles as Andy.

Christopher's noticeably quiet, but Judith doesn't seem to take note. She tells them about their wedding which took place just after the baby was born.

She invites Amy and Andy to join them, but Stewart interrupts with the need for a a few more wedding pictures before the banquet room opens up.

Andy puts his arm around Amy as they follow Stewart to meet up with Jake and Victoria. "Are you okay?" he asks.

"Believe it or not, I'm fine," Amy replies. "I've thought about an encounter with him since our last meeting, but he really means nothing to me now, there are just no feelings at all."

Andy gives her a quick peck on the cheek, "I'm glad. By the way, have I told you how much I love you today?"

After cocktail hour, everyone moves into the dining room for an excellent meal of beef wellington with all the trimmings. It's a refreshing change from turkey. The dessert is the wedding cake and it is served after the speeches are completed.

After dinner and speeches, Al and Ed take control of the mike. Since Jake and Victoria have so many household items, many of those present have pooled their gift of money and bought tickets for a two week cruise to present to the newlyweds. Jake and Victoria are ecstatic since they haven't made plans for a honeymoon, thinking they'd just spend time getting their new house put together. They received possession and the keys to their new home earlier in the week and Victoria's stuff arrived from Toronto yesterday. They had planned to go on their honeymoon later, but a cruise is an excellent idea and they're truly grateful for this wonderful gift from their friends and families.

More pictures are taken as they cut their cake. The guests are thrilled with the different flavours of the cake. Everyone enjoys the opportunity to sample the layers of the cake as the toasts and speeches have all finished and coffee and tea is served.

With the music starting, the bride and groom take the floor. Jake and Victoria glow as they glide around the dance floor.

As Amy and Andy dance, Andy whispers in her ear, "Just 140 more sleeps and this will be our night."

Amy nods her head in agreement. "I've got to be honest, during the entire ceremony, I was thinking about how ours will be."

On several occasions Amy feels Christopher starring at her. She realizes she has no feelings for him. Amy holds Andy tight as they dance. The music goes long into the night and Amy and Andy leave with Ed to Riverside to stay overnight rather than drive back to the city. Andy sleeps in Jake's old room and Amy goes back to her room.

Chapter Thirty One

With their holidays over, both Amy and Andy get back into their routines. Andy starts his new job in the new police white collar crimes unit. The month of January moves forward quickly and the city is in a deep freeze with more snow and cold weather.

Andy puts all the outside Christmas decorations away, both for Amy and his mom. They have formed a routine of eating dinner together, playing games or working out in the exercise room with Tai Chi and Taekwondo. Sometimes on the weekends they go out to visit Amy's dad and play with Finnegan. Finnegan has matured and become an important part of Ed's life.

Andy's happy with his new job. Being in charge of his unit and handling white collar crime suits him. It's a new division of the Calgary Police Force, so there's a lot of liaison meetings between other departments and the local RCMP detachments. Andy's excited about the job and has put in many hours of overtime to get the new unit up and operational.

Amy's back at work with a mountain of reports and files to handle. The beginning of the New Year marks many new changes for her department. She has one more doctor on staff; however, she's had two of her rotational doctors leave for permanent positions in new hospitals and has two new replacements to deal with. The new doctors are working well with her team and she's surprised at how quickly the adjustments have been made.

Jake and Victoria are back from their cruise and have moved into their new home. Victoria's been busy unpacking the storage crates containing Jake's grandparents' furniture. Most are still packed in their original containers since Jake had never bothered unpacking them in his condo. Cheryl and her two assistants have met with Victoria to create a design plan for her to work with. Cheryl's pretty much retired from her design business but has come to work out the ideas, letting the assistants take on the actual work.

January moves into February and February into March. Amy has sent out the wedding invitations and has carefully created lists on the computer to track address changes, replies to the invitations and telephone numbers. It helps her stay on track. The lists for the wedding have started to dwindle as the days get closer. Amy enjoys crossing off each item from the list.

Andy continues to track the days to the wedding, reminding Amy every morning when he calls her.

Chapter Thirty Two

This year, Easter is late and happens to fall on her regular weekend off. Amy has also started to count the days left till her wedding. There is just a month left until the big day

The bridesmaid, flower girl and ring bearer outfits have all arrived. Amy has checked on her own dress and found that Josie's had numerous pink crystals sewn on the front of the wedding dress. She's also incorporated the pink stones into the train and along the lace trim at the hem line. Amy's thrilled with the results.

Amy's brought home all the outfits and they carefully line the closet in one of the spare bedrooms.

Together Amy, Andy and her dad spend Easter Day with Andy's family. The family joins together for the special Easter sunrise breakfast at the church. After church, before they walk across the street to Grace's house, Ed gives Amy a small box.

Puzzled, she looks at him, "Go ahead and open it. It's something your mom left for me to give you for your wedding."

Amy opens the box and inside, covered in tissue paper, Amy finds the special gift. She looks back at her dad, her eyes fill with tears.

"It's the veil and headpiece your mom wore at our wedding. I found it in the closet the other day and realized you need to have it. I think it might need some work. It doesn't look as fresh as when your mother wore it on our 25th anniversary. Maybe you can get Grace or Joyce to help you fix it."

Amy gently lifts the package out of the box and removes the tissue that surrounds it. Inside, the veil has yellowed and the tiara has tarnished. Amy holds it up. "Dad, it's beautiful."

The tiara is exactly what Amy's dress needs. Remembering her mother's love of all things pink, it's not surprising to see pink stones in her tiara. Starting at the base the tiara are two small rows of rhinestones. There are two smaller circles of rhinestones and dime size pink stones secured in each center, flanking each side of the headpiece. In the middle, in all its grandeur, sits a rhinestone encrusted pink heart about the size of a quarter. Loops of rhinestones run along the top of the side circles to the summit of the tiara, finishing off with a small five point star which is completely smothered in much smaller rhinestones. The veil is attached behind the tiara with two combs to hold it in place.

"I know it doesn't look like much now, but I hope you can fix it up. I remember how beautiful it looked on your mother; she took my breath away when I saw her walk down the aisle."

"Dad, it's perfect and it's from mom. With some silver cleaner and jewellery cleaner the tiara will sparkle again. I'm not too sure about the veil." Amy has trouble speaking with the lump she feels right now. Even though her wedding gown is totally different from her mother's dress this is just perfect.

"Thank you so much, Dad. I love you." Amy kisses him on the cheek.

She gently folds the tissue paper back around it and puts it back into the box.

Together they walk across the street for Easter Dinner. Ed leaves Finnegan at Amy's house since he tends to turn on his charm and with those big sad eyes he always nets big rewards from everyone. It's become apparent it's too much food for his tummy. Finnegan watches them from the side panel of Amy's front door, prepared to guard the house as instructed by his loving master.

Chapter Thirty Three

Amy has carried over her one week of holidays from last year, adding it to her four weeks this year. She plans to take the week before the wedding to allow her to handle all the last minute details. Jake and Amy have discussed taking two weeks for a honeymoon, but haven't decided where they'd like to go. Amy wants to have at least a week after they return from their honeymoon before she has to go back to work.

Amy is busy sprucing up her yard and setting out her plants as she does every spring. Normally, she spends several weeks making sure her plantings are perfect, but this year, she only has a few days since she's so busy with wedding details. Even with her many lists and her organization it seems something is always popping up that requires her attention.

Andy starts moving his things over to the house and Amy's been busy making sure there's space for everything. Andy has found someone to rent his house; Cst. Calvin Carter and his new bride are ready to move in. Since they don't have much in the way of furniture and belongings, Andy's offered to leave most of his furniture behind for them.

Together, Amy and Andy have walked through Andy's house, as Amy wants to be sure Andy's not leaving anything special behind. To Andy these things really don't mean a lot, he's just looking forward to their married life together. But Amy wants to be sure Andy has no regrets about leaving things behind.

Jake's informed her that men think about these things differently. "I felt the same way about my stuff. It just doesn't matter what Victoria wants to do with things, I love her and stuff is just stuff."

"But, aren't there things you want to keep that are special to you?" Amy pushes.

"Sure, but it's stuff from our grandparents and Victoria loves those things. My old football, hockey equipment and golf clubs, things like that, but most of it belongs out in the garage. But, listen, Sis, you're putting too much thought into this, believe me," Jake stresses to Amy.

With that, Amy calms down; since it's the same thing Andy's told her several times, she realizes men certainly are from Mars.

Time passes quickly and before she knows it, it's the last day of work before her wedding. Joan and Cindy are both scheduled to arrive over the weekend. Both of them want to help Amy with all the last minute details and running around that they know from experience will occur.

Grace pops over to bring back Ann's headpiece. She's polished the silver, cleaned the rhinestones and replaced the veil material with a sparkly white crystal organza fabric. Josie ordered a miniature version of the trim lace for Grace to hand stitch around the entire veil finishing it off perfectly.

"What an unbelievable difference; it doesn't look like the same headpiece." Amy's surprised. "I know you understand how much this means to me." She hugs Grace.

"Let's check it out against your parents' wedding pictures to see how it looked on your mom," Grace suggests.

With that, Amy gets out the album that she and Jake had custom made for their parents' 50th anniversary, just before her mom died. They sit for a few minutes and check out the pictures of Ann and Ed on their wedding day and at their 25th anniversary. The headpiece looks as good as it did then.

Grace suggests they should take some measurements in the main sanctuary of the church for Katherine. She called earlier in the week to check the width of the altar table. She wants them to measure the top to make sure there is room for the candles, Ann's Bible and the flower arrangement that Katherine's making.

As they drive up to the church, Amy sees several cars in the parking lot. "Maybe we should come back later; it looks like something might be going on."

"Probably choir practice, we can be quick – in and out," Grace replies.

As they walk into the main foyer Amy is surprised to see all her friends and family.

"Surprise, surprise!" Grace giggles. Grace has worked in secret with Amy's friends and her job was to get Amy to the bridal shower.

Amy can't believe her eyes. It seems half of Riverside's here, along with most of the staff at the hospital.

"Sure hope there are no emergencies tonight," Amy jokes, "Is there anyone left at the hospital tonight?"

Amy's surprised at how everyone kept this such a secret. Many near slips are exposed and Amy realizes why there were so many strange happenings during this past week.

Dozens of women have joined together to participate in the shower. Everyone moves downstairs into the banquet room. There's a table groaning with fancy desserts and squares. At the front of the room, there's a table with wedding ribbons and bells decorating it. Sitting alongside is a table full of gifts and cards.

All of the wedding party have worked together to organize games and skits. They tell stories about each other's wedding adventures and everyone laughs and giggles at the stories.

Amy opens her gifts, and many of gifts include fancy nightgowns with matching bras and panties. She receives several sets from her bridesmaids. In anticipation of a wonderful honeymoon, several gifts are travel items.

Amy's overwhelmed by the thoughtfulness of her friends and family. All in all, everyone has a great time and at the end of the night Andy arrives to help carry gifts out to the car to deliver them back to Amy's house.

Later that evening Amy shows Andy many of the great presents she's received. She keeps the lingerie as a surprise for after they are married. They're both grateful for the generosity of their friends and family. Andy confesses he's been part of the plan and that it's been difficult not to let something slip out.

Andy heads back across the street to help his mother with a couple of jobs she needs him to do.

After Andy leaves Amy gets right to work sending out thank you cards, something she knows her mom will be happy to see her doing.

Chapter Thirty Four

The week passes quickly. Amy has the girls come to try on their outfits and make sure everything's ready to go. The dresses are all neatly hanging at Amy's house, including the shoes and underwear that the girls have brought to the house; everything is ready for the wedding. The men's tuxedos have all arrived and are waiting at Andy's place. The men are getting ready over there while the women and children prepare at Amy's house.

Amy spends Wednesday afternoon making sure the yard's organized and presentable. She weeds and mows. The house has been cleaned, thanks to Judy the cleaning lady, from top to bottom.

The appointments for hair and makeup have been made. Amy's doubled checks her lists to make sure has not forgotten anything.

The rehearsal goes off without a snag; Andy and Amy go over their vows and everyone practices walking down the aisle. Ed has given Pastor Trevor Ann's Bible to use for the Bible verses. It's just one more way Ed ensures Ann's presence.

The church is a beautiful old building. The main sanctuary has twenty foot oak ceilings with 15 foot stain glass windows row upon row, each depicting a story from the Bible, with the Old Testament on one side and the New Testament on the other. The front window depicts a floor to ceiling cross with stain glass blocks reflecting all the colours included in the various Bible scenes. Surrounding the cross is more oak. It's a long straight walk from the back foyer to the front on a beautiful blue carpet. The church is amazing even without decorations, but the decorating crew have spent several hours adding their decorative touches to compliment the scene and not take away from the grandeur of the room.

Katherine and her team of decorating assistants (mostly made up of Amy's family) have made everyone leave the church while they set up. They want Amy to be as surprised as Victoria was at her wedding.

Grace has everyone over to her place for the rehearsal dinner. She hosts a huge family style barbecue in the back yard. She's made tons of potato salad, cole slaw, and baked beans with apple pie and ice cream for dessert. Ed and Jake help Andy with the steaks and hamburgers.

The schedule for the next morning is reviewed so that everyone knows what time to be where. Amy's confident she's handled everything. She's read all of wedding planning books she's received and incorporated all the details that she and Andy want into their wedding. She's worked hard to make sure many of the items in her mom's letter have been included.

Amy's cousin Zack and Andy's brother-in-law Phil have taken on the task of co-masters of ceremonies. They've been huddled up in Richard's office for several evenings. Apparently they had so much fun at Christmas that they've developed a strong friendship. Both are jokesters who love to laugh and they've taken on the responsibility with great zeal. Amy's a little concerned, but Andy's reassured her that things will be just fine.

As Ed leaves, he asks Andy and Amy to walk him out to his truck.

"Amy, I asked Andy to hold off on your plans for your honeymoon because I wanted to give you something special," Ed explains as they walk the short distance down the street to his truck.

"Dad, you've done so much for me. Hey, wait a minute." Amy stops as she finally registers her father's last statement. "You've been discussing our honeymoon with Andy!" her voice raises slightly.

"Actually, the day I asked your father for permission to marry you his only request of me was not make any honeymoon plans without discussing it with him first," Andy interjects.

"Honey, I wanted to give you something very special. It was special to your mother and me so I want it to be special for you." With that, Ed reaches into the glove box of the truck and produces a large envelope.

He hands it to Andy who in turn passes it to Amy. "Sweetheart, here's our honeymoon arrangement."

"Do you know what's in here?" Amy asks Andy.

"No, only that it was on your mother's list for your father to handle," Andy says smiling.

Amy opens the envelope and her eyes grow wide. Andy leans over to see what she's reading. He has a similar response.

"You're giving us the same trip you and mom had for your 25th wedding anniversary." Amy's shocked. "Dad, this is too much."

"Actually, I loved doing it, but I wasn't alone." He motions for Andy and Amy to look behind them.

Their entire wedding party is standing behind them.

Jake speaks first "Actually sis, Victoria and I received a similar package. We were sworn to secrecy so as not to ruin the surprise. We're planning to take the Paris trip from Dad this fall."

Going to tears, Amy hugs her father. "You're my little girl, I loved every minute I put into these plans. It brought back wonderful memories for me and I'm more grateful that your mother, through her lists, suggested this project for me to take on. I pray you two have as great a time as your mother and I did. I'm grateful for everyone's input and there are a few extras that I added to make sure I put all the financial gifts from everyone here into the package, including an extra week for you to spend touring the wineries of France."

Everyone moves in for a series of hugs and kisses. Amy's so overwhelmed by this she's speechless. Andy thanks Ed along with his mother and everyone else for such an amazing and special gift.

Ed confirms that he completed most of the trip based on the directions Ann had left him in his list. Amy continues to be surprised by the number of things her mother had put into her lists before she died. Obviously her list to her husband was in greater detail than the lengthy lists she left for her and Jake.

"Now we're completely ready for our wedding," Andy happily announces. "It's been tough to keep being so indecisive about plans for our honeymoon, but a promise is a promise."

Andy and Amy are ready for their day. Hand in hand they decide to take a walk to enjoy the evening and reflect on the day's events. As they walk, the scents of spring abound, with the heavenly aroma of flowering May day trees and the scent of freshly mowed grass. They continue to discuss their honeymoon plans. For their wedding night, they've decided not to stay at the bridal suite at the Greenwood, but to come back home to spend their first night together in their own home. It's their little secret.

As they reach the house, they decide to enjoy the warmth and beauty of the spring night further by sitting out on the love seat on the back deck.

They review the contents of their honeymoon package; it's the same 19th century luxury spa hotel, with a romantic dinner at the Eiffel Tower that Ann always raved about, a day with a car and driver to tour the Palace of Versailles, and dinner at the Hotel Trianon Palace Versailles Waldorf Astoria Hotel restaurant Le Gordon Ramsay au Trianon. There is also a tour of several popular vineyards that include seven different bed and breakfast locations. As they study the package, they realize the time and effort that Ed put into completing these plans. This trip's a spectacular honeymoon and they're both humbled by the work Ed's put into these arrangements and the money he and the rest of the wedding party contributed.

It's late and before Andy leaves he pulls out a small package.

"My grandmother gave this to me before she died. At the time, I had no idea why, but now I understand." Andy hands it to Amy.

The small wooden box opens easily and reveals a simple pair of pearl earrings. A single pearl is surrounded by a circle of diamonds. Amy smiles at Andy. "I wasn't sure which earrings to wear, but of course, these are the ones." Amy kisses Andy.

"It's been a long countdown, but now, as Jennifer would say, we have one more sleep to go."

Andy holds Amy in his arms as they reflect on their plans for tomorrow.

Chapter Thirty Five

The morning of her wedding, Amy wakes up to Andy's call. "Good morning my beautiful bride, I love you."

"Hello yourself," Amy answers as she leans over to check the time. "What have you got planned for the day to keep yourself occupied while all of us ladies are making ourselves beautiful."

"Think we might hit the golf course since it sounds like your dad's bringing his team early so they can join us," Andy replies.

"Well don't be late to the church," Amy quips.

"Not a chance, I've been counting the days for too long. See you at the church and remember I love you."

"I love you more," Amy replies.

She heads to the shower. She sings *Love me Tender* as she goes through her daily routine. Hair damp, she pulls it up into a pony tail. With her jogging pants on, she looks for a button down shirt so she doesn't mess up her hair. Amy changes the sheets on the bed; she has a wonderful fragrant powder that she shakes over the new Egyptian sheet set she received at her bridal shower from Andy's sisters. The 1200 thread count sheets feel like silk as she takes her time to smooth them out. She tidies up the room; it needs to be perfect for tonight.

With their honeymoon plans finalized, Amy pulls out the suitcases, one for her and a slightly smaller one for Andy. She'd already made a list, actually several lists, of what to bring depending on their final destination. With military precision Amy packs her suitcase. She's done a fair bit of travelling over the years and has learned how to pack and what to pack. For Paris, she chooses light summer dresses, shawls, comfortable sandals, slacks, tops and two special evening dresses. It all fits nicely in the suitcase with room to spare for the special items she knows she'll find to bring home. She also has a list made up for packing Andy's suitcase. She and Andy made up his list and she quickly starts organizing his suitcase. He needs to double check it before she locks it up. She carefully tucks her suitcase back into her closet with Andy's suitcase sitting on top waiting for final inspection.

With the bedding in the washer and the suitcases packed, Amy heads downstairs to check her wedding to-do list one more time. She knows it off by heart, but checking it helps calm her down. She decides to read the newspaper while she waits for Joan, Cindy, Faith, Sherry and Grace to join her for their trip over to the beauty spa. The others are meeting them there.

During the past months, Amy's tried several hair styles to try to decide how to wear her hair. Finding her perfect dress has been so much easier than trying to decide what to do with her mop of strawberry blonde hair. In the end, with Andy's suggestion, she decides to have her hair curled into dozens of ringlets, with the hair pulled back at the sides and gently falling down her back.

Grace and her girls arrive and they head off to meet up with Sophie and Victoria. Jennifer's also going to meet them to get her hair done as well. Carrie's not sure how the little one will handle having her hair primped, but Jennifer's been determined that she wants her long hair curled like Amy's. Jennifer has an envious head of hair, slightly more blonde than her mother, with a hint of natural curl. She'll wear a small tiara with her hair in the same style as Amy's.

Amy has her hair done first with Lisa, her regular stylist. While Lisa handles Amy, Sonya takes on Jennifer. Since she has a daughter almost the same age, it's decided Sonya has the most patience and is familiar with the issues a little one faces. Just to be on the safe side, Carrie brings her small DVD player with the Disney Cinderella movie, Jennifer's favourite.

Everyone has a complete spa treatment, including pedicure, manicure, hair styling, and makeup. Surprisingly, Jennifer's been a perfect angel the whole time. The staff provides cheese, cracker, meat and fruit trays along with a variety of different refreshments for the bridal party.

It's afternoon when they arrive back at Amy's house. They order in Chinese food and quickly eat, being careful not to mess up the makeup and hair.

Andy has been busy sending text messages to Amy throughout the day and the latest update from him advises the men are also having Chinese, since they're now back from golfing and getting themselves organized.

Once lunch is finished, everyone goes upstairs and starts the process of dressing for the wedding. Grace runs across the street to quickly change and arrives back just as Stewart, the photographer appears. She's found a very elegant long skirt and short jacket outfit with a matching lace top in a very soft sea foam green colour with silver threads running through the lace. She looks very smart and is happy with her outfit.

Stewart took the wedding pictures for Jake and Victoria and Amy fell in love with the unique quality of his shots. Without question, Amy booked him for their wedding. She was so pleased that he was available.

With the bridesmaids all dressed, they turn their attention to Amy. She has her dress in the spare room where it's been safely tucked away. She's checked the dress everyday for three weeks. Today's the day and without much fanfare she quickly slips into her brand new lace under garments and Sophie and Victoria help her step into her gown. She feels the same way and has no regrets; to Amy, it's the perfect dress.

The full skirt fans out and the zipper is hidden in the back by a series of small buttons that Sophie quickly does up. Several small pink rhinestones now adorn the front panel of the dress and fall into a striking pattern around the hemline of lace. The train has its share of pink rhinestones as well. Amy doesn't put the train on right away, waiting instead until she has her headpiece in place. Once the headpiece is on, she quickly puts on the elegant earrings Andy gave her last night. She decides not to wear a necklace; the scalloped neckline of the dress is all she needs.

Stewart quietly enters and continues to snap pictures as Amy gets ready. Jennifer twists and turns in her dress, showing off the sparkles and rhinestones. She's thrilled to be part of the group.

At the top of the staircase, Grace shows the girls how to attach the train to Amy's gown. With a bridesmaid strategically placed on alternate stairs, starting with Jennifer at the bottom, Amy comes down four steps and Grace helps Stewart arrange her train so it tumbles down the remaining stairs. After several pictures, Stewart takes more of Amy alone on the stairs. Even more pictures of the girls are taken in the living room, and Grace announces the limousine has arrived. With perfect timing, Katherine arrives with the bouquets and Ed. For the weekend, Finnegan is having a sleep over with Sharon Talbot who's pleased to see that her little runt puppy has grown up into a well mannered dog.

"Wow, that's cutting it close," she laughs as she opens the back end of her SUV. Inside, the fragrance of flowers escapes.

Katherine takes out Amy's bridal bouquet. "I hope you like this," she says as she passes it to Amy.

Amy's in awe; it's the most beautiful arrangement she's ever seen. Twelve perfect pink sweetheart roses with three silver grey coloured calla lilies cascade down with white stephanotis and green ivy tumbling down the front of her bouquet. She'd always wanted a cascading bouquet, but this is more elegant that even her wildest dreams.

Katherine stands back for a moment. "You're the most breathtaking bride I've ever seen," she declares.

Katherine pulls a tissue out of her pocket as the tears flow. "It's hard to believe my beautiful little Goddaughter's all grown up."

"Aunty, please don't cry. You'll make me cry and I don't want Andy to see me with messed up makeup."

Stewart kindly steps in with a small joke and has Katherine stand next to Amy for a few shots. Amy hugs her aunt. "You're amazing and I love you."

"Let's not get all mushy and mess up the makeup, ladies," Grace jokes.

With that, Katherine hands out the bridesmaids bouquets. A smaller round version of Amy's bouquet each contains white and pink roses with one grey-silver calla lily is handed out to each of the four lovely ladies and slightly smaller versions to the two junior bridesmaids. She passes Grace's corsage over to Amy to pin on. Stewart holds her bouquet as she puts the corsage on Grace; they stop for pictures of Grace and Amy together.

"Hey, what about me?" Jennifer shouts out. "Did you forget me, Grandma?"

"No, sweetheart, I'd never forget you. I made a very special arrangement for my little pumpkin."

"Do you like my dress, see how it spins around." Jennifer twirls around Amy and the girls. "Look at me!"

"Come here, and take your flowers." Katherine hands her a tiny bouquet with two miniature pink and white roses. It's the perfect size for tiny hands.

Jennifer loves her flowers.

Ed and the limousine driver have been patiently waiting. "Amy, we need to leave, we're going to be late." Ed ushers the girls towards the car.

Cindy, Joan and the younger girls get in first. Grace is next and takes Jennifer's hand as she helps the little girl into the car. Victoria and Sophie follow.

Ed and Katherine help gather up Amy's train and Amy slowly gets into the car. Ed piles the train around the floor. He hops into the front with the driver.

Going to the chapel and I'm gonna get married is the song playing on the stereo and everyone sings along as they head to the church.

Chapter Thirty Six

As the wedding party limo pulls up in front of the church, the last of the guests begin moving inside. Stewart's already arrived, and he has positioned his camera to snap Amy as Ed helps her out of the car.

It's such a beautiful day, the sun's shining bright in the sky and the trees around the church are in full bloom and bow down to Amy in all their splendour. Even the air's quiet so as not to disturb the bride's hair.

As Amy stands by the car, arranging herself, she sees a penny on the cement; Ed has seen it and picks it up. He squeezes it into her hand. She holds it with her flowers.

As they enter the foyer, they move quickly to the room just to the side waiting for their cue. Grace leaves the wedding party to join the men. She'll walk her son down the aisle just as Ed will walk his daughter. Grace has dreamed of this moment since Andy was born. She's had her moments of regret that her beloved Richard's not here to share her joy, but she's determined to keep a smile on her face.

Alex's wife Emma has a Shania Twain voice and as the men slowly make their way down the aisle, she sings *Endless Love*. All the men take their places at the front. Slowly, Grace and Andy walk to the front of the church. Andy escorts his mother to her place in the front pew, giving her a kiss before moving to the front of the church.

Emma finishes the song and waits as the music is cued. She turns, ready to sing as the music soundtrack starts. A full orchestra plays the soundtrack of *From This Moment On*. Slowly the girls move forward, each walking as they'd rehearsed. Jordan and James walk side by side, coached by their mother who sits proudly in the second row.

The boys look dashing in their grey tuxedos with pink vests and bow ties. They each carry a small white pillow with pink tassels. Placed on the centre of one pillow, Amy has placed her wedding band, securing it with a safety pin and she's done the same with the second pillow with Andy's band. Beside each ring she's sewn a small dinky car to keep the boys entertained during the service.

Faith and Sherry enter next, moving at the same pace as they were shown at the rehearsal. Jennifer walks down the aisle. She looks left and right and smiles at her family as they smile and encourage her forward.

Amy can see the decorations in the church. Just as with Victoria's wedding, Katherine has magically transformed the church. Floral corsages of white and pink roses are tied together with flowing layers of organza made into pink and white ribbons, adorning each pew. A huge archway of twinkle lights, more organza and even more flowers form the entrance which everyone has walked through. At the front of the church, huge flower arrangements standing on four foot crystal pedestals flank the stairs up to the altar. Sitting on the altar table is a magnificent white rose arrangement positioned slightly to one side. The other side has three candles, two tall white candles in silver holders and one large pink candle in the middle. Front and center is Ann's Bible. Within the program is a note at the bottom of the page that reminds all those in attendance that the white floral arrangement is in remembrance of those who are not present. It's the same tribute that Jake and Victoria followed for their wedding. On either side of the altar stand two enormous twelve candle silver candelabras. The alternating pink and white candles gently flicker in the air.

It's now the final verse and Emma lifts her voice as Amy stands at the entrance of the sanctuary. Andy gazes at his bride as Amy enters the room. She stops for an instant to take in the room. Ed, holding her hand, gently moves her forward. As they make the long walk down the aisle, Amy locks her eyes with Andy. He gives her his special reassuring grin and she takes a deep breath and continues to make her way to the front. Emma has spent hours practising to make sure she can make the song last until Amy gets to the front and as Amy stops at the bottom of the row of steps at the front, Emma finishes the last words to her song.

Ed stops and waits as Andy moves forward to meet them. Amy reaches over and quickly kisses her father's cheek. A tiny tear trickles down Ed's check as he returns a kiss on his daughter's cheek. He takes her hand and places it gently into Andy's outstretched palm along with the penny Amy is still holding. Andy sees the penny and smiles at Amy.

Together Andy and Amy take the last four steps together to the centre of the stage where Pastor Trevor is waiting.

"I am beginning today with two scripture readings, the first from Genesis 2:24 and repeated again in Ephesians 5:31 '*For this reason a man will leave his father and mother and be united to his wife and they will become one flesh*'. Andy and Amy, as you understand, today starts a new beginning in your lives. Today is the wedding, but it only lasts the day. Your marriage is for the rest of your lives. You'll both start back to school, becoming students of the school of marriage. Today you begin the learning process to learn to love each other in a deeper way. You'll join together to become one, but you will not lose your individuality. Becoming one does not happen overnight. Every day for the rest of your lives you'll learn and become better at marriage as you share your lives together. You'll learn to lean on one another, love each other, share your lives with each other and take each other into consideration. There's no room for selfishness in marriage. Marriage is a school of love."

As Pastor Trevor continues with the service, he quotes the verses of love from the Bible. They are verses Amy and Andy have recited to each other in their pre-marriage classes.

"Before Amy and Andy recite their vows to each other, I must tell you all that I had the privilege of attending a service about marriage a few years back. Now, with your permission, I would like to share what I learned that day so long ago. I'd like everyone here to take a few minutes to close your eyes and hold your spouse's hand. If you're alone and do not have a spouse, hold your own hand and visualize yourself with your spouse. Men, I want you to think about these words as a renewal of your wedding vows.

"My lovely companion, I take you to be my wedded wife, to have and to hold from this day forward. When you are happy with me, and even when you are so mad at me that I tremble in fear, when I have lots of money and when I am broke, when you are sick and can't do things around the house, when I leave the toilet seat up or when I make supper for you, and when you make me feel like the most important person in the world. To love you with gratefulness till God takes me home."

"Now women, it's your turn. Repeat after me, 'My loving husband, I take you today to have and to hold from this day forward, when things go my way and when they don't, when you listen to me and when you ignore me, when you have a good job and when you are struggling, when you are tired and irritable and want me to wait on you hand and foot, when you leave wet towels and dirty clothes on the floor and when you feel so good you sweep me off my feet. I love you and look to you with gracefulness till death do us part'."

As Pastor Trevor continues to speak, there's a stir by those sitting in the front row of the church. The two little ring bearers have managed to remove the rings and passed them to Andy, who eagerly takes them from the two boys. Having figured out how to take the little cars off of their pillows, Jordan and James go down on their bellies to play cars. This can only be seen by the front rows and those standing at the front of the church. Stewart has captured this on his camera and chuckles to himself.

"Amy Elizabeth Green Murray will you take Andrew Richard Henderson to be your lawfully wedded husband?" Pastor Trevor quietly moves his feet out of the path of the little cars and continues on with the service.

Amy and Andy recite their vows to each other and exchange their rings. They move around the two little boys and their cars towards the Unity candles where they take the single lit candles and together light the big candle as a symbol of their new lives together.

As they sign the register, Emma sings another song. This song she dedicates to Amy in remembrance of Amy's mother, *A Song for My Daughter* by Ray Allaire. As she finishes, she sees many eyes glistening with tears both for the beauty of the song and the singer and for Amy and Ann.

Having completed all the legal requirements, Pastor Trevor has the couple stand in front of the church facing their guests. "Amy and Andy, in the presence of God and as authorized by the Province of Alberta, I can now legally declare you are husband and wife. Andy you may kiss your beautiful bride."

Andy leans forward and whispers, "Amy, I love you with all my heart and soul." He kisses his gorgeous bride.

"Ladies and gentlemen, may I introduce to you Amy and Andy Henderson." The guests erupt in loud applause and cheers. Amy and Andy head down the aisle to go outside into the warm spring sun.

The wedding party spends some time outside, greeting their guests and receiving the congratulatory hugs and well wishes.

Watching the time, Grace organizes the wedding party to head back to Amy's back yard for some pictures and then off to the Rock Gardens for more outdoor pictures. It's the perfect day for pictures, no wind, not too many bugs and lots of beautiful light and flowering trees and plants.

Finally, Andy and Amy have a few minutes alone in the limo on the way back to Amy's house. Andy puts the penny back into Amy's hand and kisses her.

"This is probably the only time we are going to have alone for the rest of the day. I just want to tell you how beautiful you look. The dress is perfect and I love you so much."

They laugh about the boys playing with their toy cars and decide it is a story they plan to share at each of the twin's own weddings when they grow up.

Chapter Thirty Seven

The guests head over to the Greenwood for cocktail hour and appetizers. The area is set up outside the main banquet hall where the doors remain closed to the guests. Katherine meets up with the wedding party as they arrive outside and she takes Amy and Andy through the side entrances so they can see Katherine's family gift of yet more decorations and flowers before their guests enter.

They stand in complete disbelief.

The empty banquet room that they first saw has been completely transformed. Round tables have been decked out on either side of the polished hardwood dance floor. Chairs have been outfitted in white covers with huge bows of pink satin tied at the back of each. As the center piece for each table, three foot tall clear crystal glass vases with pink roses, white calla lilies and tall gladiolas are majestically placed on round glass mirrors with small battery operated twinkle lights surrounding them. At each place setting sits a thimble size sterling silver three layer wedding cake name card holder. Each name is centered on a small card with engraved pink bows and dark grey print. Sitting right next to it is a tiny crystal bell with a pink bow tied around the handle. Next to the bell a guest gift favour has been placed. There are two guest gift favours, one is a gourmet coffee container decked out in a black tuxedo with a tiny heart shaped coffee spoon attached with a grey bow, and the other a similar gourmet tea container in white organza with pink trim, again with the same tiny heart shaped teaspoon attached with a pink bow.

The bride and groom and their attendances will sit at rectangular tables facing their guests. Ceiling to floor white sheer draperies cover the wall behind the head tables creating the illusion of a large picture window. There are a series of pink floor lights placed behind the draperies. The pink light showers the room in an overall pink glow. The two large standing candelabras from the church have been moved and now flank each side of this area. Dozens of tiny tea lights stand in a row down the center of the table. Silver stands to hold all of the bouquets have been set out and will be featured as the head table floral arrangements.

The main entrance of the room features the large archway that stood at the back of the church earlier today. Katherine and her team have set it up so each guest enters through the arches. Two small flood lights also with pink bulbs add a pink glow on the archway. It looks enchanting with the twinkle lights, fresh flowers and crystal organza covering the white wooden arch. Each guest is asked to pose for pictures as they enter.

Carrie's husband Brett, who loves to play with his camera, has volunteered to take pictures of each guest arriving through the archway.

Katherine guides them to the cake table. They picked a cake from the same bakery that made Jake and Victoria's cake. The wedding cake is set front and center on a round table with two glass candle holders on either side. The white table cloth has pink organza gathered around the skirt of the table and two big satin bows on each side.

The cake is a four layer cake with white icing and edible pink roses and grey catta lilies strategically placed around each layer. Written on each layer are the words that have been incorporated into their wedding, from their vows, to their table arrangements, ***Sharing together one love one lifetime***. On the top 8 inch round in edible dark grey calligraphy is the word 'Sharing.' On the next 12 inch round is the word 'together', and on the third 16 round reads 'one love'. The bottom 20 inch round features the words 'one lifetime'. The top of the cake has a small porcelain bride and groom. The groom is a police officer complete with hat and badge. He has the bride in his arms holding a tiny pink bouquet.

Another table off to the side holds the white floral arrangement from the church. In the middle of that table is a miniature wishing well decked out in pink and white satin ribbons and bows.

Amy and Andy are overjoyed with the room. Katherine's pleased with the results as well. Amy gives her a big hug and Andy hugs her, lifting her up into the air. Happy that she's succeeded in her task and glad they love her efforts, Katherine heads off to join her family in the cocktail room. She leaves Amy and Andy to enjoy the room before everyone heads in to eat.

Amy and Andy spend a few minutes taking in all aspects of the room. They are amazed and grateful for this fabulous gift Katherine and her family have given them. Stewart comes in and quickly takes several pictures of the happy couple before the room fills up.

They leave shortly before the cocktail hour is completed, the same way they came in. They go around to the main entrance where the rest of the bridal party is waiting.

Their arrival works in perfect harmony with the day's schedule. The main banquet room is opened up and guests slowly make their way in and find their seats. The guests are impressed with the decorations. Brett is busy taking pictures as each guest entered the room. Carrie helps with film and the second camera. They welcome each guest. Their twin daughters, Vanessa and Victoria sit nearby at another table with a picture frame containing a large 16 x 20 inch pale pink coloured mat with a small picture space of 8 x 12. They have several black and grey pens and are busy getting each guest to sign the mat. Once the mat has all of the guest signatures, Carrie and the girls will insert a picture from earlier today that they've printed from Carrie's small digital camera. It's the girls' gift to the bride and groom.

Chapter Thirty Eight

Zack and Phil begin to ask the guests to find their places. They've spent hours preparing for today and are looking forward to a fun time, mostly at the expense of the bride and groom.

They carry in a large wheel that has been divided like a pie into forty different slices; each slice contains the name of a couple present today. Many of the guests have puzzled looks as they watch this strange item pass them by. It's definitely homemade and very curious. Since both of these gentlemen are known by their families and friends to be very creative, everyone's looking forward to a good time.

Zack and Phil take their places at the podium and invite everyone to take their places since the bridal party have arrived. They explain that on the wheel are the names of various couples in attendance tonight, personally chosen by the Masters of Ceremonies. The crystal bells will be rang as a signal for the bride and groom to kiss, but with a twist. Zack and Phil will take turns spinning the wheel, the name of the couple appearing where the wheel stops will provide a live demonstration of the proper methods for kissing.

The DJ's set up his equipment and is playing background music while the guests take their places. On cue from Zack, the Hawaiian Wedding Song starts to play and the bridal party come out slowly, one couple at a time, first Jason and Joan, next Shawn and Cindy, Jake and Victoria, and finally Sophie and Steve. The junior bridesmaids, the little ring bearers and the flower girl bring up the rear.

Just as the bride and groom make their entrance and right on cue, the DJ changes the music. The theme song to the TV show from the 1970's Married with Children suddenly fills the room. This is a complete surprise for Amy and Andy, but as everyone laughs and claps to the music, Amy and Andy move in time to the music as they make their way to the front.

Amy's been unsure about whether she should leave her train on for the reception, but Grace suggests she enter with it on and just before she sits, Grace will quickly come up and help her remove the train. They've actually practiced a couple of times and discover a shortcut to get it separated from the dress in just a matter of seconds. Sure enough, no glitches and Grace takes the train back to her table, folds it up and puts it into a storage bin that has been tucked under the tablecloth. It happens so quickly most aren't even aware of the change.

Amy and Andy know they're in for a great night with an entrance like this and Phil and Zack are not planning to let them down. Zack's surprised them all with his one of a kind suit. He's ordered an outfit from LoudMouth Golf, a brand made famous by professional golfer John Daly. The outfit has caused quite a stir. The pants are disco balls on a black background. Circles of red, pink green, orange, lime, purple, blue, and grey cover the pants. The jacket matches. It's bright and colourful and Zack loves it. He's teamed it up with a black shirt and pink tie.

Not to be outdone, Phil's also ordered his outfit from the same place. His coat of many colours consists of a patchwork of different patterns of plaids, checks, flowers, and a range of colours from reds, pinks, purples, oranges, greens, browns and blues. He's optioned for the matching pants to co-ordinate his outfit. Like Zack, he chooses a black shirt and hot pink tie.

Before the bride and groom are seated, the first crystal bells ring out and Phil spins the wheel. Al and Joyce are the couple the wheel stops at and without much fanfare; Al puts Joyce on his knee and plants a big kiss right on her lips. Andy and Amy follow with great gusto as they mimic Al and Joyce. Each couple try to outdo the previous every time the wheel spins and Andy and Amy enjoy watching the other couples and have great fun, much to the delight of Phil and Zack and of course all the guests.

The jokes and laughter continues as the introductions are made. Pastor Trevor is called upon to say grace. Once grace is said, the four course meal starts. The first course is a choice of either tomato feta soup or Tuscan roaster garlic soup. Between each course, jokes and stories are shared by the dynamic MC team.

The second course is a choice between a wonderful summer greens salad with sun dried tomato vinaigrette and crumbled goat cheese and oven toasted pine nuts or Caprese, which is a house made mozzarella layered between ripe tomatoes with fresh basil and shaved onions dressed with balsamic vinaigrette.

The fourth course is another choice between lemon and herb roasted chicken breast served with herbed fonduta sauce, baby roasted potatoes and fresh asparagus spears and strips of carrots or thick prime rib roast served with creamy gorgonzola mashed potatoes, green beans and carrots slices and red wine demi glace with horseradish on the side.

Each course is a masterpiece of creation as the chef has made sure to design his plates to match the splendour of the room. The final course, dessert has been kept simple. It's a choice of Nocello blueberry bread pudding enhanced with white chocolate and served with fresh whipped cream and glazed fruit, or Crème Brule garnished with kiwi and strawberries. They will have the wedding cake as a second dessert with more tea and coffee after the wedding cake is cut.

Tea and coffee completed the meal with everyone sitting back with full tummies to relax and enjoy the much anticipated program they expect Zack and Phil to produce. Without disappointment the lights go down and a giant screen rolls out at the back of the room, just in front of the archway. The projector from the ceiling drops down to bring, through pictures, the life and times of Amy and Andy. Jake and Victoria worked together with Zack and Phil, scouring through the hundreds of pictures to match the various stages in this couple's lives. Fortunately Grace loves the camera as much as Ann, so there are enough pictures to satisfy the requirements of this group for their presentation.

From birth to the loss of their first teeth, to their first cars, the lives of Amy and Andy are shared with everyone. Amy's first car, Merv, was her pride and joy. It survived her teen years with minor bumps. One picture taken by Mr. Hatfield, the school principal showed poor Merv with a giant Band-Aid taped across a huge dint in the front driver's side when Amy accidentally hit a car as she was coming out of the school parking lot. Andy had a parallel situation with his first truck, the Green Hornet, which also faced similar pain at the expense of another truck. And so their lives went on right up to the pictures on the night of their engagement. Speeches and toasts, welcomes to the family, all with lots of laughs and jokes continue at the expense of the happy bride and groom.

Amy and Andy love every minute of the program and make comments back and forth to the guests.

After enough time to settle everyone's full bellies, it's time to cut the cake. The bride and groom cheerfully hold the knife into the first cut while Stewart and other camera happy guests click dozens and dozens of pictures. Andy shares his bite of cake with Amy. The servers very quickly passed out slices of cake to everyone, with lots of options for second and third helpings.

With dinner finished, toasts completed and all the jokes and laughter done, the DJ starts the music as servers quickly remove the rest of the cutlery and dishes from the tables. Andy and Amy chose a song from Ann's IPod collection, an Elvis favourite, *I Can't Help Falling In Love with You*. With Amy's train gone, Amy floats around the room wrapped in Andy's arms. As they entertain the crowd with their skills in ballroom dancing, they truly enjoy these special moments together and alone on the dance floor.

The next dance Amy dances with her father, alone on the dance floor to the song by John McDermott, *Dance with me Daughter*.

The third dance features Grace and Andy. It's a beautiful song written by a mother to her son. Grace found this song on the internet and Emma has agreed to sing once again today. It's called *The Man You've Become* written by Gloria Sklerov & Barbara Rothstein. Grace has tears in her eyes as she dances with her son around the room.

Finally all the wedding party join together on the dance floor with Ann Murray and her love song, *Can I Have This Dance*. With this, everyone's invited to join together on the dance floor.

Andy and Amy take turns dancing with most of their guests and then visit each table and thank each person personally for sharing their wedding day. They thank Katherine and her family both publicly and privately several times. They appreciate all the friends and relatives who have helped to make such an amazing day.

Throughout the night they manage to have time together to dance and share this special day. It's well after midnight, when Andy steals his bride away. He's been watching the time since he made special arrangements to have the limousine pick them up at 1AM to take them home to spend their first night together in their own place.

Grace and Ed see Amy and Andy just as they're ready to make their escape. They quietly follow their children to the door.

"I assume you're not staying here tonight," Ed surprises them.

"We thought we could make it out without being spotted," Andy laughs. Andy doesn't answer the question; the limo is evidence of their plans.

"We saw you two sneak out and had to say goodnight one more time." Ed smiles. "I know you've had a great time and I'm so happy for both of you."

"Awe Dad," Amy tears up, "It's been the best day of my life, this dress, the wedding gift of a honeymoon, all our family, all our friends, the jokes and laughter, and Dad you're the best." She reaches up to kiss him one last time before they leave.

Andy hugs Ed, "thanks for your daughter, I love her with all my heart, you know that."

Amy puts her arms around Grace. "You're the best too. Thanks for everything you've done."

"Can we impose on you to join us for breakfast before you leave on your honeymoon?" Grace's a bit hesitant to ask.

"Most definitely, we thought we'd come back here to meet you guys for brunch. Our plane doesn't leave until 4:15 PM and we need to be there two hours early, so can we meet around 11:00 or so." Andy suggests.

"It's been a long day and we want to relax and not have to hurry in the morning." Amy suggests.

"Besides, I've not finished packing yet," Andy chimes in.

"That sounds great," Ed replies. "Grace and I will pack all your gifts and things into the hotel storage room until tomorrow and then after you two leave, we'll get the boys to help us load everything up and take to the house tomorrow afternoon."

"Thanks Dad." Amy gives him and Grace each one last hug before they hop into the limousine.

The ride home's short and when they arrive, Amy unlocks the door and Andy picks her up and carries her into the house. Laughing together, they go upstairs. As husband and wife, they start their new life together.

Chapter Thirty Nine

Amy opens her eyes, it's just pre-dawn, she feels the warmth of Andy beside her, she's glad she listened to her mom's facts of life lectures and waited for her honeymoon to share her love with her husband. Now content and happy, she cuddles down next to Andy and goes back to sleep. She realizes this is the best place in the world to be, in the warm protective arms of her husband. She smiles at her sleeping husband.

A few hours later, Amy awakes to find Andy watching her.

"I know, I'm a mess in the morning," Amy self consciously pushes her hair around.

"Are you kidding, you are the most beautiful in the morning. I've been laying here admiring the view." With that, he pulls her into his arms and kisses her. He realized he has a lot of work to get Amy to understand how much he really loves her and how truly beautiful she is both on the outside and the inside.

Amy pulls away and looks deep into Andy's eyes, "So you mean if I get fat and ugly you'll still love me."

"I'd love you no matter what; you're beautiful from the inside out." Andy spends time showing Amy his love.

Much later, Andy checks his watch and is surprised at how quickly time passes. "Wow, look at the time, we've got to finish getting packed. I've got to get everything secured. We have to meet our family for brunch."

Amy laughs at her husband as she hops out of bed and heads to the bathroom. A few seconds later, Andy joins her in the shower.

"Now I understand the logic of the size of this shower," Amy smiles as Andy helps her wash her hair.

A short time later, Amy is dressed and ready. She's chosen a soft lilac coloured pant suit that she found when she was out shopping a few weeks ago. She decided it would be perfect for their honeymoon and for travelling. The colour and style looks fabulous on and Amy's pleased that it fits her so well. She felt beautiful when she tried it on and she knows she looks good today. The material is a stretch satin polyester/spandex blend. It has a ruffled collar with V neckline and one button front. The pants have pencil thin legs and are extremely comfortable. She's put a sleeveless white top underneath. Amy adds a comfortable pair of white pumps.

While she's been getting ready, Andy finishes packing his suitcase and has carried them both out to the car. He's checked the house and done all the necessary things to ensure the house will be secure while they're gone. He knows his mom will check the house regularly and he's made arrangements with one of the neighbour's teenage boys to mow the lawn.

Amy's put together her travel carry-on and is finally ready to leave. She takes a few minutes to tidy up the bedroom and bathroom. She's made arrangements for Judy to come in and clean just before they get home so everything will be clean and fresh.

"Are you ready?" Andy comes around the corner and stops as he sees his beautiful wife picking up her bag.

"You sound like the perfect husband," she smiles and walks towards him.

"Wow, you look spectacular, you were beautiful yesterday as my bride, but today, as my wife, you look even better" He takes her in his arms and kisses her.

They're interrupted by the ringing of Andy's cell phone.

"Sorry to interrupt you son, but we're just wondering if you still plan to join us for brunch." Grace asks.

"Hey, do you have a camera in this house?" Andy replies.

"No, but I was a bride once myself." She giggles.

Andy checks his watch, "Actually we're just leaving the house now, so we'll see you in about 15 minutes."

Andy hangs up. "I guess we better get going. It appears we're going to be late for brunch."

Laughing, they get into the car and head over to the hotel restaurant for brunch.

Chapter Forty

Hand in hand, Andy and Amy enter to be greeted by Grace and Ed. Hugs are exchanged and they head into the dining room to eat brunch. Andy and Amy are surprised to see their wedding party and many family members gathered together. They're greeted by clapping and cheers.

Everyone's happy to be together one more time before the happy couple leave on their honeymoon.

Amy realizes she's starving and is pleased when she finally reaches the brunch buffet table. She loads up her plate and heads to the table with Grace and Ed. Andy's filled his plate and is already eating.

"I'm sorry I didn't wait, sweetheart, but I'm famished." Andy gets up to pull out her chair.

"You'd think you chopped wood all day." Ed jokes.

"Well, we didn't have anything to eat since supper last night. I danced the night away." Andy replied as he put another pile of pancakes into his mouth. "Besides, you know what they say about airplane food."

Grace opens a big bag and shows Amy. "Dear, I took all the cards last night from your wishing well. You might want to open some of them before you leave."

She peers into the bag, "That looks like too many to read now, maybe just leave them at your place till we get back," she suggests.

"With the boys to help, we're going to unload your gifts in the family room at your place later today," Ed tells them.

"Thanks Dad, I'm not sure what we'd do without all your help." Amy smiles and works hard to keep tears from flowing.

As soon as Amy and Andy finish eating, they spend the next two hours visiting their family and friends who have decided to spend time with each other before they all start to head back to their respective homes.

Shortly before it's time to leave for the airport, they're saying good bye to the last ones in the dining room.

With final hugs and good byes, Grace and Ed drive the newlyweds to the airport with Andy's car. They return back to the hotel with the plan for Grace to drive the car home and put it in the garage until they return. Ed, with Phil and George's help finish loading the truck, Phil drives with Ed over to Andy and Amy's house. George meets them and they unload all the gifts into the house for Amy and Andy to deal with when they get back from Paris.

Chapter Forty One

Leaving their parents, Amy and Andy head towards the international check in. They are looking forward to their trip together. With luggage checked, they wander through the airport until it is time to clear security and go to their boarding gate.

Once on board the plane, Amy and Andy settle in for their trip. The stewardess, having been alerted the happy couple are on their honeymoon, brings them glasses of champagne. First class is an amazing part of the plane and neither have had the privilege of sitting there before so they check out all the bells and whistles that are provided.

As the plane takes off, they snuggle down in their seats. Andy put his arm around Amy; this is going to be a wonderful time alone together. Amy has plans to send thank you notes to all their friends and family during the flight over, but she decides maybe on the way home. They watch Calgary lights grow dim and sit back and enjoy the flight. During an excellent dinner, they discuss their plans, adventure and the excitement of visiting Paris together.

Chapter Forty Two

The sun is high in the sky, the air is so quiet and still, Amy smiles as she hears the crunch of the fall leaves under her feet. It's a beautiful autumn Saturday. She's come back as she has always done on the anniversary date. It's hard to believe it's been seven years since Ann's funeral. Amy put the bouquet of pink roses into the vase cemented next to her headstone.

She drops down on the ground as she has done so many times. So much has changed these last few years and Amy reflects on how she's grown in that time. She's emerged from a sad and unhappy woman to a busy and happy wife and mother. She remembers the love she witnessed growing up and has taken the lessons her mom taught her into her own life. When she married Andy, she loved him with all her heart. She had no idea how much her love would grow. She'd wondered if she'd have enough love for her babies, but she's learned her love is as endless as the open sky above her.

A gentle breeze caresses her shoulders and she smiles, believing with all her heart that it's a hug from her mom. With the starting point of the letter and lists she left Amy when she died, Ann must be proud to see that Amy's finally completed every single item on the list. As a lesson, Amy now has her own lists. She knows her mom's watching over her and now as a mother herself she knows how proud Ann is of the woman she's become.

Amy's a happily married woman having recently celebrated their sixth wedding anniversary. She's kept her job as Head of Cardiology. Now, as a mother of twins, Mary Ann and Elizabeth Grace, Amy looks over at the two beautiful babies snuggled down in the stroller.

Sitting in the shade of the stroller is Casey, Finnegan's cousin. They added Casey to their family after Amy suffered her miscarriage on their second wedding anniversary. Andy brought Casey home as a companion hoping to help fill the void and pain in their lives. Casey did indeed help both of them heal. Amy received a third and final letter from Ann when she first became pregnant. Ann left her the story of her own pregnancies and miscarriages. It was this final letter that helped Amy through her own miscarriage. It was during that difficult time that Amy finally came to understand the dream she'd had so often growing up. She's convinced it was a message from her birth parents, both heart beats were those of her dying father and mother. The security she felt after coming into the bright light was after her birth when she was wrapped and gently placed into Ann's waiting arms. She believes her own little boy is safe and secure in her mother's arms with all three beautiful people to look after him until someday she's reunited with him.

The pain Andy and Amy suffer lessened when the twins came into their lives. Andy was so protective and Amy was so careful during her entire pregnancy, terrified they would lose again. Everyone was so happy and excited when Mary Ann and Elizabeth Grace made their débuted, just a couple of weeks ahead of schedule.

When the twins came home from the hospital, Casey, much like Finnegan, shared her heart and even her doggy toys with them. The girls return Casey's affection with their own hugs and kisses.

For now, the girls have fallen asleep on the walk over from her dad's apartment, which is close by. They still have afternoon naps and the excitement of running around their Grandpa's house has exhausted them. The girls will be celebrating their 3rd birthdays in a couple of weeks.

Amy's been lucky to find a wonderful nanny, Rosie. Pastor Trevor helped her immigrate to Canada after receiving a distress call from his Mexican missionary friends. Rosie's husband was a Mexican drug enforcement agent and he'd been killed by the Drug Cartel. Rosie's own life was in danger and she needed a safe place to start over. With the help of the church and some friends of Andy's from the Canadian RCMP Drug Agency, Rosie came to Canada and started a new life as their nanny. She's helped bring two of her friends from Mexico and they all share accommodation in Andy's house.

Rosie loves the two girls and watches over them while Amy and Andy are both at work. She's become an important part of their family.

Amy's exhausted, but it's an emotional exhaustion. Today, Andy and Jake are helping her father move the rest of his things over to his new apartment in the newly constructed seniors' complex just a couple of blocks from the cemetery. The years are starting to take their toll on him. He walks with a cane since his recent hip replacement. His new place is right next to Al's apartment. Both now widowers, they've decided their yards and houses are just too much of a burden.

Ed planned to sell the house, but Amy and Jake purchased it with plans to rent it out. They found a nice young couple with small children who will take care of it almost as well as their parents have. They've left a lot of the furniture since Ed's new place is a small two bedroom place with one living room and a kitchen with eating area. It's small, but as Ed says, it's big enough for him and Finnegan.

Victoria has stayed at the apartment, supervising the move. She and Jake have had their share of highs and lows as they have faced the challenges of life growing stronger each day in their love for each other through the power of prayer and their never ending faith in God.

Amy looks across the cemetery rows and sees the headstones for Joyce and Bruce and Connie. There have been many losses over the past years and Amy misses her mother's friends. They'd become substitute mothers to her over the years. Joyce died last year after a very short battle with breast cancer. Bruce and Connie were killed in a terrible collision coming back from visiting their son and his family. A logging truck lost control and hit the couple's car head on.

So many changes, and now with her dad moving into a senior's apartment complex, she realizes change is just another part of life. Amy also knows that her dad's looking forward to the day when he joins his wife and can once again hold her in his arms. It's not his time yet, but Amy sees he's slowing down. The arrival of the grandchildren has given him a diversion from the loss of his friends over the years, but the years seem to be passing quickly.

Amy reaches over to adjust one of the roses and finds a penny lying next to the vase. She smiles upwardly and picks up the penny. She'll take it home and put it into the jar of pennies in her room. Over the years, she's created quite a collection. She hears the grass crunch and turns to see Andy walking across the lawn towards her. She smiles and waves.

"A penny for your thoughts." Andy grins. "You look like you're deep in thought."

"I'm just sitting here reflecting on my life." Amy answers.

"I saw you and figured you'd probably need some help to get up." Andy takes her hand and helps her up.

Amy rubs her swollen belly; their unborn son has started bouncing around in recognition of his father's voice. Carter Richard Edward will be making his début in a few short weeks.

"I hadn't got that far yet, but you're right, I would've had to call you." Amy reaches over and plants a kiss on his lips. "Thanks for giving me some space today, it's hard to see dad leave the house and someone else ready to move in."

Andy takes a Kleenex out of the stroller and gently dabs a tear as it falls down her face. "I know, but your dad really is excited about his decision."

"I know, you're right, but it's another sign that he's getting old."

"Hey, we're all getting old, before long our kids are going to be pushing us in our strollers." Laughing he takes hold of Amy's hand and together they push the stroller back to the complex.

As they walk along the sidewalk, Amy spots another coin and struggles as she bends down to pick it up, another penny from heaven.

THE END

Acknowledgements

Like many writers, I look close to home for my inspiration and story lines. My niece saw her family in the first book and because all of my family is so dear to my heart, they will see bits and pieces of the family woven into the rest of this series of books.

For example, my nephew's LoudMouth graduation suit was such a show stopper it had to be included in my story. His outfit will continue to be the talk of his grad class at every reunion they have. You guys are the greatest and I love you all. Your energy and excitement for life is contagious and your stories keep me wanting to hear more.

I want to thank my family- my husband, my son, my daughter and my grandchildren for their patience as I dedicated so much of my time to these books. Again my daughter and daughter-in-law are my strength and sounding boards as I bounce story lines and ideas to them. Alisa especially guides me with her wall charts and spreadsheets to help me keep track of my characters and for her suggestions on future projects and story lines. I am grateful for all the times at their home in Houston, Texas which gave me the chance to finish this book.

Special thanks to my friend Rhonda and her daughter Karen for taking time to read the book and helping me with the cover. The Canadian pennies on the cover would not have been possible without the assistance of Ray over at Sundre Great West Publishing. I want to acknowledge my proof reader, Alex, who provided me with her suggestions and her review.

The folks at FriesenPress provided me with great assistance and their evaluation provided me with motivation to move the story to a better place.

My most important acknowledgment is for my Saviour and Lord. My relationship with God keeps me moving forward through all of life's trials and tribulations. I cannot begin to imagine life without God; He has carried me many times and given me the courage and love to keep me going when I thought my world was ending. He is my rock and my strength, through Him all things are possible.

Coming Soon

In my next book, Trust Your Heart, you can discover more about Jake as his story unfolds. The lost of his fiancé, starting a new law practise, and finding his strength after his mother's death will challenge both his character and his faith to move forward. When he finds another opportunity to love, he moves past his fear of losing a second time and finds the courage to love again. When his wife faces the fight to survive cancer and makes life changing decisions, Jake must face his own anguish. Will Jake's love for his wife endure all things?

A Song For My Daughter

By Ray Allaire

Just once upon a yesterday
I held you in my arms
You grew into a little girl
with lovely childhood charms
Now it seems I only turned around
And I see you by his side
Oh, I can't believe my eyes today
My daughter is a bride
I guess somehow I always knew
This day would soon be here
Still I wonder as I look at you
What became of all the years
And no words could ever quite express
The way I feel inside
Oh, I can't believe my eyes today
My daughter is a bride
All the laughter and the teardrops
The sunshine and the rain
I would relive every moment, Dear
If I could bring them all back again
But now, my love, the time has come
To send you on your way
So I wish you every happiness
And the blessings of this day
And I hope the love I've given you
Will forever be your guide
Oh, I can't believe my eyes today
My daughter - Oh, I can't believe my eyes
My daughter - Oh, my angel and my pride
My daughter is a bride

Dance With Me Daughter

By John McDermott

*These are the thoughts of a father
On the wedding day of his daughter
As his mind wanders back to the first time he held her
He looks at her now, the same pride in his eyes
As onto the dance floor they glide
This is the dance of the bride and her father
Dance with me daughter of mine
On this your wedding day
Dance with me daughter of mine
You'll soon be going away
I loved you since you first began
Now you've found a new man
But I love you so, and this you must know
That my love won't falter
So dance with me daughter
Beautiful daughter of mine
We walk down the aisle
On my face there's a smile
But deep in my heart there's a tear
Our friends and relations are here in the church
With smiles on their faces they stare
As we walk t'ward the man who has stolen your heart
And to whom I must give you away
But I wish you love and happiness too
On this your wedding day
Dance with me daughter of mine
You'll soon be going away
I loved you since you first began*

Now you've found a new man
But I love you so, and this you must know
That my love won't falter
So dance with me daughter
Beautiful daughter of mine
The dance has begun
We twirl around the floor
But I know you're not my little girl anymore
A lovely young woman has taken her place
And there's happiness written all over her face
But always remember although we must part
You may leave my arms but never my heart
Dance with me daughter of mine
You'll soon be going away
I loved you since you first began
Now you've found a new man
But I love you so, and this you must know
That my love won't falter
So dance with me daughter
Beautiful daughter of mine

The Man You've Become

By Gloria Sklerov and Barbara Rothstein

Big wheels, hot wheels
Little trucks and cars
Skinned knees, climbing trees
Whishing on the stars
Moments may be lost
Somewhere in time
But the sweetest memories
Are never left behind
Now you've grown so fine
And come so far..
I'm so proud of who you are
The man you've become
Thrilled to share your deepest joy
To know you've found the one
For the great things you will do
I'll be blesssed
Because you are my son
But I'll always see the boy
In the man you've become
School days, sleep aways
Driving all alone
Phone calls, shopping malls
Late coming home
It was hard to know
When to let you spread your wings
When to let you go

*To face the challenges life brings
But you've grown so fine
And come so far…
I'm so proud of who you are
The man you've become
Thrilled to share your deepest joy
To know you've found the one
For the great things you will do
I'll be blessed because you're my son
But I will always see the boy
I see the little boy
I'll always see the boy
In the man you've become*

Maureen' Ham Sauce Recipe

2 eggs, beaten well

1 cup white sugar

1 tbsp. dry mustard

2/3 cup white vinegar

Mix together and place in the top of a double boiler

Cook until thick (much the same as lemon pie filling)

Serve as a side dish to baked ham or like Andy and Ed, anything you think of

Yield: One Pint

CPSIA information can be obtained at www.ICGtesting.com
Printed in the USA
LVOW05s1314230713

344088LV00002B/32/P